A Pretty Game

Jill Turner Claybrook

maple avenue
publishing

Copyright © 2024 by Jill Turner Claybrook

Published by Maple Avenue Publishing

All rights reserved. No part of this publication may be reproduced, stored in a retrieval system, or transmitted in any form or by any means, electronic, mechanical, photocopying, recording, scanning, or otherwise, without written permission from the author. It is illegal to copy this book, post it to a website, or distribute it by any other means without written permission.

First Edition

ISBN-13: 979-8-9899415-2-0

To my mom

CHAPTER ONE
Playing the Game

Wren Amberton was good at playing games.

Cards. Croquet. Chess. Those were the types of games she always enjoyed. Always won. But there were other games in her life she seemed destined to lose. As she picked at a scratch in her family's dining table and stared at her younger sister, she struggled to play the game she was usually best at. A game she called *How Well Can Wren Pretend Not to Care*.

When the midwife had placed *Eilliana* in their mother's arms one day shy of fifteen years ago, both parents had wept. Rich, clover honey hair and smooth, creamy skin. A beauty such as her would surely bring them wealth and comfort. It wasn't long before what seemed like all of Langley called on the Ambertons to admire the loveliest child ever created. And so began Wren's days of being a nobody.

She should be grateful. Many times had she been told how lucky she was to have Eillie for a sister.

'Do you just stare at her all day?'

'What a delight it must be to look at that angel's face all the time.'

'How fortunate for someone like *you* to have a sister like *her*. Proof that you might carry good genes somewhere.'

Wren stabbed a fork into her rubbery fried egg.

"There is no need to attack your breakfast in that way, Wren," Mrs. Amberton said. "See Eillie? That is how a young lady ought to receive her sustenance."

Eillie straightened and put down her egg spoon to take up her tea.

Ugh! An angel for a younger sister. She was like a blinding light that allowed not even a shadow. Wren could be the devil herself, but no one ever considered she might be such an interesting soul.

A door slammed at the back of the house.

"She's back," Mrs. Amberton said, bolting upright. "Plucky! Plucky, do you have it?"

The middle-aged governess/housekeeper/lady's maid pushed into the room through the servant's entrance, her face bright red and a tailor's bag filling her arms.

"Yes, ma'am," she said between heavy breaths. "Mrs. Gusset said she did it just as you instructed."

"Oh, thank heavens. Take it up to my room." Mrs. Amberton took a calming sip of tea while Plucky lumbered from the room, shrugging to keep a hold on the overstuffed bag. "I should have been extremely upset if it were not finished. I am sure we all remember what happened to me at last year's ball." She looked to her husband, waited in vain for a response, then took a bite of toast. "Mrs. Gusset swore to me my gown would be ready this time, but she is known to exaggerate her abilities. And with everyone from the farmer's daughter to the viscount's mother going tomorrow, she was bound to be behind. It was wise we got your gown early, Eillie dearest. What stress!"

Eillie nodded, her pretty curls bouncing with her head.

A Pretty Game

Wren slapped another cut of ham onto her plate.

A ball on Eillie's birthday. What luck! It was almost as if the chamber had planned it. Wren could hear them now. 'When is that pretty Amberton girl's birthday?' 'Why, it's in the beginning of September, a whole month after the usual date of our ball.' 'Well, push it back, man! What can you be thinking holding the ball before she is fifteen!'

Wren's own coming out had only been eight weeks ago, just after her seventeenth birthday. In a rushed decision to make way for Eillie, it had been to a small neighborhood party where sweets and eligible young men had been scarce and stinky cheese and port had been abundant. Her mother had assumed that if the gentlemen got their intake of food and drink, one or two might be induced to play a game of cards with Wren.

But the tables had always been full and not once was she invited to sit beside a prospective partner, foxed or not. She had spent the entire evening at her mother's side, listening to mindless chatter such as how many strings of pearls the late Duchess of Rockstell had owned and who in the neighborhood had ordered the ugly bolt of fabric at the dressmaker's.

She huffed out a breath.

"One mustn't breathe like a wild horse, dearest."

When Mr. Amberton excused his family from the table, Wren retreated to the sanctuary of her own room and shut the door. A rustling greeted her from the corner.

"All right, PJ," she cooed to the pigeon whose full name was Prince Jeonfigmigpigeon II.

She went to the small table supporting the bird's cage and picked up a pencil and a slip of pre-cut paper to scribble out a note to her best friend.

Dearest Lyn,

Good morning! I hope you slept well. I, myself, had a fitful night's sleep. Such a dream I had. Translate this one for me: My neck was as long as a rutuki antelope, and I bounced around like one, stepping on people's toes and nibbling their hair.

I'm sure it means something.

Love,

Wren

She rolled the note and tucked it into a tiny canister. Lifting the door of the cage, she wrapped one hand around PJ's weightless body and drew him out. With sure movements, the canister was fastened to a skinny leg and the window unlatched. The bird flexed in her hand, anxious to get his breakfast at Lyn's. She stroked his back several times, gave him a quick kiss, then opened her hands to watch him fly away. The morning was already warm, and Wren hoped it wouldn't break its promise to be a beautiful day.

With a heavy sigh, she flopped onto her bed. Tomorrow's Tremdor Town Ball was to be her first dance, too. Closing her eyes, she worked her way through the coming evening for the hundredth time—the great hall dressed in its finest, the scent of summer flowers romantic and fresh. Colorful gowns shimmering in the soft candlelight and tables full of cake.

It will be fun, she lied to herself.

How different she would feel if she could walk into the great hall on her elder brother's arm. The evening would be guaranteed enjoyable if Luke were with her instead of at sea. But then again, with so many in attendance she was sure to dance. A tiny thrill sparked in her stomach. Would young Mr. Robert Starly be there?

A Pretty Game

Wren briefly pressed her fingers into her eyes, then turned to look at the bright pink gown hanging on her wardrobe. It was nothing like Eillie's elegant sapphire gown and not at all to Wren's taste. And she had to use rags to fill the bust. But it was pretty—satin with beads along the sleeves. Better than the old, refashioned dress of her mother's she had been forced to wear to the neighborhood party.

Still, Wren could not look at it without wincing. Mrs. Amberton must have felt a prick of guilt ordering such an extravagant dress for her youngest daughter and leaving the eldest to her own hand-me-downs. The pink dress was a symbol of her mother's vanity, not affection.

A muffled thump sounded in the wardrobe. Wren shot up.

"Whoever's hiding in my skirts better show himself before I pick up the hot iron from my fire." There wasn't a fireplace in her room, but her eight-year-old brother evidently had forgotten.

The right door flew open, and a boy with amber curls and blue eyes spilled out. "Do not poke me, oh one who holds my fate. It is only I, Sir Charley."

"And what, sir, are you doing in my room?"

He scrambled to his feet and looked around for the absent fireplace. He scowled. "I was only waiting to see you turn into a witch."

A smile threatened Wren's lips. Continuing the ruse she had begun six months ago, she leaned forward and whispered, "You know I only turn into a witch on moonless nights."

"Yeah, I was going to wait. I need to see it. I might not explain it right if I don't. And I need it for act twenty-seven of my latest work or it will be sunk."

"Well, you don't need to hide in there. I'll tell you next time I go into the woods. I've been needing the toes of a brilliant playwright.

5

And that's a very fine tongue you have inside your mouth."

Wide-eyed, he shut his lips over his gappy teeth. "Never mind, I'll just make it up," he said quickly and dashed out.

With her room secured, Wren moved for the low, padded stool at her vanity. For just a moment she analyzed the green damask patterned cloth before her. Slowly, she reached out and tugged the cover. It fell away to reveal her reflection.

If she were asked what made her face homely, she would not have an answer. Thankfully, no one had asked her since she was eight, and at that age, one really isn't expected to give any sort of intelligent reply. Her dark hair was dull and straight but not an unfortunate shade. And her brown eyes were expressive—or so she liked to think.

Truly, when she analyzed each of her features one at a time, they weren't so bad. But as a whole, they just didn't...blend. She had always assumed the Divine Governor simply hated her, and it just showed through her countenance. Why the heavens should hold her in contempt, she didn't know. She did set fire to the church belfry once, but it couldn't be helped. She had to drop the burning songbook before it blistered her hand. At nine years old, how could she have known Luke was joking when he said holy books didn't burn?

Wren shook her head and re-covered the mirror. Several wrinkled papers fell to the floor as she took up her most recent purchase—a book about invertebrates of the southern continent—and opened it to the page marker.

Wren used to get all of Luke's old schoolbooks, and he would go through them with her, sharing what extra tidbits he had learned. But the books had stopped coming when he finished secondary school over a year ago and joined the King's Navy, leaving her to acquire books on her own. Which was just as well. She much preferred pages of science and adventure to lectures on economics and political philosophy.

In her late perusal of her new book the night before, she had found a species of crab she especially liked the look of. With yellow armor and long, thorny legs, it looked like something Charley might make up. Or Lyn. Try as she might, the creatures Wren sketched from her mind never came out right. Copying suited her best. She rummaged through the drawer, pushing aside broken pastels and stiff paintbrushes, until she found her favorite pencil. She had just begun to sketch the curved line of the shell when there was a knock at her door.

"Wren," Plucky said. "Your father wants you."

"Me?"

The door opened. "You. He's in one of his moods so best not dally."

Reluctantly, Wren dropped her pencil and followed Plucky down the stairs. Mr. Amberton was found seated in his study, the only part of the house he really knew. If he had been asked to get his own socks, he would not have been able to accomplish it. Fortunately, he never was and remained blissfully unaware of his ignorance in his own house.

"Ah, Wren, here you are. I have a favor to ask of you."

"A favor? Of me?"

"Yes, your mother tells me that you often go about visiting poor souls. Is this true?"

"Yes, Papa. But I don't know that I go often—maybe once or twice a week, just small rounds. Why? Am I not supposed to?"

"No, no. If you choose to spend your time with people in vermin-infested places, I shall not stop you. So long as you don't bring any home with you."

"Vermin?"

"No, people." He glanced at the newspaper on his desk for a moment and eyed a few notes, seeming to forget she was in the room anxiously waiting to hear what it was he wanted from her.

She filled the minutes by inspecting his various dusty books and no-touchy knick-knacks from where she stood. An inhale brought in the smell of old garlic and musty earth. She could account for neither, but where the window was never opened, maybe the smells were just what came off her father.

Finally, he looked up again. "And you go on these visits alone? Unchaperoned?"

"Yes." She rubbed her ankle with the opposite foot. "Mum says I do not need one."

He checked her over quickly. "No, I don't suppose you do. Continue as you have. But I want you to put my cousin and his wife on your little route. The Adleys have recently taken up residence at Ebdor Cottage. She's unwell and likely to die soon—gone mad, I understand. And he has never been able to manage anything in his life. So if you would pay them a visit, help out around the house and what have you, you would do a service to your family."

Wren was rather shocked. She had not known they had any family living nearby. Nor that her father would care about them. "Of course, I'd be happy to. Shall I take some of Cook's bread or some—?"

"Certainly not. We cannot feed the neighborhood. What a silly— just take yourself. That will have to be enough."

"Yes, Papa." Wren ducked into a quick curtsy and turned to quit the room.

"Oh, and Wren," he said, sounding as if what he was about to say was an afterthought, "I think my cousin has fallen into a little wealth with his work and some nonsense papers he wrote up. They have no children to pass anything to. So if you could…feign a heavy dose of concern and friendship, we might be able to inherit when the old man goes. There now, be a good girl and run along. No sense standing there anymore. Shut the door behind you."

Wren felt a whoosh of heat in her chest and hurried from the room. "Feign concern and friendship!" she said under her breath. "What does he think me? An actress going about pretending to care? Why, I should hate to see the vomit of a gown he would pick out for me. Probably a poofy concoction in a violent shade of fuchsia with puce roses trying to strangle me."

The muttering continued as she stomped up the stairs. She threw open her wardrobe and snatched her short jacket from its hook.

"If I were Eillie he would have at least invited me to sit and told me something wonderful about myself." She thrust her bonnet onto her head, jilting the dangling, crinkled ribbons. Before leaving the house, she dropped into the kitchen and snatched a newly baked loaf of bread. She would not show up at a cousin's home empty handed. Plucky had taught her better than that.

As she marched down the road to the remote Ebdor Cottage, some winding mile and a half away, she was forced to admit that going about the neighborhood was not a completely noble endeavor. She was pleased to care for the uncared for and to relieve any suffering her plain hands could. And she was interested in learning about all sorts of ailments.

But more than anything, it was an escape. She could have been green with festering wounds and the people on her little routes would still be happy to take her bread or have her sweep their floors. In truth, the visits made her small world just a little bit bigger.

Regardless, the insult from her father dug its ugly claws in deep for the first half of her walk. She might not be an angel, but she certainly didn't have to *feign* concern.

By the time she reached her destination, however, her lungs were full of filtered air from the woods and her father's words had become just another hurt locked in the chest she tried never to open. She hadn't been out this way in some time—the cottage being well off the main road and having been uninhabited for a year at least. She had forgotten how beautiful it was.

Ebdor Cottage nestled in the middle of a grove like a satisfied little bird, its blue-gray stone sturdy and thatched roof clean. Flowers skirted the walls, bursting from the beds in a wild way—yellow, purple, and pink blooms breaking up the green. Hollyhock canes as tall as a man poked out from the masses and the grass in the yard brushed Wren's shins under her skirt.

No, it would not be difficult to visit this place often. Next time she might even bring her watercolor things.

A family of finches flitted about the eaves, but otherwise the home sat silent and still. Wren wondered if they might be napping inside and tried to casually peek through the pristine windows. Glimpsing no hints, she decided to take the risk and knock.

Within a short time, shuffles came from inside and a voice called, "A moment. Just a moment!" Presently, the thick, hand-carved door opened, and Wren was greeted by a slender man with neatly combed gray hair and large, silver-rimmed spectacles pushed up crookedly to his forehead.

"Yes?" he asked.

"Uh, hello. Mr. Adley?"

"Yes?"

"I'm Wren. Amberton. George Amberton's daughter."

A moment passed as she waited for recognition to set in, but it didn't come.

"We're cousins," she said finally.

"Cousins! Oh, you don't say. Well, this is happy indeed. Come in, come in. Ann! Ann, we have a cousin here to see us. Yes, come in, right in here. Right here. Sit down. Yes, do sit right there. Well," he said, taking the seat across from her, "this is such a nice—Ann! Come in here! We have a cousin!" He smiled widely at Wren, and she couldn't help noticing the flecks of brown stuck in his teeth. A bump sounded from another room, and he gave a start. "Ann! Come—just a moment dear Miss…er…Cousin. Just a moment."

He dashed out of the room, leaving Wren to study it freely. Books and books filled shelves on either side of the little fireplace. The volumes were stuffed haphazardly in their places, both vertically and sideways, piled on top of others or nearly blocking more from view. None were dusty but most were very worn. On the coffee table were piles of peanut shells. *Ah*. Peanut skins explained the brown flecks in his teeth. The rest of the room was tidy and absent of any sort of adornment, aside from several portraits hanging above the mantel and one large rug beneath the comfortable furniture.

Mr. Adley returned with a delicate-looking woman shuffling at his side. She beamed at Wren and held out her thin hands.

"Oh, it's you!" she said. "You have finally come to see us. We have missed you, haven't we…um…"

"No, love. This is our first time meeting her." He smiled at his wife who frowned in return. "But she is here to see us now. Come, let's sit. Sit down, dear." He reached up and pushed on the woman's shoulders until she lowered to the cushions. "Sit, that's right. So we are cousins.

You say your father is named George? Yes, I seem to remember having a cousin named George. I did not know this is where he ended up."

"My father inherited our home from my grandfather before I was born," Wren said, trying to sound simply informative. "He has always lived here."

"Has he? Oh, well I must have visited a time or two. Perhaps that is why I was instantly so fond of the area."

"And how long have you been here? A couple weeks?"

"Quite near six months I believe, haven't we, dear?" He brushed a few loose strands of gray-streaked auburn hair from her face. "This has been our home nearly half a year?"

"I don't live here," Mrs. Adley replied. She looked at Wren and smiled. "How nice of you to have us in your home."

"No, sweet one. She is visiting *us*. This is our home. Remember? You remember, don't you? See our pictures there on the wall?"

"Oh," she said quietly and looked at her hands.

Mad, Mr. Amberton had said. Wren had nearly forgotten. When she pictured someone who was 'mad' she envisioned wild hair and rantings and shredding of furniture, like in the novels she read. Mrs. Adley's upright form was tidy—her hair neatly pulled back in a simple bun and her dress clean. Mad.

Suddenly Wren recalled the weight on her lap. "I brought you some bread. It might be a bit big—I didn't know if you employed a housekeeper or…"

"No. It's just the two of us here. Just how we like it, right love?"

Mrs. Adley smiled absently and tried to get up, but her husband grabbed her by the arm, rooting her back in place.

Wren shifted a little. "Well, it dries out slowly and…" She rolled the loaf into his outstretched hands.

"We will enjoy it, thank you. Yes, I've tried making our own bread, but it always comes out quite a lump. Yes, very much a lump, doesn't it dear?"

The little room fell silent, and the sound of four different clocks, each counting to its own rhythm, ticked in Wren's ears. Mr. Adley sat comfortably with his wife's hand in his, while the woman looked around the room with great concern. When her eyes fell on Wren, they softened and for a fleeting moment Wren thought she glimpsed a different woman. One with keen, understanding eyes that seemed to examine Wren's soul. Then the woman was Mrs. Adley again, a pinched expression with fretful eyes. Suddenly she laughed as if the funniest thing had been spoken.

Wren shifted uncomfortably in the soft chair again as the laughter faded into tears.

Mr. Adley jolted forward and handed his wife his handkerchief. "There, sweet one, don't cry. We're all right. Everything is all right." He looked back at Wren. "I'm afraid my wife is not well today. She is usually the best of hostesses, aren't you Mrs. Adley. You always like to take care of the house and see that our guests are comfortable. Why don't you go get the tea things, hm? That will cheer you up. Go on now."

Wren winced as Mrs. Adley leaned away from him shaking her head, stammering about not being in her house.

"Actually, I should be going," Wren nearly shouted. "Er, my mum will want me back."

A lie, of course. She doubted Mrs. Amberton noticed she had left.

"Oh going, yes, yes." Mr. Adley rose to his feet. "Well, I am so pleased to have met a cousin. I really was unaware we had any family here or else I should have come to call on your father. We keep to ourselves, me and Mrs. Adley. She doesn't care for crowds anymore, and well, I only care for what she does. But do come again. You're a sight for sore eyes with your pretty…bread and your…yes do come again. We should like it."

Wren turned at the door. Her curious gaze roved over the bright little entryway and strayed down the hall, stopping on a door to the right with a small table pushed in front of it. She stared a moment, and when she snapped her attention back to Mr. Adley, he was watching her carefully.

"I beg your pardon," she said with a blush. "What?"

"You'll come to us again, won't you?"

"Er, yes, I'd be happy to," she said, bobbing a curtsy.

He let her out with a wide smile and gracious thanks.

Instead of going directly home, Wren took the long road (passing the woods of "Pirate Pond" as she always called it) and made a couple more stops. Along this road, there lived only the Clamps and a widow—Mrs. Tapps, the latter only in need of idle chatter and the former in need of almost everything but. Hours later, Wren set off for home feeling exhausted, having held Mrs. Clamp's crying baby for half an hour while reading to the other six and having helped harvest vegetables from an unruly garden for the better part of the afternoon.

Thoughts of Ebdor Cottage and its residents kept Wren busy the entire walk home. Six months! The couple had lived there nearly six months, and no one had ever mentioned to her the cottage had been taken. And by cousins, no less. She planned to visit them again very soon, hoping to satisfy several curiosities. Was Mrs. Adley truly mad? What were all those books on the shelves about? And what was the use of a door if a table were kept in front of it?

CHAPTER TWO
Ribbons and Rivalry

Dearest Lyn,

Are you ready for tonight? My mum has great expectations. She is hoping to have Eillie married off to the wealthiest gentleman in attendance by noon tomorrow. I'm sorry for him, his wife will never make a bit of sense. But he'll have the consolation of a pretty face, I'll grant that. I wish you well in your preparations.

Love,

Wren

The warm water crab sketch was coming along nicely. Shading all the shelled nooks and crannies was tricky, but Wren was pleased with it so far. She set down her pencil and sifted through her morning sketches. She had found a particularly beautiful web in the old, stone barn, and its occupant had not yet run off. She stopped on her drawing of the weaver spider.

Plucky had complimented the details of the penciled spider after coming to "fetch her from the chicken poop." Wren didn't bother reminding Plucky that there were no chickens in the loft. Only pigeons. And while they had made a wreck of the place with loose feathers and forgotten roosts, Wren enjoyed the company of the wild birds.

And they didn't seem to mind her, either.

Wren's bedroom door popped open. "Eillie needs to go to the milliner's for ribbon," Mrs. Amberton said. "I need you to chaperon."

"But Mum, I—"

"Wren. I am up to my elbows in yards and thread. My gown was not redone to my liking, and I must fix it up myself. I need Plucky to help me and your father is out. Well, what are you sitting there for, chit? Get up! Come on, come on."

Wren shoved away from her desk. Without a word, she grabbed her jacket and bonnet, marched past her mother, and stomped down the stairs.

"Step lightly, dearest. Don't want to damage the wood."

Eillie was already waiting for her on the outside stoop, lovely as ever. A soft pink dress draped perfectly over her body and her golden curls gleamed despite being tucked under the shade of her bonnet.

Not blinded by the beauty, Wren brushed past her, heading for the open gate in the tall hedge surrounding their quaint property. Eillie's quick, light steps soon caught her and silently they began the journey toward town, just over a mile down the sunbathed road that had long ago cut its path through the Tremdor woods.

"Thank you for attending me, Wren," Eillie finally said. "I really am desperate to get a thicker ribbon for my hair. I don't seem to have a single one that will work. Plucky thinks I should wear it in braids around my crown, but I think I would like curls, pinned loosely, with a thick blue ribbon for color. Or maybe some little flowers—like baby's breath or something. What do you think?"

I think you'd receive ten proposals tonight even if you styled your hair into a chicken, Wren thought bitterly. Aloud, she said, "Do whatever pleases you most, Eillie."

A Pretty Game

Her sister didn't speak for a moment. Then, "But everyone will be admiring me tonight. I need to wear it whatever style is most flattering. You have an eye for such things. How shall I wear it?"

Wren sighed. "With the ribbon, I suppose, since we are walking into town to get it."

Eillie flashed her dazzling smile. "Right then. So I shall."

The two sisters reached the shop, and a long strip of blue satin the exact shade of Eillie's eyes was cut. The shopkeeper gushed over the match and repeatedly exclaimed how delighted she was to provide Miss Eillie with the perfect accessory for her first ball. Before Eillie handed over her coin, Wren was out the door.

Outside, a thick, unapologetic smell wafted from the community stable, and the wide streets of Tremdor moved with their typical pleasantry—clopping hooves, humming talk, shop bells tinkling. Wren wondered if Lyn happened to be in town.

A glance up the street proved worthwhile when her gaze snagged on a young gentleman astride a sleek coal-black thoroughbred. Their eyes met, and she put out her hand in a little wave. He turned his horse, and when he was near enough to be heard, touched his hat.

"Miss Amberton."

Wren smiled. "Gideon. You used to share the same piece of sickle root candy with me. I think that allows you to use my given name."

Gideon Brayford's dark eyebrows relaxed beneath the shadow of his brim. "Beg your pardon, Wren. I guess my schooling has chipped off my country manners."

"If your schooling teaches you to forget a friend, then I don't know the use of it."

"True." His reserved smile was a sad comparison to what she expected. Her elder brother's best friend from boyhood, she had been used to seeing Gideon's wide smile often. She hoped he hadn't grown completely humorless like his father had been.

The shop bell jingled, and Eillie stepped out saying something to Wren about being left behind. She froze mid-sentence, realizing she was interrupting, and dropped into a curtsy. Gideon's eyes shifted to her, and for a moment Wren thought she saw him lose himself. But he recovered and looked back to her.

"Will you be at the dance tonight?" he asked.

"Yes. Will you?"

"I will. And you, Miss Eillie? I understand tonight is to be your coming out."

"Yes, my lord. I'm a skein of yarn wound really tight and coming unraveled in anticipation!"

Wren glanced sideways at her sister.

"I look forward to seeing you both then." Gideon gave them a farewell nod. "Good morning to you."

Eillie squinted to watch him go. "That was Lord Garwick, wasn't it? I didn't know him until he spoke and even then I wasn't sure. He is looking well." She smiled coyly at Wren. "I think the extra eight thousand pounds has improved his looks."

Wren ground her teeth. "He looks exactly the same as he did four years ago, never mind his annual income."

It was true. Regardless of his polished attire, money and the title of Viscount of Garwick had not changed his looks. His eyebrows were still too thick and naturally brooding, and his hands large and rough. Through his years away at school, he had managed to retain the look of a boy who worked farmland alongside his tenants.

A chorus of girls bounded to the front of the milliner's.

"Hello, Miss Eillie!"

A Pretty Game

"Can't wait to see your dress at the ball tonight, Eillie. If we weren't great friends, I'm sure I would hate you."

"Will you wear your hair in curls? I don't want to do the same and be outdone."

A few gentlemen passed and cooed at her as well, and yet another pair stopped her to exclaim their excitement to see her tonight.

Without waiting for them to finish, Wren marched ahead, arms stiff at her sides. Within a few seconds, Eillie broke off conversation and hurried to join her, dashing Wren's dream to leave her behind forever. It always seemed no matter how fast she moved her feet, her sister remained only several graceful steps behind.

Wren quickened her pace.

Eillie did, too.

Wren quickened it some more and soon they were both hanging onto their bonnets in a shockingly unladylike race. When they blew through the hedge gate, both girls were gasping for breath.

"Pirates!" Charley shouted from the walnut tree. A pile of green-hulled nuts rained down on their heads. Eillie and Wren laughed and counterattacked, igniting a war.

"Charley! Stop that!" Mrs. Amberton yelled from the window. "You'll bruise your sister!"

Eillie swallowed her laughter and hurried inside. Wren knew she wasn't the sister their mother worried about, so she returned fire just long enough to render the boy desperately clinging to his branch. Satisfied with the duel, she scrambled into the house before he could recover and ran up the stairs two at a time.

"Wren, please. Ascend like a lady."

"I only look like a lady, Mum," she called back. "Really I'm half Saldavian mountain goat." She smiled at her own joke and added,

"That's why I wear a bonnet. To hide my horns."

Once in her room, she removed her horn cover and tossed it to the bed. With a sigh of relief, she unbuttoned her jacket and plunked down at her desk. Her sketches had waited.

A half-hour before the ball, with all manner of bustle on the other side of her door, Wren began her own laborious toilette: wash the graphite from her hands and put on her dress. Four minutes from the time she started, she was ready. She sat at her desk again and stared at the cloth covered mirror. There wasn't much use looking underneath. She knew what she would see. But…

A knock sounded at her door. "Come in, Plucky."

The door creaked open, and Eillie surprised Wren by stepping into the room. Her gold curls were piled on top of her head and clustered around her face in a perfect frame. The light blue ribbon was a lovely contrast to the deep blue satin gown with a high waist, modish neckline, and dainty sleeves.

Despite herself, Wren gasped. "Eillie, you look…really nice."

"Thanks." Her blue eyes brightened, forcing a small smile from Wren. Eillie stepped forward. "I'm so nervous, I hope I don't show it. I had Plucky help me early so I would have time to help you." She put out both hands. "If that's all right. I would have been here sooner, but my hands have been shaking so, and my hair wasn't doing what I wanted and Mum kept fussing with it. But now she's running late, so we have time to do something with you."

"Oh. Great, that's—er, thanks, but there's really nothing—"

Before Wren could finish, Eillie's nimble fingers set to work. She pulled out the knobby little bun on Wren's head and braided, twisted, and pinned. She finished by tucking little white flowers in strategic places and pulling a few tendrils loose about Wren's face.

"There. I think this is a very becoming style for you Wren." Eillie uncovered the mirror.

Wren looked side to side and almost agreed. It was fancier than she would ever request herself, but she did like it.

Trying not to look too pleased, she cleared her throat. "Thanks." Now, if only her gown wasn't so terribly bright and washing all color from her face. She got up from her chair. "I hear Papa calling, we should go."

She grabbed her favorite shawl from her bedpost and wrapped it around her shoulders. The olive green wasn't a pretty contrast to the pink, but she hoped it would tone down the eye-scorching dress. Eillie pulled a small case from her reticule and lingered behind for just a moment, then joined Wren's descent to their waiting parents.

"Eillie! Oh dearest, take those horrible things off."

Wren startled and looked back at her sister. A round pair of gold-rimmed spectacles sat on her nose and looped around her ears.

"But Mum, Papa just got them for me, and I see so well with them. I won't know who is coming toward—"

Mrs. Amberton reached up and plucked the offending accessory from Eillie's face. She patted her cheek with her other hand. "They cover your lovely face. We cannot have that tonight."

"Your mum is correct, Eillie," said Mr. Amberton. "They mar your face. Keep them to yourself for a time. Once you are married you may wear them whenever you like."

"But—"

"Enough! I will smash them to pieces if they're going to cause such a fuss. Out, all of you."

The thin man ushered them through the door and ducked under the frame to join them.

"Hark!" Charley shouted from an upper window. "What beauty I see below me. How hast the beasts disguised themselves so well?"

"To bed, boy!" Mr. Amberton roared. "And no more of your writing nonsense."

Charley disappeared from view as the rest of the family climbed into the family barouche. Wren felt the seat crack a little more beneath their weight and tried to think light thoughts so as not to fall through. With everyone seated and nobody comfortable, the groundskeeper/stableman/groom, Mr. Forner, snapped the reins. They were off—one daughter hoping it was to be the best night of her life, and the other quite terrified it would be the worst.

CHAPTER THREE
Wren Who

The ride was short, and Wren considered it silly to even take the carriage. She could have walked and arrived at the same moment as her family. But the light, sweetly scented breeze across her face was refreshing, and it did make her feel a little fancier, imagining the wheels didn't creak and the leather wasn't worn.

They arrived at the ball a fashionable three minutes late and were greeted at the door by the unpleasant scent of burning tallow and the tuning screeches of the musicians. A number of families were already present in the old, dim hall, and Mr. Thorte—the chairman of the ball—was hastily directing better candle placement.

Wren felt her heart leap when she spotted the Starlys—a relatively new family in town—standing by the single flower-laden cake table.

It was not completely unheard of for a young gentleman of Langley to be engaged by the time he was out of university, at which time he either began apprenticeship for his profession or gained access to his personal income through the family trust. For some, this was around twenty, for others twenty-two. And of course some gentlemen felt this to be rather hasty and waited many years more for the right match to come along, while others chose never to engage themselves at all.

The younger Mr. Starly was finally home from university for good—his father only requiring a two-year study from him—and Wren had a secret hope he was of the hasty kind.

He was all the things she admired. Tall and handsome. Educated. Handsome. And tall. Well-spoken, too. Or so she assumed. They had never actually been in conversation, but she once heard him speak with her father about the fine pea soup he had eaten at a Ferriton City party. He had sounded amazingly informed. And he *had* spoken to her that one time on the street when she, feeling very brave, had casually stepped into his path.

"Sorry, I didn't see you there," he had said. Not the response she hoped for, but at least he had shown manners by acknowledging he had not seen her. That was more than most people she had known her whole life had done.

The young man of interest glanced across the floor and spotted her family. His face lit up, and he immediately made his way toward them. Wren gave herself a quick once over, hoping the wadded rags under her dress weren't obvious.

"Mr. Amberton. Good evening. Your family is looking well."

"Of course," her father replied stiffly.

The young man pressed his lips together and bowed awkwardly. "Ah, Mrs. Amberton, ravishing as ever." Wren's mother responded with a playful swat of her fan. Starly turned, and Wren watched with a sinking heart as his eyes took in her sister. "And Miss Eilliana. You are…an angel." He stood dazed for a moment then cleared his throat and looked around. "A bang-up room for your little town. Nothing like that found in Ferriton, of course, but it will do."

"I understand we have your mother to thank for there being a dinner tonight," Mrs. Amberton said.

A Pretty Game

"Yes, all the balls in Ferriton hold a dinner. It was good of Mr. Thorte to turn toward the trend." He beamed, obviously pleased. The elder Mr. Starly called to him from across the room. The young man held up a hand to his father, then swung around to face Eillie. "Miss Eillie. I came early hoping to be the first to secure you for a dance. Please tell me I'm not to be bobbed."

Eillie giggled and nodded. "I'd be so joyous—er—honored to dance. With you. Sir."

He grinned like a schoolboy and gave a bow before retreating to his family.

Wren gently shook her head and closed her eyes to the world. She didn't know what she had expected. Why should this evening be different than any other time in her life? She wished she had chosen to wear her gray shawl rather than the green. Perhaps it would have made more of an impression.

"Wren," came a bold voice from behind. She felt her shoulders relax and spun around.

"Lyn!" The two girls embraced, and Wren stepped back to admire her best friend of four years. Lyn's graceful frame was draped in a bright yellow silk that perfectly complimented her skin tone. Her brown eyes glowed with excitement and her thick, ebony hair was braided and wrapped elegantly around the back of her head. "You are a vision," Wren said. "I am so glad you are here."

"Me, too," Lyn breathed. "Our first dance! My mum even talked my father into coming. He said he would come only if he could pick his own shoes. So, there they are."

Wren leaned around Lyn and saw her friend's white-haired father dressed in his finest black coat and white breeches with his country's traditional colorfully embroidered slippers on his feet. Wren laughed and admitted she would trade her plain dancing slippers for his. He caught the last words and grinned as he joined them.

"You like my shoes, Wren?" he said with an accent.

"Yes, Mr. Pak. I admire them very much. I am glad you are comfortable."

He shrugged. "I am never comfortable at parties—never in nine years. But I come to make my girls happy. Enjoy," he said with a bow and hurried to catch up with his social, Langlish wife who was already five families ahead.

Presently, the floor was thumping to the rhythm of dancing feet. Wren was first asked to dance by Mr. Pak and then—after sitting out two dances—by gawky Mr. Robbins. Her cheeks burned when the young gentleman let slip that his mother had told him to ask her. When the music ended, she hurried from the floor feeling like she would rather not dance at all if she was only to be humored with her friend's father or because-my-mum-told-me-to partners.

She took a chair on the lighter side of the room. Lyn was moving down the set with a beaming Captain Bofferd, and Eillie, of course, was bouncing joyously with Mr. Starly. Several times Eillie bumped into another couple or stumbled into an innocent bystander. Wren smirked wickedly at these little mishaps until she heard two women remarking what a marvelous dancer the younger Miss Amberton was and how beautiful she was engaged in any activity. Wren sat back with her arms folded across her chest.

"Rest them, dearest. Rest them," Mrs. Amberton said softly as she passed behind her.

Wren rolled her eyes and untwined her arms so one arm laid gently over the other. The dancing continued for an hour before dinner was announced. It was a squeeze to fit the crowd into the adjoining room.

A Pretty Game

The tables were tightly packed, and attendees had to shuffle sideways to weave between the chairs. Several tables were lined only with benches and some unfortunate women had the awkward task of hiking up their dresses to climb over their seats.

The young Mr. Bert Toone pulled out a chair for Lyn, then seated himself beside her and conveniently across from Eillie. Wren had known him for as long she could remember, though she doubted his memory of her went back very far. He wasn't handsome, but he did have a happy disposition. She wouldn't have minded being next to him and censured herself for feeling jealous of her charming friend. Before the table filled, Wren took the chair on Lyn's other side.

She leaned over to say something clever, but Lyn was already absorbed in a conversation with Toone, Eillie, and Starly, who seemed to be adhered to Eillie's side. She knew her friend wasn't conscious of it, but Wren felt as if Lyn's slight turn of her shoulder were a brick wall isolating her from their talk. Wren turned to her left to find Miss Lucy Brayford, which was by no means a comfort.

With striking features, Gideon's elder sister possessed a feminine version of his thick eyebrows with even more critical eyes. Wren couldn't remember her ever laughing as a child, and while Luke, Wren, and Gideon played in the woods and fields, Lucy would sit inside and deconstruct whatever it was her needle made until it was absolutely perfect.

Tonight she had what must be the feathers of an entire bird fanned in her hair. Her scarlet gown was hemmed in black lace, and a thick ruby necklace wrapped around her neck. If Wren were the imagining kind and imagined a vampire cat queen, she would look a lot like Lucy Brayford.

Wren scratched her ear and focused on her plate hoping the entire evening would pass without her being required to speak to Lucy.

"Well, Miss Amberton," Lucy purred. "You are looking…clean."

"Er, thank you, Luuu—Miss Brayford. Your feathers are very fine. What kind of bird are they from?"

The young lady stiffened. "How should I know? They didn't arrive *on* the dead thing."

"No, of course not. But some people like to know, so I thought—anyway, I would guess them to be feathers from the Poppito bird. Very sought after—very fine in form but stout enough to last several headpieces. You probably knew that though. But those are usually not—"

"How very interesting," Lucy said and turned away to speak with the young man on her other side.

Wren felt her cheeks warm and swept her eyes around the table. No one had noticed her be slighted.

As the meager courses came and went, Wren listened to the chatter around her. She was puzzled by the nonsensical things Eillie kept saying, though each utterance stirred considerable laughter from the boys. Lyn was wholly engrossed in the conversation, and Lucy never once deigned to acknowledge Wren again.

In fact, Wren was very sure she could have left the room and no one would have noticed. She entertained herself by thinking of all the things she could get away with—drinking from any cup within reach, eating with her fingers, leaning back in her chair like a man. Her favorite idea was hopping up onto the table and strutting down it like a chicken. The only person who would notice would be Mrs. Amberton. 'A lady doesn't strut like a chicken,' she would say. Then Wren would reply, 'No, Mum,' and crow like a rooster.

All these thoughts were fun for a time, but her heart was nearly in her feet by the time pudding was served.

She could tell witless jokes like Eillie. And if she were pretty like Eillie, they would be funny instead of nonsense. She could have smart conversation with Mr. Toone. And if she were poised like Lyn, it would be interesting. She could ignore everyone in the room, and if she were dressed like Lucy, she would be regarded as regal. Instead, she was not funny, not interesting, and drowning in fabric.

Mercifully, the meal did end. Like a clumsy duckling waddling after the swans, Wren tailed her table companions into the dance hall. It was very tempting to run for the main door, but instead she followed as if on a leash. Yes, she would go in and sit by Lyn again and be her sad little puppy friend.

Groups formed around the room waiting for the music to recommence, and Wren found herself standing with her mother and sister, Mrs. Starly, and Lyn. Mrs. Starly asked Lyn about her harp and inquired whether Eillie was at all musical.

"Oh, yes! Eilliana is so gifted at the piano. She has been dutifully practicing Movement Four by Bastoff. Do you know it?"

"Oh, Mum, please—" Eillie whispered.

But Mrs. Starly didn't hear. "Why yes. My son is very fond of that one."

"Sure he is." Wren ducked her head. She hadn't meant to say that out loud. Only Lyn seemed to notice and pressed her lips together to hide her smile.

"Tell me, Miss Eilliana. How else are you fond of spending your time?"

Starly joined them, and the rest of the time carried on as before with not a word spoken to Wren and much raving about Eillie and her pretty dress and fine hair and great sense of humor and remarkable musical talent. Wren felt herself shrinking further into obscurity.

The dancing began and once more the room was bursting with merriment. Wren slumped into her former chair and settled in to wait for the night to end. She even kept her arms folded across her middle after Mrs. Amberton discreetly reminded her to "rest them." How could she uncross them? They kept her insides from falling out as she watched Mr. Robert Starly swoon over her sister and whisper in her ear. It was painful and humiliating.

Song after song rattled from the instruments. Staring at the floor, Wren watched the stockings and skirts meld together in a kinetic display of color. Suddenly a fine pair of shoes disrupted her view.

"Will you favor me with a dance, Miss Amberton?"

Wren looked up to behold a miracle. It was none other than her Mr. Starly, his hand held out. She looked about to make sure he wasn't talking to Eillie, but Eillie was already on the dance floor.

She nodded and with her heart climbing into her throat, placed her hand in his. Oh gracious! She couldn't even speak. Her tongue felt like lead in her mouth and her pulse was nearly choking her.

The music began, and she was relieved to hear it was a minuet. A stately dance in a rough country setting might have been laughable at any other time, but it was a boon tonight. She would not have to dance herself out of breath. This was her chance. Conversation!

Don't be a ninny, she scolded herself. *Find your voice. Let him hear you.* "I am drawing a crab," she blurted out as they stepped forward, inches apart.

He turned his head slightly. "Are you? That is…unique."

"Yes, this species of crab is very unique. We have nothing like it in all of Langley."

"Hm."

A Pretty Game

They turned to move down the line on opposite sides. Her mind scrambled to think of something better. Something more intriguing. The weather? No, overdone. Cross-stitching? If she wanted to bore him to death. Hats? She was too clever to discuss hats.

No sooner had they reunited at the base of the set than her mouth betrayed her once again. "There is a black fever epidemic on the far continent, and many are dying."

"Oh?" he said uncomfortably. "Well, I shall stay away from that part of the world then."

"Yes, that's a good idea. You don't want your toes...to...rot." *What?* What was she saying? Oh! She should never have left her seat. Turning him down would have been less mortifying than forcing her scattered thoughts on him. Another turn down the line. How much longer until this was over?

He stepped forward, so close she could smell his woodsy shaving soap. He cleared his throat. "Your sister is an angel."

Wren's whole chest deflated. How fortunate she had the stuffing. "Yes. I know."

"Does she ever mention me?"

"No." Wren looked up to see clear disappointment in his handsome face. Finding a little bit of mercy, she added, "But she doesn't really talk about any other gentleman either."

A spark rekindled in his eyes. The music ended, and the couples politely applauded.

"Thank you. You have given me hope!"

Wren nodded and hurried away to find her mother. A headache was beginning to form behind her eyes, and she felt herself sweating through her satin.

She found Mrs. Amberton by the cake table, her hand on Eillie's arm. "Even though it's your birthday, love, you really should put down the cake."

No sooner had Eillie's plate touched the tablecloth than another besotted young man appeared at her elbow requesting a dance. Mrs. Amberton glowed as she watched her be whisked away.

"What a delightful evening," she sighed. "Wouldn't you agree, Wren? Just look—why what is the matter, dearest? You have no color. Are you ill?"

"Maybe." *Or maybe it's just this horrid dress.* "I really am not feeling well, Mum. I'd like to go home."

"Home? But it is only the third hour." Mrs. Amberton looked anxiously around the room. "No, we can't go. You—oh! Giddy—I mean Lord Garwick. Lord Garwick hasn't even come yet. He is expected, you know. His mother said he is just waiting for a great friend of his to arrive. The boy has been away so long. Don't you—"

"Please! Mum. I'd rather go."

"Well, we can't just run out."

"I know. I mean for you to stay. Eillie and Papa and you. Stay. The walk isn't far. I'll be fine."

"Well," Mrs. Amberton glanced around with a *tsk*, "all right. If you're sure you can't stay."

Wren assured her mother she could not. She retrieved her shawl, bid a surprised Lyn good evening, then bolted out into the night.

The open air was a welcome reprieve from the stuffy dance hall. Music and laughter haunted her a good distance down the road before the evening grew still of everything but the natural sounds of the world. The crickets were gone to sleep, but a nearby stream still babbled somewhere under the cover of trees and an owl occasionally interrupted the water's thoughts.

Wren picked up a handful of pebbles and absently dropped a few one by one. It didn't feel unreasonable to want to be noticed. To have people laugh at your jokes no matter how silly or ask you to dance regardless of how you moved. It didn't feel unreasonable to wish to be in Eillie's shoes for just one night.

Wren flung the remaining pebbles into the woods.

CHAPTER FOUR
Thief

Dear Lyn,

We are all in an uproar! This morning it was discovered that Eillie has only five good bonnets. Only FIVE, Lyn! What would happen to her creamy skin if she were to lose one in the wind, a couple to fire, and the last two to robbers on the highway?! It is unthinkable. I shall cry bitter tears tonight just thinking about it.

Your outraged friend,
Wren

Several days passed uneventfully from the night of the ball, other than Wren's second visit to little Ebdor Cottage. Mrs. Adley had beamed when Wren entered the home as if she had seen her hundreds of times. "Oh, it's you!" she had said as Wren placed her hand in the trembling one.

Wren had also been excited to learn that Mr. Adley was a *scientist*. A biologist to be exact. And he was very delighted to learn that Wren had tried to make herself acquainted with the living worlds surrounding them, worlds that often went unnoticed by their fellow human beings. He showed her specimens in bottles (ticks, water flies, partially developed birds) and stiffly dried lizards and snakes, most from out of the country. He had an entire parlor devoted to his studies that he allowed Wren to enter and ask as many questions as she liked.

While they puttered about the scientific room, Mrs. Adley made faces at the dead creatures and absently organized stacks of papers and books that Mr. Adley then had to search for to show Wren. "Where did that paper go, sweet one? I had it here a moment ago, and your tricky little hands have taken it up." His wife would then break into tears, and he would pat her hand and assure her he would find whatever it was that had gone missing.

As Wren again made the trek to Ebdor Cottage, she worked hard to direct her thoughts. Her blood still churned whenever she remembered the way Starly had danced with Eillie, so she constantly kept her mind busy with other things. Like mollusks. No one could be sad while thinking of mollusks. But all snails and squid were forgotten when she arrived at the cottage to find Mrs. Adley out in the yard, pacing back and forth with flowers crushed in one hand.

"Mrs. Adley! Are you all right?"

The woman looked up and startled as if Wren were a bear, then rushed forward. "Where were you? I was lost. Where were you!"

"I'm sorry, ma'am. I've just come from home. Where is your husband?"

"I haven't got a husband. But they're coming. Any moment!"

"Who's coming? Where is Mr. Adley?"

"Gone. He's gone, and they're coming!"

Wren looked around. She called out for Mr. Adley several times but heard no response.

"I'm sure Mr. Adley is here somewhere," she finally said, hoping she was not mistaken. She took Mrs. Adley gently by the arm and led her inside.

Everything appeared to be in perfect order within the home, aside from the front door being swung wide open. She could see signs of Mr. Adley having been there at least that morning, with smoldering coals in the fireplace and fresh, half-eaten toast atop an open book of ink splotched scribbles.

Wren removed her outdoor-wear and dropped everything onto the settee. "Do you remember where Mr. Adley went?"

"Of course I do," Mrs. Adley said with irritation. "Where *were* you? I was so frightened."

"I'm sorry. Really sorry. I didn't know you would be alone. So…where is he then?"

"Where is who?"

Wren scratched below her ear and looked the room over again. "I guess he'll be back eventually," she said, more to herself. "Should we get tea?"

Mrs. Adley muttered something inaudible and shook her head, slowly easing onto a dainty chair set before the hearth.

Wren rocked on her heels and scrunched her lips to the side. The little cottage was not as comfortable without Mr. Adley. She knew she was welcome in the sitting room, but Mr. Adley might not approve of her wandering about his house just yet. The kitchen and tea were better left unfound.

But there had to be something for the two of them to do. Wren was about to suggest a game of checkers when suddenly Mrs. Adley shot up and burst into her fretful tears. Wren remained still hoping the woman would sit back down, but instead she hurried out of the room.

"Um, nope. Just come back in here and sit, ma'am. Uh, Mrs. Adley?" Wren caught hold of a frail arm.

"No!" Mrs. Adley shouted, shaking off Wren's hand. "I want to...I need...lost. Where is it?"

Wren followed her down the hall where Mrs. Adley pulled at the door blocked by the little table. Wren watched her work her hands around the table, as if she knew it shouldn't be there but couldn't figure out how to move it. After several attempts, she successfully pushed it out of the way, a vase wobbling atop it, and again tugged at the knob.

"You have to turn it," Wren said.

Mrs. Adley muttered some more and covered her face with one hand. "I can just—we can find the thing. Then..."

"The thing?"

Mrs. Adley looked at her intently. "Yes, you know. If we find it."

Hoping it was the right thing to do, Wren reached out and tried the knob. Locked.

"I'm sorry, Mrs. Adley. I can't open it. It's locked." She gently took the woman by the arm again. "Let's go sit down."

"Stop!" Mrs. Adley said. "Don't. I just want to fix..." Her sentence faded into mutterings.

Wren decided not to pull at her again and looked around for something to distract her with. "Oh, what pretty flowers," she said, pointing to the full vase. "We should move them to the sitting room so you can enjoy them there."

Wren picked up the vase and heard a little metallic clang. A key gleamed on the table. She glanced at the brass knob. It looked like a fit. She knew it would be wrong. She knew she should leave it and take her friend and the flowers back to the sitting room. But before she considered any ramifications, the key was in the lock, the knob turning in her hand.

Mrs. Adley immediately pushed past Wren and disappeared into the dark. Seconds later, heavy drapes were pulled back and sunlight burst through the windowpanes, revealing a bright room completely lined with white painted shelves.

The library. But it was not a typical one. The shelves supported not only books but also odd glass pieces and vessels, bowls, and bottles. Hundreds of bottles. Bottles of dried leaves, stems, berries, powders, liquids. Each one tagged with white paper and clearly labeled in a pretty hand, many of the words unfamiliar to Wren. Papers were pinned to the walls displaying lists and drawings, and an assortment of coils of metals lined a sideboard. In the center of the room was a tall, mahogany desk supporting one large pot with several smaller vessels, a scale, and candles.

Mrs. Adley bustled about, happily collecting bottles in her arm and arranging them on the work surface. She dug through drawers and pulled out various tools.

Wren studied her new friend. Never had Mrs. Adley been more animated. So alive. Surely this must be a room meant for her own particular use. Or had been at one time. Slowly Wren stepped up to the desk and turned several pages of a large notebook that had been carelessly left open. What looked like recipes filled the pages with notes scrawled at the bottom. Wren read through one.

> *4 potentilla seeds, fermented*
> *1 g sun bleached poppy seeds*
> *1 g iron flecks*
> *3 g dogwood bark, crushed*
> *5 g powdered horesham, soaked in floirian solution*
> *50 mg pure fladimum*

A Pretty Game

150 mL chicken blood
100 mL spring water

Cooked first five ingredients to 200 degrees C exactly, under pressure using the Borris method. Added fladium. Results: Clear for several minutes. Was able to recall breakfast. A horrendous headache.

"You're a witch!" Wren shrieked.

Mrs. Adley's hands paused a moment, then carried on fumbling with the bottles and vessels. Wren almost made herself leave the room, but curiosity clamped her feet like thick mud. She thumbed through the book some more.

Heart Strength. Cure for Insomnia. Window Cleaner.

Many of the pages had strange symbols or were crossed with a thick, red X.

Beard Thickener. Spider Repellent. Stomach Biome Build. Beauty: Have to the Have Not.

Wren stopped. The latter begged for a closer look. It was one of the pages with a red X, but all the words could easily be made out.

"Have to the have not," she said aloud. "What does this mean, Mrs. Adley?"

The woman looked at the page. "Sour milk to sugar. The thing with what it wants. I have it. Or he does. Just a thing…"

Her chatter went on long after Wren stopped attending. Sour milk to sugar. Have to the have not. If anyone was a have not, Wren was. She had no grace, no style, and no beauty. Could it be possible? A recipe to turn her sour looks into something sweet.

"Does the red X mean it doesn't work?"

Mrs. Adley laughed. "Work, work, work. Busy like a beaver."

Wren scratched her ear and began scouring the semi-alphabetized shelves for the ingredients listed.

Crushed rose petals, in red.

Florlock needle extract—Clow Method.

Each one was placed on the table as it was found.

Dried alyssum buds.

Snapdragon root treated with haderium.

Gamnesium.

Gel of sheep's eye (here she gagged).

First drops of rainwater, blessed.

Powdered gold. (This bottle was very small and took some minutes to find.)

When everything but the 'hair from the have' was on the table, Wren stared at the bottles. What if this was all she needed to solve her troubles? What if these little bottles would give her beauty like Eillie naturally possessed? She could catch the eye of Starly, perhaps. Then he would look at her as she really was—intelligent and fun. She was those things, right? All she lacked was the face. And grace and style. But those could be learned. Beauty could not be.

She hurried from the room and returned with the lidded basket she had brought with her.

"Mrs. Adley," she whispered. "Might I borrow these bottles? I promise to return them, though a little emptier than they are now. And this burner and pot? And measuring glass?"

Mrs. Adley shook her head and mumbled a few things before she smiled at Wren. Good enough. Wren loaded the bottles into her basket, then reached for a pencil to copy down the formula.

"Bup, bup, bup!"

Wren whirled around to see Mr. Adley coming at her. He took her by the shoulders and gave her a shake.

"Do not speak a word of this room, understand, Miss Wren? Not a word." He released her and dragged a hand over his face. "I should not have left. I shouldn't have done it."

Wren gripped her basket. Had he seen her loading the bottles? "I- I didn't mean—she was out in the yard and so upset. I—"

"She was out? Oh, gracious. She knows she is supposed to stay inside. What were you doing outside, Mrs. Adley?" He reeled back at Wren before his wife reacted. "But what can *you* be thinking coming in here? Have you no manners? Have you no thoughts in your head?"

"I didn't mean to find the key. I didn't mean any harm, honest! She just wanted so badly to come in."

His face softened and his shoulders deflated, returning him to his regular stature. "I see. Yes, of course she did." He looked at his wife scratching a clean pen across some paper. A sadness filled his eyes. "And why shouldn't she? Her life's work is in here."

"Life's work?" Wren asked. "So she *is* a witch."

He clamped a dirty hand over her mouth and swooped his face close to hers. "Don't speak that word in this house. If she hears you…fits. It will be fits." He dropped his hand.

"But the bottles. And the pots. If she's not a wiii—person who makes spells and potions, what is all this?"

He put his hands on his hips and stared affectionately at his wife as she fumbled with lids. "Mrs. Adley is an *alchemist.*"

"An alchemist?"

"Yes. Oh, you are so young, Miss Wren. I'm afraid one your age should not have to keep secrets like this. We'll have to mix up that one—uh—drink. Then it will be as if none of this ever happened—"

"You mean I'll forget? Oh, no, I don't need to forget," she said hastily. "I can keep secrets. Really I can. Hardly anyone talks to me anyway. I promise I won't tell a soul." She looked at him pleadingly, and he sighed and turned away in submission. Wren grinned. "So, what is the difference between an alchemist and a you know what?"

He whirled back around. "My dear, we are people of science. Not imaginary magic. Concepts and concrete thinking are what we do. I chose to study life, and Mrs. Adley chose the science of perfection."

"Perfection."

"Yes, yes. The natural world holds all the secrets to purifying and perfecting imperfect things. You know, lead to gold. Frailty to strength. Mortality to immortality. Mrs. Adley believed it's all here."

"Oh." Wren looked around the room.

"Not here here. Here below the heavens, I mean. One just has to find the right formulas and correct methods." He strode over to his wife and looked over her thin shoulder. "She was close, I think. She was close. Mind like a crocodile's jaws, this one. Nothing ever escaped once it went in."

"What happened?"

"I don't know," he said quietly. "Well, the human body is not made to last forever, Miss Wren. In its current, unrefined state, see. Death comes when the heart fails. Or when disease overpowers its organs. But sometimes the mind wears out before the rest of it. Don't know why. And I don't know why it had to be hers." His voice cracked, and he cleared his throat. "But we are going to keep searching, aren't we, my dear love? We are going to find it. See here, I've brought you back some hogswollop and chapwick roots. But we'll work on this later."

Mrs. Adley stopped "writing" and stared at the blank desk before her. A single tear slipped down her cheek before a laugh filled her throat. Emotions seemed to swiftly shift inside her, like a swooping flock of starlings.

"Now listen," Mr. Adley said in a low voice as he led Wren to the far corner of the room. "Listen my young friend. There for a while she dabbled in what some might call—" he cupped his hand to the side of his face and mouthed the word *witchcraft,* "—creating formulas that didn't really have a noble purpose. See, in her pursuit of the worthy, she discovered little combinations that had effects. Elixirs that made one's voice an octave lower or gels that dissolve even the toughest grime from your cookstove.

"Once we had a cat that whinnied like a horse for two years. Try hiding that from your neighbors. And she found a few with negative effects, too. Severe stomach pain or one that turned her entire eye blood red for a few days." He waved his hand in the air. "You know all sorts of results. But when she began to forget things—little things like where she put her gloves or my birthday or even just the time of day. When she began to forget, she quickened her work. Returned to the higher cause."

"Perfection."

He shook his fist vigorously. "Yes! Perfection. Perfection of the body. Of the mind. Insusceptibility to disease. Of any kind. Not a cold or influenza ever to be plagued by. Imagine a perfect heart beating in your chest and a mind that could access everything it ever learned." His excitement rose as he carried on. "A mind with a higher way of thinking that would leave all the petty things of our civilization behind. Imagine it, my dear girl! And my sweet love was going to find it! She was going to cure her own ailment." His voice cracked again, and he backed himself into a chair. But it progressed too quickly. The brainrot did. It moved too quickly.

"I thought the country air would help clear her mind. But almost as soon as we arrived, she could no longer organize herself. Couldn't collect what she needed or compare and contrast to make changes to a formula. It wasn't long before she couldn't even read or write correctly. It seems to me the Divine Governor knew she was getting close and did not want His secrets to yet be given to man. So her mind was taken."

There was no bitterness in his voice. Only grief. Mrs. Adley broke into a fine strain of sobs and threw down her pen in frustration. Her husband hopped to her side.

"Come, sweet love. Let's get some tea."

Wren stood frozen in the strange room. The soft watercolors of plants on the wall. The rows of bottles containing both the beautiful and the repulsive. And the burners and the pots and the mixing jars. She could see now it was a scientific room, not one of evil.

Suddenly she recalled her basket. And all of the Have to the Have Not bottles. She glanced down at the little notebook, still open to the red X formula. She bit her lip.

Then Starly appeared in her mind's eye. *"Your sister is an angel,"* he said before leaning into Eillie's flawless face.

Steps down the hall warned Wren Mr. Adley was returning. In the split second before he appeared, she tore the page from the book and stuffed it into her basket.

"Are you going to join us, Miss Wren?" he said at the door. "Really I think I would prefer you didn't linger in her room."

"Yes, of course. I'm sorry, I just—I admire her watercolors so much." Guilt flooded her conscience, but she coughed to rid herself of it. "Actually, I need to be going. My mum…is looking for me, I'm sure."

A Pretty Game

He locked the door behind them, and Wren hurried to escape. She made it to the stoop when he called, "What about those things?"

Wren gripped her basket. "What things?"

He pointed to the settee. "Isn't that your bonnet and things?"

"Oh!" Wren forced a laugh. "Yes, those things. In here, yes." She went into the sitting room and scooped up her belongings. Mrs. Adley sat with her hands wringing in her lap. She looked more upset than she had before they went into the room. "Goodbye, Mrs. Adley. I'll be back in a couple days."

The woman shook her head. "Sour milk to sugar. For gold. We shouldn't do it, you know. Daffodils. And eggs under the chickens for winter…"

Wren bid Mr. Adley goodbye and hurried out the door before her conscience could completely strangle her. Like a mouse fleeing a cat, Wren scurried home as fast as her legs would carry her. To her relief, the further she went from the cottage, the lighter she felt as her mind rationalized its way into tranquility. It wasn't fair for some to naturally have an abundance and others to have not a speck. Like those who inherited the wealth of a kingdom having done nothing but exit the womb. It was the same with beauty. And she had gotten none of her share. So it was only right to try for a piece, wasn't it?

Of course it was. Something great had led her to meet the Adleys. Destiny, even! She was meant to find the formula that would bring her all the happiness she had dreamed of. She had nearly rounded the tall front hedge of her home when voices carried to her ears.

"Well, I am sorry to have missed her."

Gideon. Did he have his friend with him?

"Thank you for the tea, Mrs. Amberton. You are most kind."

Without any real clear idea what she was doing, Wren tucked herself and her basket into the hedge, sticks poking into her side and tangling her hair. Gravel crunched under the weight of a horse, and Gideon appeared on the same black thoroughbred. He was without his friend. Wren suddenly regretted hiding.

"She hides in the hedge!" came a high shout.

Gideon stopped and looked about until his eyes settled in the beech tree opposite the road. Wren didn't have to look to know who was there.

"Thus I seen her dive into the green," Charley carried on. "Like a pig dives into swill. From whom dost the strange maiden hide?"

Wren watched Gideon's eyes scan the hedge until they rested on her walking boots. Slowly, she pulled herself free from the clinging branches and stood, brushing fragments from her skirts. Gideon stared for a moment, a scowl mixed with amusement on his face.

Wren waved a hand toward the hedge. "I was just—"

"Looking for spiders?" he finished for her.

"No, I—actually I was worried you had your friend with you, and I just didn't want…to be seen."

He nodded and pulled a gold watch from his pocket. The gesture made him seem oddly old for his eighteen years, and she wondered what had happened to the squire boy who threw dirt clods at her.

"I am expected back. My friend was delayed in coming and is just arriving today. He might already be there, so I better go. You weren't at the ball last week."

"No. Well, yes, but I left. I won a great deal at the tables, and several gentlemen threatened to throw me out, so I made my escape before they could get their ruddy hands on me."

He nearly smiled. "Eillie appeared to enjoy herself."

"Yep."

"Good. It's a shame when a girl's first ball is unpleasant."

"Yep." Wren had firsthand experience and wondered if Gideon really knew anything about that sort of thing.

He turned his horse again and nodded curtly before riding away. If Luke could see his friend now, he might not recognize him. She suddenly ached for her brother's arm, to have him walk her to the door and tell her about his travels. He was—

"Dost the strange maiden long for the stony beau of which she can never partake?"

With a jolt, Wren remembered the traitor in the crow's nest.

"She seemeth to wilt in the dirt, death imminent. Her tortured face remembereth-ed only by the worms that began their luncheon of her skin. No. What would be a better word for skin?"

"Flesh," she said, taking long strides to the tree.

"Yeah, flesh. Worms that eateth her fleshy flesh, and the birds that—hey! Stop that."

Wren jumped again, reaching for his ankle. He climbed higher.

"You'll make me fall!"

"Yes, and then the worms can eat your fleshy flesh. I ought to whip you for calling me out!"

He laughed. "What were you hiding for anyway? Who was that?"

Charley was too young to remember the days Gideon frequented their house, which was a shame because those days would have given the boy much material for his plays. "Just Luke's old friend. Lord Garwick, to you."

"Oh, is that all?" Charley said without any deference to title. "I thought he was a pirate who just hadn't lost his eye yet."

"Come on, get down before the birds peck out *your* eyes."

"Hey, I was going to say that about you. Don't steal my lines!"

When they entered the house, Wren was immediately summoned by Mrs. Amberton to the sitting room, which in the last four days had become something of a conservatory for Eillie's flowers.

"Giddy—rather, Lord Garwick—has just left us," Mrs. Amberton said, indicating Eillie. "I cannot believe the change. I almost don't know him. He complimented the tea and noticed my stitches in that framed piece there. And of course he was so attentive to Eillie. I'm not surprised he'd call so soon with so many gentlemen lined up to dance with her. You know he just finished his preliminary term at Starton. He's to complete four years at university. Four whole years! Imagine. And closer to home now, he—Wren! Your hair is full of sticks. Really dearest. And your dress. What must people think, you appearing I don't—go clean yourself up before dinner. I shouldn't be surprised if we have another caller for Eillie before the evening is over, with five already today. I really…"

Wren left the room without waiting for her mother's sentence to finish. It really was uncertain how long it would take to pick sticks out of her hair, and she would stay out of sight until she finished. Maybe Plucky would need to bring dinner to her room.

That night, when the house was still and darkness occupied every room, Wren crept to Eillie's door. Silently, she turned the knob and entered the room before crawling across the floor to her sister's bed.

Few people knew this about Wren—only those who played with her as a child—but she was an expert creeper. At an early age she had realized she was nearly invisible and decided to make the most of it. She practiced sneaking about the property—keeping close to the walls and memorizing the boards that squeaked, climbing into thickly

A Pretty Game

boughed trees or tucking into crevices. She may or may not have even sneaked into her parents' room to snip buttons off her father's shirts or spied on Plucky from the kitchen hamper to watch her make eyes at the delivery man.

She peeked her head over the side of the bed and found her sister sleeping peacefully with her hands tucked under one side of her matchless face and her curls cascading across her fluffy, white pillow.

Eillie did kind of look like an angel, Wren conceded.

She ducked back down and scooted to the other side of the bed. With a pair of sewing sheers she had stowed away, Wren snipped a curly lock from her sister's head. She grimaced at the blunt remains that stuck out like cut wheat stubble. Perhaps she hadn't needed to take an entire lock. But it was nothing a bonnet wouldn't cover.

Still undetected, Wren slipped from the room and back to her own. She tied the hair with a ribbon and tucked the lock into her basket. Intrigue complete, she flopped onto her bed and snuggled under her quilt.

"Now we can both be angels." The whispered words hung cold and heavy above her, and she almost heard another voice reminding her she was no angel. She tucked the blankets tighter around her shoulders and decided she would no longer speak her hopes out loud. They were much prettier unspoken.

When she discovered she couldn't sleep—her mind all astir with the glorious possibilities awaiting her—Wren threw on her boots and Luke's old great coat, covered her head in a black shawl, and climbed out her window, a basket hanging on her arm. A trellis was conveniently mounted below her window, as her parents never once worried about late-night suitors calling, and she easily reached the dewy ground.

She made for the dark barn but halted midway. The birds would surely stir, summoning Mr. Forner, who slept in an apartment on the ground floor. She couldn't go there. So into the woods she went.

The woods behind the property were completely known to her and felt no different than walking through her house, despite the fog that rolled over the earth and the spindly trees that shivered and rustled in the dark. Within minutes, she reached her destination—a small pond with a sharp bank and lots of willows around to hide her crime—er, alchemy.

She knelt down and emptied her basket, then cleared a spot for the burner and the scale she had borrowed from the kitchen. Cook wouldn't mind. She measured almost everything in her palms and rarely used the scale. Wren filled the burner font with kerosene and lit the canvas wick to have light and in preparation for her potion—or elixir rather. (Not a witch.)

Carefully, she crushed and scooped and measured, gagging again when she came to the sheep eye gel. Then she snipped the lock of hair into tiny pieces over the pot. When the whole concoction was simmering over the burner, she sat back a moment to admire her work. It was rather fun to calculate and pour, weigh and mix. She could see why Mrs. Adley would choose it for her work.

To be sure she had done it correctly, Wren carefully reread the note paper. Yes, she had followed each step precisely. It wouldn't be long now. She simply needed to wait until the liquid reduced by a third, then add the gamnesium powder and the concoction would be complete. A note indicated the mixture should be nice and thick. Wren guessed it would look something like milk pudding.

When it globbed and burped in heavy bubbles, she turned off the burner, stirred in the gamnesium (jumping when it *whoofed* with a quick, purple flame), and waited somewhat impatiently for it to cool enough to drink. Or eat, actually. It *was* thick, and she wondered if it was too thick.

The steam finally dissipated, and she lifted the bowl to her face. It smelled very…earthy. And not at all like anything one should eat. But it was for the greater good—or at least her own greater good—and she was prepared to do it. She tipped the bowl and threw back her head to allow the bitter, hairy pudding to go down her throat. She gagged but choked it down manfully.

And then she waited once more. She touched her face hoping to feel the change but could perceive nothing. However, her stomach was doing something. It twisted and began to burn as the pudding reached the pit.

Then the world around her began to swirl. Wanting only her bed, she stood. But the earth heaved up and down under her feet. She stumbled back then pitched forward several steps, slipped on the muddy bank, and disappeared into the dark pond waters.

And suddenly Wren found herself feeling like a garment soiled with grape jelly, being scrubbed against the devil's washboard by a woman whose eleven children's very lives depended on the stain coming out. Tossed and swirling, lurching and flailing. No way of knowing which way was up. She was certain she would drown. Rot! Her vanity had sent her to a cold, watery death.

Then, miraculously, her feet touched sand, and she pushed it away. A gasping breath above water, she shrugged out of her heavy coat and thrashed her way to a patch of willows, using them to drag herself forward and out of the water.

Exhaustion replaced the burning panic, and she slumped into a spinning, dreamless sleep.

CHAPTER FIVE
Riding with Idiots

When Wren opened her eyes, the sun was bright and her nightgown nearly dry. She sat up with a start and glanced around. No one in sight. Surely no one would have come across her sprawled on the ground and left her without ensuring she was not dead. No one had seen her.

Shivering with cold, she gathered all her things into the basket, fished her soggy coat from the pond, and rushed home. It was tricky to sneak around in daylight, grown as she was now, and with Mr. Forner already at work in the garden, she decided it was best to pretend she had gone out early to sketch and casually walk right in.

However, as she crossed the threshold, excitement overtook her and she scrambled for the nearest mirror, found in the sitting room.

"Am I pretty?" she said, crossing the room.

Mrs. Amberton looked up from her delicate stitches and smiled benignly. "Not conventionally, dear."

Wren looked at her reflection and drew a sharp breath.

The same. Her reflection was exactly the same as when she had left. Except her hair looked like it really had been run through the wash.

A Pretty Game

Wren dropped her basket, the bottles clinking together, and sank into a chair. Eillie briefly looked up from her book, a look of pity in her pretty smile.

How could this be? Wren wondered. *Not a single change.*

A short, mirthless laugh escaped her throat. She had choked down Eillie's hair for no purpose at all, other than a frightful experience in the pond. And no one even asked where she had been or why she was in a filthy nightgown. Why had she thought she would need an excuse for coming home after breakfast a muddy mess?

"Wren, are you going to stay home today?" Eillie asked. "I am sure one of my admirers will be along soon. Perhaps Lord Garwick will come with his friend. Or Starly and Toone. Mum says I may not go out with gentlemen alone. If you are not busy, you could come with us. It would be fun."

"Sorry, I can't," Wren said, feeling dejected and annoyed. "It's Thursday—Lyn will expect me, and I have other visits to make."

"Oh pish," Mrs. Amberton chimed in. "Going about doing good is worthy—such a great reflection on your upbringing. But Wren, dearest, you mustn't neglect your own family. Think of your sister. She has more need of you than anybody else. Three times she has been asked to go out. Three times! And she has had to refuse every time with no one here to go with her."

"You could go."

Mrs. Amberton scoffed. "Me? Don't be a ninny. Bouncing about in a barouche with a bunch of young people." She was quiet for a moment, her lips pinched as she actually considered the idea. She shook her head. "Why, it's absurd. None of the gentlemen would even attempt to woo your sister with *me* sitting there. No, you must be available to go with her should an offer come."

Wren did not have to wait long. Not an hour later, Starly was at the door with Toone and a fine barouche, and soon the four young people were bouncing down the road just as silly as Mrs. Amberton said they would.

Before she left, Wren scratched out a note to Lyn and sent PJ to find his breakfast.

Lynny-Wynny,

Going on a picnic with the beauty and her beaus. I may not make it to see you today. My deepest apologies. If you do not hear from me by tomorrow, please send a search party. I don't expect anything dramatic to happen. Only fear they will forget me and leave me to live on wild strawberries and honey.

On second thought, don't send the search party. Know that I live in sticky peace.

Your dearest friend from the wild,
Wren

Wren, of course, was seated in the back with Toone, while Eillie and Starly took the bench. Toone, seeming to have left his happy manners at home, hardly said more than a hello to Wren and sat all-a-gog, leaning forward on his seat in order to hear what was being said above them. By his tense jaw muscles and curled fists, it was clear to Wren she was not the companion he desired.

As the foursome drove through town heading toward the hills behind Garwick, Wren glared at the admiring faces they passed on the street. No one noticed of course, as they were all staring at Eillie and Starly, but Wren displayed her feelings nonetheless.

The bitter pudding was still fresh in her mind, and she did not even

A Pretty Game

try to subdue her dark mood.

"If you could just drop me off at the Pak home, I would be much obliged."

"Drop you off?" Eillie said. "And have Mum descend upon me for being out alone. No, Wren. Please stay with me."

"True," Mr. Starly agreed. "Your mother would have me basted and swanked, and never allow you to ride with me again. I'm afraid you are out of clovers, Miss Amberton. You must stay back there with Toone." He snickered, and Eillie shared in the joke.

Toone leaned back with his arms crossed and muttered a curse or two under his breath.

"I would say the same of my confinement with you if I were not a lady," Wren said airily, adjusting her skirts. She had a new resolve to practice having some poise like Lyn if she were never to have any beauty. He didn't seem to hear her in any case.

The barouche passed the road that would take them to Lyn's and continued out of town toward the rolling emerald hills of Garwick, destined for the upper hills. Low stone walls tracked the countryside, dividing fields and pasture. Most of the lower land had long ago been cleared, but every now and then, trees gathered in gossiping groups or a lone maple stood defiantly on the edge of a field.

In the distance, Wren spotted two gentlemen riding over a hill, away from the road. She sat up straighter to better see them, quite certain she knew the black horse and therefore the rider. The other must be Gideon's school friend she decided, before slumping back into the seat.

Don't see us, don't see us.

As if her thoughts had bounced right across the field, one rider turned his head, signaled to his companion, and both horses began making their way swiftly toward the road. As she feared, Gideon and friend galloped up and phased into a trot beside the rolling carriage.

"Good morning, Garwick!" Starly said brightly. "Come to admire my white ewe?"

White ewe? Wren wondered. *Did he just refer to Eillie as a woolly mammal?*

"Morning, Starly," Gideon replied. "Wren, Miss Eillie. Toone. May I introduce my friend, Mr. Reynard Casner."

Wren flickered her gaze to the young man and felt her breath catch. Young Mr. Casner was uncommonly handsome, with a strong jaw, clear blue eyes, and dark, curling hair. He made Starly look like a goat. She followed his stare to Eillie and felt all hope of being noticed crumble like stale cake.

"Where are you off to?" Gideon asked, looking to Wren.

"To the hills for a *private* picnic." Evidently Starly had also noted Mr. Casner staring at the prize seated beside him.

"Go on then," Gideon said. He looked at Wren stoically, aside from a twinkle in his eye. "Just do me the favor of keeping your eyes on Wren. I've known her to wander away and get lost."

Wren's cheeks warmed, recalling the time Gideon and Luke had been forced to search for her an entire afternoon. That was before she knew the woods and had chased an imaginary fairy until she didn't recognize a single tree. Frightened, she had curled up beside a tangle of exposed roots and cried herself to sleep. She would never forget the wash of relief when she woke to find two heroes leaning over her.

The memory evaporated when Casner glanced at her and flashed a bewildering smile. Her blush deepened.

Starly slapped the reins and straightened. "I'm sure we can handle her," he replied, as if she were an old cow.

A Pretty Game

The two horses wheeled around, and the vehicle moved on. Wren angled herself to watch the riders turn their steeds in the opposite direction and disappear into a copse of trees. A large piece of her was glad to be driving away but a tiny piece of her wished her friend and new acquaintance had been invited to follow.

The picnic proved more painful than the drive, with Toone and Starly taking turns falling over themselves to get Eillie a piece of cake or to fill her cup or to brush the dirt from her shoes. It was a true spectacle that Wren was too bitter to laugh at.

Soon she ventured a good distance away from the blanket, finding a comfortable seat on a decomposing log, and occupied herself with sketching the hills or the dragonflies and butterflies that occasionally landed on the wildflowers at her feet. She had to admit, she loved the view of the valley and was a teeny bit grateful to have been dragged to this spot.

Tremdor was in the center of it all, with its neatly packed brick homes and shops. Spiraling from there were the fields and houses and woods she had known from birth. She had left this valley but once, to see Luke off in the port city of Binton some seventy miles away. It had not been a pleasant trip. Aside from parting with her brother, the bumpy, nauseating coach ride and the dirty, bustling city relieved her of any desire to leave her country town ever again.

Off to the right, haloed with ancient maples and alders, was Garwick Manor—stately and proud. She smiled to herself recalling the time her family had been invited to a neighborhood party at the giant house and had their first taste of iced cream. Her ten-year-old self had been certain that one bowl would keep her happy forever. But forever had only lasted until she met the master of the house a half hour later.

The former Viscount of Garwick had been a harsh and reclusive man. No one had ever seen him smile. Childish rumors said it was because his teeth were green and his tongue had been cut out. But Mrs. Brayford told Gideon it was because the old man had long ago lost his young wife and child in an accident, and his pain was so great, he never wanted to lose a love again. Wren always thought the latter reason romantic, but never could quite fathom any woman loving the crotchety man.

Despite all this, he had taken a liking to Mrs. Brayford and her son. When the old viscount passed and his will was read, everything had been left to Gideon. Wren still remembered the shock in the community. It was talked of for weeks.

Wren's reminiscing and thinking was spoiled as the bursts of competing laughter from the gentlemen grew obnoxiously loud. Eillie was a vision, her legs tucked prettily to the side and her face delicately shadowed beneath her bonnet. Wren pretended not to notice Eillie's frequent glances in her direction. No doubt she was thanking the heavens she was not an unfortunate little hermit creature like her sister.

Finally, after such a length of time that Wren was certain she had developed age spots, the barouche began its crawl back to the Amberton home, everyone situated just as they had come.

Immediately after stepping through the door, Wren was summoned to her parents' bedroom to rub a newly obtained cream on Mrs. Amberton's rashy feet.

"Dr. Maphis says he has had very good success with this," Mrs. Amberton said from her bed. "I hope so because I cannot lose any more skin. I'll soon have exposed bone, I'm sure. There now. Thank you, dearest. Cover your Mum up, I feel I must rest. Did Eillie have a good time?"

A Pretty Game

"I think so. She giggled so much I thought maybe her throat was suffering spasms."

Mrs. Amberton smiled. "Never mind your sour report. I shall save hearing the details from Eillie herself at dinner."

When she was safely within the walls of her own room, Wren determined she wouldn't be heartbroken to never hear Toone laugh again nor see Starly's absurd winking. What a joke those two boys were, making complete cakes of themselves. Charley dressed up in a cravat and top hat spouting his own poetry would have made a more convincing gentleman.

She plopped down at her desk and began organizing her papers. When she reached for a stack on the far left side, her foot bumped the basket on the floor, and she was reminded of her contraband from the Adleys. She considered taking a walk—a good discussion on the eating habits of beetles sounded like just the thing. But almost as quickly as the idea formed, she decided against it. She would return their things tomorrow.

Or maybe in a couple weeks.

She continued her sorting for a few minutes before glancing up at the mirror hidden behind the green cloth. She wondered. What had Gideon's friend—Mr. Reynard Casner—seen this morning? Not that she cared. Much. She pulled off the cloth and looked at the reflection. It was all too painfully familiar. Except…

She turned her head. Except her hair didn't seem so mousy. It maybe even had a bit of gloss to it. She glanced at the window thinking it was just a trick of sunlight, but the sun was too far gone in the sky to shine straight through her window.

Hm. She threw the cloth over the mirror again and doodled until dinner. After the meal, when Mr. Amberton had disappeared into his study with a bowl of hazelnuts and Charley had been sent to bed, Mrs. Amberton, Eillie, and Wren stitched, practiced the piano, and read about barnacles, respectively.

During dinner Mrs. Amberton had probed Eillie for a complete history of their excursion, repeating all the details for Mr. Amberton as if he couldn't hear Eillie himself, and was now content to whisper to herself the compliments given to her daughter as she worked. "Just like me," she would quietly chime. Wren delved deep into her book and worked with some difficulty to block every sound from her ears. Eillie's tinkling on the piano keys was beginning to make her twitch.

"Wren!"

She looked up, startled her mother would so suddenly shout.

"Gracious, chit. Have you ears? I asked what you have done with your hair."

Wren reached up and touched her head. "N-nothing. Why? What's the matter with it?"

"It just looks…different. I wondered if maybe you had applied something—a cream or oil—to it. Whatever you have done, it is quite a pretty shade."

Wren shook her head and shrugged. Eillie looked up from the piano. Her pretty lips turned down a bit before she refocused on her music.

When Wren was under her covers for the night, she twisted a strand of hair around a finger. Perhaps the gagging and dizziness had been worth the trouble. If all the pudding gave her was a fine head of hair, that would be something. Maybe tomorrow she would have Lyn teach her how to style it better, if it was to be her best feature.

CHAPTER SIX
The Dawning of Change

The next morning, Wren awakened to a dreary sky outside her window. There surely would be no picnicking and barouche dragging today, thank the heavens. She rolled herself out of bed and put on her warm, gray frock and walking boots. The weather would keep young men from taking pretty ladies for rides, but it would not dampen her desire for venturing out of doors.

At the breakfast table, Wren felt her mother staring at her in short, critical bursts. She couldn't tell if Mrs. Amberton was trying to be discreet or if she was just easily distracted. Wren glanced at her father, who was hiding behind his wall of paper, then at Eillie, who was focused on her egg cup with both hands in her lap. She didn't look well. Perhaps the long day out in the sun had taken a toll on her delicate, perfect body.

When the eggs were cold, Mrs. Amberton broke the silence.

"Wren. You should go riding with young men more often. It has done something for your complexion. Perhaps it has boosted your confidence to receive their attentions?"

Wren snorted. "It is impossible for me to receive any attentions,

Mum, when Eillie is in the room. I assure you, no young man has given me a confidence boost."

Eillie looked up out of her trance and scowled at Wren a brief moment before pouring herself another cup of tea. Wren did not know how she could stand to drink it without any cream or sugar. Or without a scone or two. She broke into her third hot biscuit and slathered it in butter.

"Well, a mother just notices things in her children. Whatever has brought a change in you must be a handsome thing."

Wren sighed. "Perhaps it's my study of barnacles. One particular drawing did make me blush."

"Wren!" Mr. Amberton said. "Enough."

"Yes, sir," she said meekly, flashing her attention to her plate. No one ever appreciated her jokes.

After a morning spent on her knees helping in the dreaded family garden and rubbing more ointment on her mother's feet, Wren was finally released to spend her time as she wished. She gathered her drawing things and retreated to the barn loft. She was delighted to find a newly spun web in one of the open windows. When she laid in just the right spot, the nearly invisible lines became clear, and she was able to copy it almost exactly. *How can strange, skin-crawly creatures create such works of art?* she wondered looking from her paper to the web and back again.

She dropped her pen and sat up. Her fingers seemed different, her unremarkable knuckles exchanged for round, fine joints. She turned her hands over several times. And her normally dry skin was as smooth as cream. "That's odd."

Maybe her mother's rash cream really did work miracles.

Or maybe…

She touched her fingers to her face but felt no difference in her features. She pulled her hair free from its untidy bun and examined a strand. It might be different.

With hope bounding in her chest, she scrambled down from the loft and made for the hedge gate, calling to Plucky—who was beating a rug with reckless abandon—that she was going to see the Paks. The woman grunted and carried on. It wasn't Thursday, but that didn't really matter. She was welcome any day at Lyn's and had missed her regular visit yesterday anyway.

When Wren knocked on the door, she was glad to be informed by the housekeeper that Lyn was home. If anyone would notice real changes in her, it would be her dear friend.

Wren dashed up the stairs and burst through Lyn's bedroom door. Like Wren, Lyn was an artist. Unlike Wren, Lyn was an artist who created from her mind. Her walls were pinned with fantastical creatures—dragons with burning eyes, rabbits with horns, women with feathery wings. Her landscapes were places known only to her and her trees were always wild and colorful.

Lyn turned from the desk and started. "Wren! You…"

"Am I much changed?"

"Yeah," her friend barely whispered. "If you weren't wearing that outdated dress, I might not have known you."

"What do you mean?" Wren said, striding to Lyn's full-length mirror.

"I mean that style. It's terrible."

"No, I mean what do you mean you might not have known me?"

"Oh, I mean your face. It's the same. But *different.*"

Wren studied her reflection. She *was* changed. Her complexion was smoother, her cheeks rosy, and her hair glossy. Her features were the same. But *blended*. She turned to study the rest of herself. Perhaps even her figure was improved, though she couldn't be sure, the lines hiding under her heavy, shapeless frock.

"What have you done?" Lyn asked. "You haven't sold your soul, have you?"

Wren laughed merrily. "So what if I have." She turned to admire herself a little more, feeling as if she were looking at a stranger.

"Wren, you didn't."

"No, of course not. I'm afraid my poor little soul wouldn't be worth the trouble. I—" she stopped short. She had not yet confessed to anyone what she had done. That she was a thief. And perhaps a witch. To say the words out loud would make her crime very real. And Mr. Adley was quite clear he did not want his wife's work known. "That is, my cousin—the one I've been visiting—had some things. I borrowed some things to help me, and they've worked. Eee! It worked!"

Lyn whispered words foreign to Wren and added, "Wren, your face. Your body. It is not something to mess with. Not this much."

"I know." Wren left the mirror and hurried to kneel at Lyn's feet. "But Lyn. Can't you see? I'm still me. Still awkward, strange me. I'm just improved. Better. On the outside."

Lyn shook her head.

Wren breathed an exasperated cry. "It's easy for you. Look at you. You've been lovely and charming since birth. People can't help but notice you."

"People notice you."

Wren snorted and stood up. "Yeah, if I'm standing in the way of the cake table. Or if they want to get to Eillie. You can't understand."

Lyn silently turned back to her brushes.

A Pretty Game

"This will make me happy, Lyn! Can't you be happy for me?"

"Of course I can," Lyn said. "You're my best friend. When you're happy, I'm happy. But...I wish you would have left yourself alone."

"Why, so I don't outshine you?" Wren winced. "I didn't mean that. You know how my mouth works faster than my brain."

"Sometimes I think your mouth is the only thing that works," Lyn replied curtly.

"Ouch."

The corners of Lyn's lips lifted a little. "But remember when we were thirteen and, despite my discouragement, you hung yourself upside down by your feet hoping it would make you taller?"

"Yeah, I had a headache for days."

Lyn nodded. "So don't get stuck upside down trying to fix what isn't broken."

"You're very philosophical today, aren't you?"

"I'm just trying to make my point!"

Wren clapped her hands. "Fine. Every pudding-headed girl needs a friend, and that's why I have you. No more fighting. This might be the new me, so you'll just have to love my pretty little face, too."

"I will. As long as the pretty face doesn't mask my friend."

"It won't! I promise. You'll see."

Lyn nodded an acceptance and moved to sit beside Wren on her bed. "I wish you would have stayed at the ball last week. It wasn't nearly as fun knowing you weren't there."

"If I had your spirit and Eillie's looks I might have. I'm afraid I must accept I am doomed to a life of running out of parties and lurking in the shadows. A witless clump who can charm with neither smiles nor conversation."

"What do you mean? You never run out of things to say."

"You'll not argue me calling myself a clump? Never mind. But having endless things to say and saying worthwhile things are not the same. I actually told Mr. Starly that he didn't want his toes to rot off."

Lyn snorted. "Oh, Wren, you didn't."

"I did. But I shouldn't make jokes. Have you heard how your grandmother is? Is she still safe?"

Lyn's paternal grandmother still lived in her home country of Karia, on the far continent. Her family had come to Langley for the sake of her homesick mother when Lyn was nine years old, but her grandmother had insisted on staying put, choosing instead to live with extended family.

Lyn shrugged. "Last we heard. I don't think the plague will reach so far north. But it's just awful—the stories we've read. I cannot imagine it."

Wren nodded gravely. She had read about the disease and the sufferers in one of her father's papers. She took up her friend's hand and gave it a squeeze. "Don't worry. It's winding down I believe."

The rest of the afternoon was spent just how it ought to be at the Pak's—looking over Lyn's latest creations and taking Karian tea with her parents. Wren often wished her father were more like Mr. Pak. He was attentive and kind to his daughter, praising her art and playing traditional Karian games with her. He had even taught Wren to play a few, and it was always such fun.

When she returned home for dinner, Wren found her family already gathered around the table and in a very subdued mood. Eillie was not feeling well and refused to come out of her room. Mrs. Amberton, of course, was fretting over her most beloved daughter, and Mr. Amberton grumbled about his soup getting cold while waiting for Plucky to come down and bring him a spoon.

A Pretty Game

Halfway through the meal, Mrs. Amberton set down her fork. "I can hardly eat knowing Eillie is up there suffering. She won't even let me enter the room. Imagine, not letting her own mother in. I can't hear her coughing, and Plucky assures me she has no fever, so what could be ailing her? I just can't imagine it. Oh! I hope it is not that plague."

"Maybe she's just worn out from yesterday, Mum. She did an awful lot of flirting."

"Shush, child. *Flirting.*" Mrs. Amberton said the word with disgust, but a smile tugged at her lips as though she really was pleased. She picked up her fork and put a heap of mashed squash into her mouth. "That's probably it. I'm sure she is just tired, what with all the callers lately. She is only fifteen."

Wren nodded. Sometimes she forgot how young her sister really was, she had worn the mask of womanhood for such a long time. Wren felt a little poke of agitation that she didn't feel any sisterly concern for the one younger than her and tried to eke out a little feeling of compassion.

"Are the Paks well, Wren? Plucky said you went to visit them this afternoon."

Wren was surprised her mother had noticed her absence. "Yes, Mum. They were."

"Such a nice family. Mr. Pak is always so complimentary. I've always thought he had an eye for beauty, which is why it is such a mystery to me how he settled on his wife. Georgette was never as tall or handsome as I was when we were children. I suppose…well, I just think some things a mystery." She looked up and smiled before lowering her fork away from her mouth. "Why, Wren, dearest. Your coloring is rather pretty this evening."

"Thank you, Mum," Wren said softly, gratified her mother had noticed.

The rest of the evening passed quietly, with Charley having been sent to bed early as a precaution in case Eillie was indeed coming down with something and Mr. Amberton not to be seen again once he entered his study. Wren tucked herself into her worn chair by the fire with a novel while Mrs. Amberton worked on her stitching, occasionally muttering concern for Eillie and absently reminiscing about her own courting days. When the clock chimed nine, the two retired to their rooms.

Wren changed into her nightgown, admired her hair one more time, and climbed into bed. A wonderful feeling of hope tickled in her chest. How long would these changes last? She hoped long enough for her to persuade someone into an engagement, at least. She would not be displeased for Mr. Casner to take notice of her.

She stretched under her covers and began the workings of a delightful little dream in which she was riding a horse over the hills with Mr. Casner seated behind her, his arms securely wrapped around her.

In the dim light of dawn, Wren was jolted from her imaginative sleep by a dreadful scream. Momentarily paralyzed and disoriented, she pieced together the furnishings of her own room, then scrambled out of bed and dashed out into the hall. At the same moment, her father burst through his door, and Charley yelled, "I didn't do it!" from inside the upper nursery.

The sound of sobs flowed from under Eillie's door.

"Eillie!" Mr. Amberton bellowed, jiggling the knob. "What is it, precious child? Let us in!"

"No, no, no! No one shall ever see me again," came the dramatic reply.

A Pretty Game

Mrs. Amberton came rushing from behind, her cap disheveled and her shawl wrapped askew. "Eillie! What do you mean? Have you tied yourself to a beau? Oh, do not elope dearest. Think what it will do to me!"

"If she were eloping, Mum, why would she scream like that? Wouldn't she want to go quietly?"

"Oh hush, Wren! I don't know the reasons for what a girl does! Girls in love are never rational."

"Open this door." Mr. Amberton pounded his fist into the door several times. "I demand you open it!"

"No, Papa, never. No one must come in. You'll have to slip food under the door if I am to survive!"

By this time Plucky was huffing and puffing up the stairs. "What is it?" she gasped. "What is happening?"

"Get the keys, woman!" Mr. Amberton ordered.

Plucky nodded with a faint roll of her eyes, then blundered back down the stairs. Eillie continued to wail from her room, and Charley once again insisted he had done nothing wrong.

"Hush, Charley!" Mrs. Amberton called up the stairs. "No one is speaking to you!"

Presently, Plucky returned, red-faced and coughing, the door was unlocked, and the lot burst into the room. At first Wren thought it was empty. *Had* her sister eloped?

But then she spied the form of a body under the tangled blankets on the bed. Mr. Amberton strode to the bedside and ripped the pink satin covers from the mattress.

Eillie rolled to her side and tucked into a ball. "Please go away."

Mrs. Amberton threw herself at her daughter and furiously stroked her back. "What is the matter, my dove? Are you still ill? Heartsick?"

"I don't know," Eillie mumbled into her featherbed. "I don't know what's wrong with me."

As Wren observed the scene from a distance, she noted a change in her sister's hair. The perfect curls were matted and stringy. And even the light from their father's lamp failed to induce it to shine. Maybe she was more ill than anyone supposed. After some soothing talk from her mum and a few barks from her father, Eillie rolled back and sat up. Mrs. Amberton gasped.

Eillie's hair was not the only change. Her skin was sallow and splotchy (from crying, Wren was sure) and her lips unremarkable. The rest of her features were the same, but somehow different. Wren felt a hollowness form in her stomach. Eillie's features didn't *blend*.

"I knew it! I'm doomed!" Eillie choked.

"No, no love. You are just unwell. Rest is what you need. And broth." Mrs. Amberton looked her daughter over again and swallowed. "Lots of broth. Plucky, fetch some now."

"I'll go for the doctor," Mr. Amberton said exiting the room, shaking his head.

Eillie looked up at Wren and a dark shadow crossed her pale face. The two sisters locked eyes, and for a moment, Wren imagined Eillie coming at her with her claws. But instead, she sank back into her pillow and tucked into a ball. Mrs. Amberton replaced the pink blanket and ushered Wren out.

"Back into your room. We don't know what she's got. Charley! You stay up there. Don't come down until you're told!"

"Alas, a prisoner, my sheets now shackles! Shall I be beheaded or drawn and quartered? No matter—I vow to haunt in pieces!"

Back in her room, Wren stood by the door. She lifted her hands to examine the smooth skin and delicately tapered, strong nails. They looked like Eillie's. Swallowing hard, she went to the mirror, removed the cloth, and startled. The face that stared back was even lovelier than it had been the day before—perfect in every feature, every look. Her hair hung about her shoulders in soft, pretty waves.

I have stolen Eillie's face. And skin. And hair!

No, impossible.

Her hair was still darker than Eillie's, her eyes brown instead of blue, and her skin not as pink. She still looked like herself. Only altered. She had not stolen any part of her sister's body. She gasped when she realized the truth.

She had stolen Eillie's beauty!

CHAPTER SEVEN
Poker Face

My dearest Lyn,

Greetings from the Amberton Prison of Vanity. We are all in fine health except our golden-haired inmate who still locks herself away. It's too bad we don't have a tower because I think putting her up there would be a nice touch, don't you? It seems like ages since I last saw your face. I hope you have not forgotten mine.

Remember me!
Wren

Days passed with no more change in either sister. The good doctor came and went several times, unable to account for the unhealthy change in the younger girl. Adjustments to her diet were ordered, bitter tonics were taken, sunlight was barred from her room, and fever was constantly watched for.

But she remained the same. When word spread of Miss Eillie's illness, her room filled to the crown molding with flowers and gifts from neighbors and callers alike. Sheets of music were sent hoping to cheer her. Baskets of fruit were delivered that Charley ate entirely on his own. Secret love notes were smuggled through by way of Cook, but always they went mournfully into the fire unread.

A Pretty Game

This continued until finally Mr. Amberton had had enough. "She isn't ill!" he shouted one day. "We must stop fussing and try to carry on as normal. We are all going to church tomorrow and that's final!"

"But Eillie refuses to leave the yard!" Mrs. Amberton cried. "She hardly even leaves her room."

"If she doesn't want to be seen, she must go with a bag over her head!"

"But Mr. Amberton, dear. What will people think?"

"Curse what they think! I'll not have a daughter who quivers and hides because she is ugly. Wren never locked herself away, simpering and whining like a ninny. I've paid more bills to the doctor than I care for. I am done and will coddle her no more!"

Even though she resented his use of such a word to describe her—and Eillie for that matter—Wren overheard this conversation with a tiny twinge of satisfaction. It was true. *She* had never hidden herself away. *She* had never whined and cried (to anyone but herself and Lyn, anyway) about her looks.

And so, the next morning the Amberton family walked into town in the calm, early autumn air. Eillie had asked for a bag as her father had suggested, but Mrs. Amberton would not have it. "A bag can be no better than your face, dearest," she had comforted.

On the way, Eillie's sweet sniffles tried unsuccessfully to strike Wren's heart. Eillie had never felt guilty for being pretty, she told herself. Why should she?

Because Eillie came by it honestly, replied an inner voice.

Wren shrugged her shoulders under her shawl and hurried her steps to the church. The sooner this was over, the better. When the family entered the chapel and took their usual pew (center section, second bench from the front, as Mrs. Amberton wanted no one to worry whether or not they were there but also did not want to appear so pious as to sit on the very first row), a murmur whisked through the congregation. Wren ducked her head a little as she caught some of the whispers.

"Oh, she looks dreadful. What has happened?"

"So sickly! Can you believe it?"

"What could they be thinking bringing her?"

"The elder, though. What's her name? She has much improved."

The whispers continued, and Wren felt Eillie's shoulders begin to shake next to hers. A swell of indignation threatened to burst from her throat. What right had they to say such things within earshot of Eillie? It was one thing for Wren to ridicule her sister, but it was quite another for the town gossips to do so. With a scathing look over her shoulder, she reached over and took Eillie's clammy hand.

The shudders subsided, and presently the young bachelor minister stood to deliver his sermon. He began boldly, but when his gaze swept down the second pew and settled on Wren, his words stumbled and he had to clear his throat. His face reddened, and he shifted his gaze to the back of the room before continuing.

After the closing hymnal, the townsfolk filed out of the building and onto the churchyard. A small social of sorts always took place when the weather allowed, and this fine day was no exception.

"Papa," Eillie whispered. "Will you please take me home? I don't want to stay."

He nodded, and Eillie slipped her arm into his. Mrs. Amberton loudly reassured her peaked daughter she would join them after she visited with a few friends. Wren watched them go, with Charley following after, swinging and jabbing a stick like a sword, until someone called her name. Gideon came toward her with Mr. Casner at his side.

A Pretty Game

"Wren? Ah, it is you. I thought so but for a moment I wasn't sure." He lowered his voice. "Rumors said your sister had fallen ill, but I had no idea they were true. I'm sorry, I would have sent something or someone or done…something."

"I don't know what you could have done," Wren said with a shrug. "She isn't ill. Or, that is, the doctor doesn't know what has caused the change."

"Well, I'm sorry for it."

"As am I," Casner cut in. "But you, Miss Amberton, are looking well today, thankfully untouched by illness. If I might be bold, you are a rare rose among thistles."

Wren felt her cheeks warm. "Uh, thank you."

She nervously glanced about herself and found, among others, the minister, Starly, and Toone staring at her from across the yard. She adjusted her shawl, astonished to feel deeply self-conscious with such a pretty face.

"My mother is hosting a dinner party this Friday," Gideon said quietly. "Would you like to attend?"

"Me?"

Gideon's mouth tweaked into a half-smile, and he looked at her expectantly.

"Ha, obviously. Me." She lifted one shoulder. "Yeah—yes. Yes."

"Excellent!" Casner whooped above his friend's 'Good.' "I've been begging Garwick to fill his house with pretty girls for me, and he has failed miserably. But now I find myself in err, as we need not a houseful. We need only one."

Wren looked at him blankly before his meaning dawned on her. A silly sort of chortle escaped her throat, and she flicked her nails across a clammy palm.

"Well, I'm going home now," she said abruptly.

"I'll have a proper invitation sent tomorrow."

"Thank you, Gideon."

He nodded and Casner took up her hand and kissed it. "Until Friday."

Wren thought she had blushed before, but this one went clear to her toes. Reynard Casner was by far the most handsome young man she had ever seen. And so proper.

She hesitated, then turned, and hesitated again. "I'm going to go now," she informed them and hurried away as dignified as she could manage.

Just outside the church gate, another voice called out, "Hey you! I mean—Miss Amberton. Miss Amberton!"

Wren turned to see Starly running across the yard, Toone on his heels.

"Miss Amberton," he said, panting when he reached her. "You are not...going to walk home...alone, are you?"

"Well, I was. Papa has gone, and Mum will be a while yet. It's not far, you know." She took several steps before he gently touched her arm.

"Yes, but a young lady should never walk about alone. Allow me to escort you."

Wren looked down the road. "All right. If you really want to."

"Oh, I must blow the gab, I've been aching to." He held out his arm, and she took it.

Toone huffed from behind. "Me, too! I'll walk you home, too." And he slipped an arm through her other one.

And so, for the first time in her life, Wren was escorted home. Not by one young man, but two! It was at this moment that Wren felt the inkling that silly attentions from a boy might not be quite so silly if they are directed at oneself.

Starly quickly offered his condolences for Eillie's illness and Toone seconded. Then they talked on and on about the time they had spent with the height of society in Ferriton. Wren found the conversation interesting at first, piecing together what Starly said between the nearly foreign language of slang. But she soon returned to her opinion she would never be happy in a place so crowded with strangers and bricks. Starly laughed when she asked if there were any barns in the city to hide in. She took that as a no. Yes, it was certain—Tremdor Valley was still the best place in the world.

When the young men had safely delivered Wren to the hedge gate, they took their leave. Before she went through the door, shouts of surprise drew her attention back to the road, and she laughed as Charley pelted the boys with dried, husk-covered walnuts shouting, "Halt putrid scum! You'll never stealeth the crown!" She was not a little disappointed her suitors ran off without putting up a fight.

In her room, she removed her bonnet and gloves and sat down at her desk. Sunday afternoons were her favorite time for drawing. With even the small three-person staff taking it easy, the day was always peaceful. As she drew lines forming a tropical hagglefish, she felt a small something chewing at her conscience. Especially near her foot. She glanced down at the basket she had been ignoring for days.

In the chaos of Eillie's illness, her mother had forbidden anyone but Mr. Forner to leave the property. Now that the family had been out in their new state, Wren was sure she would be allowed to begin her visits again. She picked at a nick in her desk and tried in vain to forget what she had remembered.

Finally, she sighed and picked up the basket. Dinner was still a few hours away. And she couldn't avoid the Adleys forever.

On the other hand, it wasn't likely they would go anywhere. She could put them off for a few more days. No sense in spoiling the couple's Sunday afternoon.

The basket was returned to the floor.

The Adley's pleasant Sunday may not have been spoiled, but the Ambertons were not so fortunate. Eillie remained in her room the rest of the day, and even their father's thunderings could not draw her out. When Wren peeked in at her, she was hunched over her vanity sobbing. The whole house felt miserable with her.

After an early supper, Mr. Amberton stomped to his study, while Wren and Mrs. Amberton went to the sitting room. Charley bounced obnoxiously about until Wren offered to read him a book. He clambered onto the settee with her and listened intently to a story about fawns and elves. On a normal day, Mrs. Amberton would have muttered about Wren filling his head with nonsense, but tonight she didn't discourage the book. She seemed as heavy as Eillie, only without the sobs.

Just as they reached the part where the elves invaded the fawns' cave, Mr. Amberton burst into the room, giving them all a start.

"I can't have it anymore. My mind is made up. She is going away!"

"Going away? Who can you mean, Mr. Amberton?"

"Eillie, of course. I can't have her blubbering about anymore. She is going to stay with my sister in Forthshire."

"With Fanny? In Forthshire? But that's a three-day trip. No, you cannot mean it."

"But I do. I have already written her a letter and will post it tomorrow. Eillie will leave on Tuesday. The letter should still beat her there by a day or two."

"But...but what if she won't take her?"

"Fanny lives alone. Has a comfortable income. She will have her. I cannot keep her in this house anymore, whimpering and whining. I'll go mad. She is no good to me now, and it will be better for all of us if she is gone."

"But—"

"Enough! I said she is going and that's the end of it." He left the room.

Charley began to cry. "Luke is gone, and now Eillie will be, too?"

Wren gave him a little squeeze. "They will both come back. It isn't forever."

He squirmed out of her arms and ran out of the room. Mrs. Amberton leaned back in her chair, defeated. Wren glanced at her mum's somber face, then snapped her book closed. There was nothing to be done.

Two days later, Eillie and Mr. Amberton left for Rembly, the next town over where the stagecoach stopped. The poor girl cried as her little trunk was loaded into the family carriage and sobbed when she hugged her mother, Plucky, and little Charley goodbye. When she squeezed Wren in a parting embrace, Wren's heart squeezed, too. Deep down inside (way, way deep), she couldn't deny her large role in the current situation. So, she kindly told Eillie she would write.

"I've left my favorite dresses for you, Wren," Eillie said.

"Oh. No. You should take them. Really."

Eillie shook her head. "I won't need them." With her lank hair braided and twisted into a delicate bun, she took her seat and waved pitifully as they drove away.

"Such a tragic thing that has happened to my poor girl." Mrs. Amberton gulped. "And so sudden she is taken from me!"

Wren nodded. What could she say? *Yes, that hair pudding was some stuff.*

"Well, that's enough of that," her mother said abruptly, wiping Charley's eyes and then her own. "Wren, I'll need you to help in the kitchen today after you empty my latrine. Your papa has given Cook a few days off."

"But I want to go visiting today. I haven't been in over a week!"

"Well, you'll just have to get your duties done here before you get to your noble ones. I would have someone else do it. I worry the work might affect your complexion. But as you can see there is no one else here."

The rest of the morning was spent helping Plucky prepare for dinner. Trying to chop the vegetables, Wren sliced her finger with the knife twice before Plucky sentenced her to dishes instead.

"Wash them in cold. That will slow your bleeding."

"Why has Father given Cook the day off?" Wren asked, emptying a cold kettle of water into the washtub. "Don't you have enough to do?"

"Never mind that, Miss Wren. Just do your work."

She didn't like not getting an answer, but Wren could tell Plucky was in no mood for questions. After a quick lunch in the kitchen, Wren grabbed her basket and two loaves of bread, and dashed out the door. Her first stop was to the Clamp family. With half a loaf and her basket hidden in a bush, Wren rapped on the door, then walked into the rickety house with the other loaf and a half held high over her head. Six little Clamps leaped and giggled trying to reach their prize.

"Now, who has been a help to Mum?"

A Pretty Game

"Me! Me! Me!"

One little girl wrapped herself around Wren's legs, nearly tripping her. "Pretty lady, me! Me!"

"Kitty, it's me. Wren."

The little girl scrunched her nose in disbelief and a few of the boys stepped back. "No you ain't."

"Yes, I am, and I will give this to your mum to divide up." She handed the loaves to Mrs. Clamp. Disappointed groans came, but Wren relieved them by pulling a sickle stick from her pocket. "But we can divide this up right now."

She broke it into seven pieces (one for herself, of course), and sent the children outside with their treats.

Mrs. Clamp swung the baby on her hip to one side and hugged Wren. "You look different somehow. I didn't know you at first."

Wren shrugged. "I've done my hair differently."

"No, that's not it."

After a pause, Wren cleared her throat. "Well, anyway, it's just me. What do we need to get done today?"

An hour whisked by, and when Wren left the home, the floors had been swept and the three rooms tidied. Mrs. Clamp had refused to let her do any laundry or wash the doors, insisting she didn't want Wren to dry out her pretty hands.

As she took up her hidden articles, thoughts of the impending visit sprang up in her mind, and she slowly—very slowly—began her trek to the Adleys. Certainly, the bottles and the burner had to be returned. But still Wren didn't know what she was going to say—how she would explain. The crime had been easy to commit in the moment but was difficult to justify now that she had time to think.

And Wren was a thinker.

She tried not to be. Especially when it was uncomfortable. All morning her thinking had made her think of Eillie. Her sad, dull smile. Her heavy, nearly lifeless movements. She was so delicate. Eillie wasn't made of the stuff Wren was. And now Wren's thinking was making her think about admitting aloud what she had done.

An idea suddenly came into her mind. Maybe there was a remedy for Eillie in Mrs. Adley's book. Her trudging turned to striding. Yes, surely there was something that could be done that would allow Eillie to have at least something back. Her hair or glow or *something*.

It really wasn't that Wren was heartless. Once she had used Plucky's most valuable treasure—a gravy boat that had belonged to her mother—as a vessel for a baby rabbit she had found. Plucky had screamed so loudly when Wren showed her, that she dropped the gravy boat. The bunny survived the fall, but the gravy boat did not. Even though she blamed Plucky (who screams at baby bunnies?), Wren had felt guilty about that for days.

But this was different. She had suffered years of slinking in Eillie's shadow. Resentment ran deep, and Wren was not the sort to forgive quickly, conscious hurt or not.

When she arrived at the cottage, Mr. Adley greeted her as he had the very first visit. As a stranger. When she informed him who she was, he stared a moment, then mumbled, "Yes, of course it is. Beg your pardon, I see you now. Come in, Miss Wren."

With the three of them seated in the sitting room, Mr. Adley cracked at his pile of peanuts while he rattled on and on about the snakes and insect larvae he had found since their last visit. Mrs. Adley quietly moved the shells about the table, shaking her head as if casting off idea after idea of what to do with the pile. Wren nodded and tried to register his words, but her conscience would not be still.

A Pretty Game

"Mr. Adley, I've done something terrible!" she suddenly blurted out. The man looked up in surprise. Wren swallowed and tried to push more words from her throat, but they wouldn't come. She couldn't fully look up at either of them, so she looked at them through her lashes.

Mr. Adley straightened and looked from Wren to his wife then back again. "Well, go on, dear girl. What could you have possibly done to cause such an outburst? A levelheaded thing like you."

"No, don't. I don't deserve any praise."

"Why, of course you do. You have been coming to us—the only soul who does besides the grocer's boy. We look forward to your visits, don't we love?"

Mrs. Adley shook her head slightly and laughed nervously.

"Well, I'm quite certain you won't want me back once I've told you what I've done. I…" Oh! Why could she not just spit the words out? "I…have caused my sister to be sent away." She was surprised to feel a teeny bit of relief. But the whole of it was still lodged firmly in her throat.

"Sent away? But how could you have caused such a thing?"

"Well, I have taken…that is I made—I didn't really know it would—but I made…her cry."

"You made her cry?" Mr. Adley's face slipped into amusement. "Hardly seems reason to send a girl away."

Wren picked at the chair cushion. "Well, it's not, but it's hard to explain. I, um, took something that belonged to her, and she became terribly upset. And cried all the time—locking herself away in her room. And my father couldn't stand it, so he sent her to be with my aunt."

"Well, couldn't you have returned whatever it is you took?"

The basket was suddenly very heavy on Wren's lap. "Yes," she said slowly. "Well, I don't know for sure. You see...it's not really something I can just give back. Not entirely. I don't think."

"I see. You have taken her beau?"

Wren snorted. "No! Well, yes, I guess I have. But that wasn't what upset her first. And that I can't just hand back."

"Then you must find another way to make it right."

"Oh, I'm trying to. Kind of." Wren squeezed the basket handle with her hands. She couldn't be out with it. Not while the couple was sitting there across from her, smiling and looking so friendly. In an instant she concluded she would need time to explain herself. A way to tell the truth concisely. Like in a letter.

Yes, she would write them a letter and send the bottles and burner that way, with someone else. Plucky maybe. Or perhaps Mr. Forner. He would not speak a word of it to anyone. Then if Mr. Adley never wanted to see her again, he could write back and say so. That would be much less painful—receiving a letter she could burn right away rather than a tongue lashing she would never forget.

A weight lifted. "Well, I'm sure I'll figure out what to do. Thank you for your help."

"Certainly," Mr. Adley said, apparently amused. "I'm not sure what exactly I've done to warrant your thanks, but you look a good deal better than you did moments ago. Come my child, let's go have a look at my new specimens."

The following half-hour, Wren indulged in one more lecture on biology from Mr. Adley. She would miss their talks that would come to an end after the truth was revealed. Perhaps in time, he would forgive her and allow her back.

Mrs. Adley wandered into the study and puttered around just as usual. For the last five minutes or so, she sat beside Wren, holding her hand and squeezing it periodically. Wren was very sorry to have to let the frail hand go when she and her basket went out the door.

She had planned to go straight to her desk to write the wretched letter when she arrived home, but she found a spiderweb up in the barn she wanted to draw. Then Mr. Forner was pulling shriveled plants from the garden and looked as if he needed assistance. After she finished with that, she asked her mother if she needed more cream on her feet, and then after that she volunteered to dust the walls for Plucky, which took a considerable amount of time and made her dreadfully tired. After dinner, she had only enough energy to unstitch her mother's latest disaster. Tucked in bed that night, she solemnly promised herself to start the letter just as soon as dawn made an appearance.

But when the sun came up the next morning, the smell of breakfast was too tempting to allow any time for sitting at a desk, and the basket was tucked far, far under her bed.

For safe keeping, of course.

CHAPTER EIGHT
Something Amiss

When Wren walked into the dining room for breakfast Thursday morning, a large bouquet of pink roses sat on the table.

"It's from Mr. Casner!" Mrs. Amberton said significantly. "Here's the note."

She handed Wren a little card of thick, creamy paper. The front was printed with MR. REYNARD F. CASNER in gold and on the back, scrawled in a strong hand, were the words, *'Anxious to see you tomorrow.'*

"Mrs. Thorte said he is a near relation of the Duke of Mendshire, who, as you know, has never married!"

"Nor produced an heir," Mr. Amberton said quietly from behind his newspaper.

"I have no idea who—"

"Hush, Wren!" Mrs. Amberton dropped her hands onto the table. "I wasn't finished. And I will not have a daughter of mine proudly displaying her ignorance of noble society. At least pretend to know something. A nod is sufficient. Anyway, he's very handsome."

"The duke?"

"No, Mr. Casner. Really, Wren, keep up. He is fourth in line for the dukedom, but still there is a chance."

Wren pursed her lips, trying not to laugh. Dukedom.

"You must have made quite an impression on the young man, just like Eillie would have." Mrs. Amberton choked up a little as she scraped a knife over her toast. "I hope she makes it safely to your aunt's, our poor little girl."

"I'm sure she will, Mum."

"Never mind. I don't like to think about it. Sit down. There's a good girl. Oh! No, dearest. No scones. Ah, no ham either. I think you should stick to tea and an egg."

"Why?"

Her mother adjusted herself in her seat. "I just think that's what a girl should eat. There now, do as I say."

Three minutes later, Wren finished her breakfast and asked to be excused. As she readied herself to walk to Lyn's for her weekly Thursday visit—her stomach still rumbling with hunger—she thought of the stops she should make on the way. She hadn't been to see the widow Mrs. Harper and her sister Miss Nelly for some time. And old Mr. Barter would probably like some walnuts to husk for winter.

Perhaps it was a good thing to have such a small breakfast. Leaving this early, she should have time to stop at both houses.

Before she escaped out the door, her mother reminded her she needed to be home in time to help prepare supper. She also called something about a daughter of hers not walking alone, but Wren pretended not to hear. It had never mattered before whether she was accompanied or alone. Why should it now?

The walnut tree had been freely dropping its fruit for a week now, and Wren set to work filling a sack she had stolen from the kitchen.

"The strange maiden has become so fair," Charley called from the tree as she busied herself about the yard. "By witchcraft, to be sure! What blood hath she drank to transform into someone new?"

"Mermaid, obviously," she said without looking up.

"Mermaid," he whispered. "Of course." He slipped down a few branches. "Where did you get it?"

"From Luke. He sent me a vial on a pigeon."

"Luke hunts mermaids?!"

"Well, what did you think he was out there doing? Protecting Langley's seas?"

He nodded as if it all made sense now. A laugh almost escaped Wren's lips, but then her little brother's expression turned to sadness so suddenly she forgot all about it.

"What's wrong?"

He tossed a walnut husk to the ground. "Nothing." Wren gave him a look, and he sighed. "I just wish he would come home and tell me his stories. And I want Eillie, too. Nobody puts peppermint candies under my pillow anymore."

"Peppermint candies? Eillie did that?"

"Yeah, or she used to. Not after she got sick. I haven't had any for over a week. Do you think she'll come home soon?"

Wren rubbed a foot on her ankle. "I don't know, Charley. She might be gone for quite a while." She turned her attention back to her task and dropped a few more handfuls into her sack. "I have to go. But I'll be back later, all right?"

He nodded and climbed back up to his perch several branches higher.

So Eillie put candies under their brother's pillow. Wren had no idea Eillie had ever thought of Charley. She felt for a coin in her

A Pretty Game

pocket and determined she would buy a few candies for him.

She found Mr. Barter at home and was glad to hand over the bag of nuts. "I shall have Bitty set to husking them right away, thank you, Miss Amberton," said the nearly blind old man. Wren was pleased she had thought of him this morning. He would have been disappointed if she had failed to bring him this autumn offering.

Mrs. Harper was not found at home, but Miss Nelly was, and once Wren was able to convince her of her identity, the delicately featured, frizzy-haired woman welcomed Wren into their small parlor to visit.

"My sister is calling on Mrs. Brayford today. At *Garwick*," she added impressively. "Such thick friends they are. I stayed home as I am not sure what I would do in that large house. So grand. I'd get lost, I'm sure. You know Miss Lucy Brayford, don't you? Very gracious but so very fine. I get fizzles in my stomach next to her. But most of all I'd be nervous to walk on the floors. I'd have to take off my shoes, as they are not very fine and surely would damage the woods and carpets. Sister said I mustn't go if I was to take off my shoes. She would be mortified. And then I had to agree that walking around Garwick lost with stocking feet would be most obscene. So here I am, at home, as you see. But it's a good thing I stayed because I would have missed your visit, and I always enjoy your visits. How is your family getting on? You know, Sunday your sister looked quite unwell. Has she much improved?"

"My sister has gone to stay with our aunt in Forthshire. My father is hoping the air there will do her good."

"Oh yes, Forthshire. That is the best place to go if one is unwell. I wish my sister would take me again." Miss Nelly proceeded to explain her numerous ailments, and Wren ticked off the list in her head knowing the speech was almost finished when the woman got to the chronic numbness in her right little toe. After that, the conversation predictably moved to shoe styles that pinch one's feet and on to the dangers of walking too often.

"Sitting is safest. You really must be careful to not wear out your feet before you're twenty-five, Miss Amberton." She let out a high, sweet laugh. "Miss Amberton. I still cannot believe it is you. But it is such a sweet surprise to have you here in our home. Yes, Sister will be sorry to have missed you, but she was so pleased to be invited for a day at Garwick."

"I'm sure she was, Miss Nelly. Well, I better be going. Please tell Mrs. Harper that I stopped by."

"Oh, of course. I wouldn't want to keep you."

After twenty minutes more of Nelly soliloquies, Wren successfully extracted herself from the house. She had forgotten that visits with the sisters—or even one of the sisters—were never short. It was nearly lunchtime, and she had hoped to spend the bulk of her day with Lyn. The afternoon would have to do now.

The Pak's housekeeper opened the door for Wren and dutifully ushered her into the sitting room.

"Can't I just go up to her room?"

The woman flicked her eyes toward the hall then back again. "No miss. Mrs. Pak prefers visitors remain downstairs. I'll fetch Miss Pak directly."

The woman swished away before Wren could remind her she had been in the home hundreds of times and was allowed upstairs. But it was only a minute before she heard Lyn's light steps coming down the stairs. When she entered the room, she abruptly stopped.

"Wren? Why didn't you just come up?"

"I tried, but Ms. Poole wouldn't let me. Said I had to wait here."

A Pretty Game

Lyn laughed. "Come on. She told me there was a fine young lady to see me. She suggested you might be the younger Miss Brayford."

Wren returned the laugh and examined her plain dress. "Gideon's little sister? Didn't she know me?"

"I guess not. But you are so very changed," Lyn said, as she led her friend out of the formal room and up the stairs. When she closed the door, she turned quickly and pressed her back against it. "Wren, please tell me. What have you done?"

Wren shrugged. "Nothing. Can't a person change?"

"Yes, but you've done more than a little changing. And in a very short time. And your notes. Poor Eillie. Your father really sent her away then?"

"Yes, hopefully the sea air will make her feel better. She shouldn't have been so dramatic."

Lyn snorted. "That's a thing for you to say. How many times have I heard your drama? But Wren, I don't believe you. You have changed and so has Eillie. It's almost as if you've…" Her words trailed off without any sign of more coming.

"As if I've what?" Wren prompted slowly.

"It's stupid. But it's almost as if you've…switched. Something." She shook her head. "Really, what have you done?"

"Nothing! Stop asking me." Wren didn't like lying to her friend. It was something she had never done before. But if there was a time to lie, this felt like the right one. Lyn was the only one who had linked the two sisters' fates, and Wren wasn't going to be cast back down into the pit of shame—she had just crawled out. "I have just learned how to care for my skin and hair. Eillie is unwell. Going to Forthshire will help her improve." She rubbed her foot on her ankle. "Have you created anything new and exciting lately?"

Lyn considered her a moment longer—a hard, discerning look in her eyes. Then she relaxed and crossed the room. "I had a dream the other night. Of a creature, a small bird that turned into a dragon, of sorts. Look here."

Wren took the pages Lyn held out and shuffled through them. The first piece was a small bird with a round belly and blank eyes, done in black ink.

"I like how you've shaded the feathers."

The next was a watercolor swirl of purple, yellow, black, and blue, with spaces left white indicating sparkle and light. In the storm of color, Wren could make out feathers and blank eyes.

She flipped to the third page and gasped. The creature created at Lyn's fingertips was not really a dragon, but Wren could see why her friend would describe it as such. It was a winged beast, beautiful and bold in the same colors of the swirling magic. It was feathered, with large talons and a beak more like a hawk than the little bird in the first picture. The eyes were fierce, nearly left white with a pale blue washed sparingly over them.

"It's amazing, Lyn! How do you come up with such fantastical things?"

Lyn beamed in her modest way. "I told you, I dreamt it up. Most come that way. This one was quick, one that came just as I was waking up, so I didn't get to see what the great beast would do. You like it then?"

"I love it. I love everything you paint. But this is exceptional."

"Thanks. Now tell me, what little real-world creatures have you been studying lately?"

Wren pulled her book from the basket she had borrowed from Eillie's room and began showing off the crabs and barnacles. A lunch was brought up after a time, as the girls showed no inclination of leaving the room. Wren inhaled her portion, then savored the little sesame treats that had been put on the tray for dessert.

When Wren had received her invitation for the Friday dinner party from Mrs. Brayford, she was pleased to see it allowed for a guest. Of course Lyn was to fill that position, and they spent a good deal of time discussing their plan for attending the Garwick party and wondering what it would be like.

"Do you think most of the guests will be locals?" Lyn asked.

"It's hard to say. I know Mrs. Brayford has many friends. Friends from all over the country. I think she keeps very busy with visits and parties when she goes to Ferriton. That's what it sounds like from what Mum says anyway."

"I'm glad my papa does not like Ferriton. It sounds exhausting."

"But you do so well in gatherings. You love a good party."

"Yes. I like parties that are full of people I *know*. Meeting new people is tiresome. I guess I get that from my father."

"Or maybe it came about when you moved over here without knowing anyone?"

Lyn listed her head. "Maybe. It was awful living with my aunt those few years—so many people in and out. Oh! That reminds me. Mother has planned for us to go visit my aunt in the spring. In Preston, for two or three weeks, depending on how long Papa lasts. Just thinking about it makes my stomach turn. Will you come?"

"Of course! How could I resist a trip that makes you want to vomit? I can think of nothing that would please me more."

"Excellent," Lyn said with a grin. "If you knew my aunt, you might not be so willing. So I am glad you don't. It will be dreadful, but with you there, it will be tolerable."

"I do what I can to make life less dreadful for those I love." Poor crumpled Eillie flashed into her mind, making Wren's breath catch. It was good she had been sent away. Soon Wren wouldn't think of her so often.

The clock in Mr. Pak's study downstairs chimed three o'clock through the floor, and Wren got to her feet. "I had better go." Before she went out the door, Lyn tucked the newly created beast portrait into her basket.

"Since you like it so much. Take it home and have it framed."

Wren smiled. "It will be passed down to my children's children!"

When she arrived home, Wren went directly to her room. After taking off her bonnet, she pulled Lyn's painting out to study it once more. Such talent her friend possessed. But looking at the painting again, she felt a stirring inside. As if it spoke to her in some cryptic way. Art often does for those who truly appreciate it. Slowly, she pinned Lyn's painting to her wall, then sat down at her desk.

Looking at her new reflection once more, she wondered how far Eillie's journey had taken her today. A minute later, the green cloth was thrown over the mirror.

CHAPTER NINE

Beautying

Loveliest Lyn,

Did you awaken this morning prepared to dazzle the fancies? Of course you did. I hope you will spare some time to help make me presentable. I have a stunning idea for my hair, though I want it to be a surprise. I shall, however, grant you a clue. Think wild bird nest goddess. Do you by chance have a horde of sticks and feathers I may borrow? Unrelated to the surprise, of course.

Wren

Friday morning Wren returned to Ebdor Cottage, anxious to somehow make things right even though the Adleys had no idea she had committed a wrong. They shelled peanuts together and talked over Mr. Adley's collection of pinned butterflies. Mrs. Adley smiled the entire visit, laughing at peculiar times and nodding and commenting as if what she said was completely relevant to their discussion. Mr. Adley occasionally chided her for interrupting and tried unsuccessfully to get her to get their tea.

"Well, never mind the tea, love." He turned to Wren. "She is out of sorts today. One of these days she'll return to herself. My wife is the best of hostesses. You'll soon see. She has always done everything to make our visitors feel at home. You know, in our former home in Ferriton, we hosted a dinner party for Lord Borion—he's very well known in scientific circles—and Mrs. Adley organized the whole party herself, not a bit intimidated to host so many well-known names. Such a meal she planned—roasted goose, chestnut stuffing, asparagus. An excellent pudding for dessert. We had music and talk afterward, and it seemed to me no one would ever go home! She received many compliments for the evening and several cards afterward. Of course she hosted many evenings such as that one, but it has always stood out in my mind as her very best."

He smiled fondly at his wife, with a dreamlike gleam in his eye. "I can still see her chatting away, arguing her points with such eloquence, and graciously listening to those who made fools of themselves by disagreeing with her. Didn't you, love? You never needed me to come to your rescue. But she always wanted me beside her anyway." He was quiet for a time, unwilling to share any more of his thoughts and wiping his eyes a time or two. Finally, he picked up another tray. "Well, now. Here's a specimen—a rare beetle from Kandobera."

Wren felt much more at ease by the end of this visit and felt no more dread at attending to the couple again. On her way home before lunch, she stopped at the Clamp home. Mrs. Clamp seemed determined to keep Wren from doing anything strenuous, though Wren could see the woman was exhausted. She had caught a terrible sounding cough. After several failed attempts to do something more than hold the baby, she decided to take her leave. An unpleasant feeling in the bottom of her stomach accompanied her the entire way home. Why was Mrs. Clamp refusing her help so suddenly?

As the day progressed, new nerves collected in her stomach until she felt as if the wadded mass would burst. She had felt nervous before

A Pretty Game

the other large gatherings she had attended, but this time was different. Lyn's question of who would be at the party had grown into a monstrous concern in Wren's head. What if she fell? What if she dribbled her soup? What if someone noticed her slouching or crossing her arms? Or worst of all, what if she bored everyone with her facts?

Without Eillie to style her hair, Wren scampered over to the Paks' to make Lyn do it. Mrs. Amberton tried to persuade her Plucky's work would do, but Wren insisted. She was in such a state, she needed her friend with her as soon as possible.

"Well, don't forget your manners at Garwick," Mrs. Amberton had called after her. "And, mind, don't eat too much. Keep your portions small, dearest. Your figure, remember. And no cheese! You'll stink!"

The girls dressed and primped, laughed and praised one another. It wasn't long before Wren was dressed and completely at ease in one of Eillie's muslins she had left—a pretty, light green gown in the cut Wren liked most with just the right amount of embellishments on the sleeves. And Lyn was lovely in a maroon dress her father had ordered made specially for her.

They played a game of Takka with Mr. Pak while they waited for the Amberton family's barouche. When it finally arrived, Mr. Forner handed them in and away they went. The road twisted and weaved through the countryside, climbing its way to Garwick Manor, nestled in the center of its expansive park.

Even though she felt a great fondness for the land they rolled through, she almost wished it had not fallen to Gideon. The more Wren became aware of the workings of their world, the more she understood just what her friend had gotten himself into. He hadn't always been a painfully serious boy, but experience had made him different.

The Brayfords were an old family that had managed to maintain status but could not say the same about their wealth. By the time Gideon's father became squire of Brayford Hall, they were near ruin. And try as he might, the rigid squire had not been able to recover the family before his death. Gideon was twelve years old when the heavy responsibility of caring for his mother and two sisters, as well as the Brayford Estate, was placed on his shoulders. At fourteen, he ascended to Viscount of Garwick, a stroke of Providence that saved not only his family, but also Brayford farms on the east side of the county where Wren's family lived. He could have sold the entire property—relegating the tenants to a new, unknown master—but had chosen not to.

By nature, Gideon was a hard worker, and Wren had no doubt he took all of his collected roles seriously. She could barely manage her brushes and books. She could not fathom how Gideon managed so many acres and lives. And yet if there were such wealth for her own family to fall into, she felt sure she would take it—whatever the demands. Then Luke could leave the navy and come home.

The carriage arrived at the massive steps of Garwick. Another carriage pulling away just ahead of them glided silently as if on water, and Wren blushed at her own creaking wheels. Suddenly Starly was before them, his hand held out.

"Miss Amberton. Miss Pak. How delightful you are both here. I had no idea. You look smashing, Miss Amberton! Like a cake I wouldn't hesitate to gobble up."

Wren squirmed a little, glancing at Lyn who had to press her lips together to suppress her laughter. "Thank you, Mr. Starly," Wren said as sincerely as she could. "Fortunately for me—and for you, I imagine—Mrs. Brayford is not known to go shy on the cakes. There will be no need to *gobble me up*."

A Pretty Game

A snort escaped Lyn, and her laughter was buried into her glove.

Starly seemed not to notice and handed each of them out. As Mr. Forner creaked away, Wren took Starly's offered arm, then linked her other arm with Lyn's, and the threesome passed through the open double doors.

Garwick really was a beautiful old mansion. The doors and trim were made of rich, dark wood—well cared for with a sheen of fresh oil—and the walls were either papered with tasteful patterns in mild yellow and green or painted with cream and robin-egg blue, all a beautiful contrast to the wood, sparing the house from feeling oppressive. The main staircase was made of the same dark wood with ornately carved banisters and the entryway floor a polished marble that carried down the hall. Wren liked the click of the manservant's heels as he guided the new arrivals to the drawing room to await the announcement of dinner.

A crowd had already gathered, and Wren felt her throat tighten when eyes began to focus in her direction. She was both pleased to be admired and terrified to actually be seen. *I'll get used to it,* she reassured herself. *Maybe even before the evening is through.*

Mrs. Brayford, Lucy, and Gideon stood at the door to greet their guests. Mrs. Brayford had taken on formal airs since her son's rise to nobility, but Wren noticed the same warm spark in her eyes.

"Miss Pak. Miss Amberton. Young Mr. Starly. We are so pleased to welcome you this evening. We hope you enjoy yourselves."

Each guest curtsied or bowed as proper and thanked their hostess.

Gideon's welcome was brief but friendly, and Lucy's was chilled as usual with only a perfunctory curtsy.

With the host greetings over, Wren swept her gaze around the room again for any face she might know. When her eyes fell on Casner, she could tell he had been waiting for her to spy him. He beamed and made his way toward them. Starly tightened Wren's arm to his side, but she managed to wiggle it loose.

"Good evening, Miss Amberton. Have you come to rescue me from an evening of boredom?"

"Probably not. Have you been introduced to my friend, Miss Pak? Lyn, this is Mr. Casner, Gideon's good school friend."

Casner turned to Lyn and bowed. "A great pleasure, Miss Pak." He glanced at the other young man and bowed slightly. "Starly. I believe your mother was looking for you. Best find her."

"Thank you, Mr. Casner," Starly said coolly. He turned to Wren and whispered, "Do not fear, my sweet. I will leave you with this bellswagger but not long. Until then."

As he oozed away, Wren felt a keen sense of relief.

"Conceited fop," Casner muttered under his breath. "Judging by the look on your face, Miss Amberton, I take it you are not fond of being fawned over."

Wren felt her cheeks warm. Did she wear her feelings so clearly?

He smiled knowingly at her, then pointed. "Will you ladies accompany me to that window seat over there? I think we will find ourselves quite out of the way."

Still arm in arm, Lyn and Wren crossed the room with him and seated themselves on the plush cushion while he remained standing.

"I haven't been introduced to many who are here tonight, and I feel rather out of place. Forgive me, as I think I might be glued to your sides this evening. For my own comfort, of course."

He glanced over the gathering crowd, and Lyn took advantage of his turned head. "Say something," she mouthed, her eyes wide.

"Oh," Wren began strongly, "Um...no need to apologize. We are

A Pretty Game

happy to entertain you, Mr. Casner."

He flashed a blinding grin. "Entertain me, will you?"

"Er, I mean keep you company." The door wasn't far, a good sprint would get her there before she could say anything more. Then again, many times had she heard Eillie say silly things only to have everyone praise and adore her. And Wren, herself, was no silly girl. "Uh, Mr. Casner. You are attending Starton, are you not?"

"I am. My second year, just ahead of Garwick. Have you interest in study, Miss Amberton?"

"I have an interest in improvement of the mind, yes. Most of what I know, I've learned on my own."

"Naturally. It isn't hard to see you have that kind of spirit in you. So, what improvements have you made then?"

Wren caught herself picking at the cushion and placed both hands in her lap. "Well, I only had a governess for four years," (A half-truth. Plucky wasn't an official governess but served as one well while she folded linens and mended stockings), "so I learned all the basics from her. Just regular stuff. And then when Luke—my brother—finished with his schoolbooks, he passed them to me. And I have recently become acquainted with a biologist and have learned a great deal from him. I find biology very interesting."

"Do you? I'm afraid I might find myself feeling very stupid in our conversations, Miss Amberton. I, myself, have never been a student of heavy science. Just very basic. I wouldn't have the drive to know more than how to read if my mother didn't push me."

"How could you not have an interest in knowing how your world works? Don't you have any curiosity?"

He smirked and lowered his handsome head toward her. "I find it is growing by the second."

Suddenly Wren wished for a fan. She cleared her throat. "Lyn is an artist. You should see some of the things she creates."

He leaned away, still dazzling the room with his smile, and voiced an interest in seeing her work. The footman announced dinner was served, and Casner held out an arm to each girl. As she slipped hers into Casner's, Wren felt a sweet shiver slip down her back. She would not walk alone this time.

The long dining table was covered in such grandeur that Wren wasn't sure there was even a table under it all. Heaps of colorful fruits and flowers commanded the eye, highlighted by tall, cream-colored candles set in gleaming, gold candelabras. The porcelain dinnerware was the finest she had ever seen, white and trimmed with hand-painted gold leaves.

She was a little disappointed that Casner was seated across the table and several places down but grateful Mrs. Brayford had seated her next to Lyn and away from the frosty Lucy.

The elderly gentleman on her right introduced himself as Lord Figi. When she introduced herself and Lyn, Wren was not surprised when he leaned away and stated he had never heard of either family. But he smiled and complimented them politely. His wife called his attention from down the table, and he turned away.

"There are so many I don't know," Lyn whispered. "I wonder where they all came from."

"From away! I'm sure they are staying here at the house. I wonder how many guest bedrooms are in this place. Twelve at least."

"Makes me glad our circle is small."

"Me, too." Wren stole a peek at Gideon, who sat rather miserably at the head of the table. "Do you think they eat like this always?"

"I don't know." Lyn looked the table up and down. "It's lovely, but

A Pretty Game

it seems like a waste to decorate a table with so much fruit."

"Oh, it isn't wasted. They feed what's left to the pigs who then get fat and end up on the table. Full circle."

Lyn laughed. "Wren, really."

Wren joined in. She glanced up the table again and found Gideon looking back with his barely discernible smile. He hadn't heard her, had he? She tried to remember how loudly she had spoken.

Throughout the meal, Wren felt a number of pairs of eyes on her. Starly looked dismayed at being eight seats away from her on the other side and kept nodding at her every time she happened to look his way. Several times she caught Lucy and two other young ladies giving her cold, calculating stares and felt herself shrink a little each time. But then she would look at Casner, trapped in conversation with a chatty Lady Thomas. His dramatic faces when the old woman wasn't looking his way made Wren snicker.

Adhering to post-meal custom, the women temporarily parted from the gentlemen at Mrs. Brayford's word and gathered in the drawing room. Wren surely would have felt like a crab in the desert without Lyn by her side. There were so many ribbons and feathers, curls and jewels. And there was a heavy feeling in the air. A palpable sensation that only a room holding jealous women can create.

Lucy was the first to speak. "Miss Amberton, you are much improved since our last meeting. So changed I cannot quite account for it. Come, won't you tell us your secret."

"My secret?" Wren looked around the room and realized every eye was upon her—some kindly intrigued, others not so charitable.

"Surely there is some secret to getting your hair to shine like that. Or your complexion to have evened so." She smiled, but it burned into Wren. "Do tell us."

"Well," Wren began. She wanted to say something like she had begun a nightly routine of rubbing chicken poop on her face and applying a mask made out of crushed beetles and toenail clippings to her hair, but a kind nod from Mrs. Brayford prevented her. "I seem to have just come into my own, I suppose."

Lucy's smile dimmed.

"Very convenient for you, I'm sure," the granite face finally said. She then turned to the other girls surrounding her and struck up a conversation about the selection of fabrics in town. The rest of the room followed suit and filled with low rumbles of more pleasant conversation.

"Who spit in her tea?" Lyn whispered.

"She's always been this way," Wren whispered back. "I think she likes me now even less than she did when I spilled my homemade mushroom and worm slurry down her dress."

Lyn snickered. "I don't blame her for nursing a grudge, then. But still Wren. She is trying to pin you to the wall. I am surprised you almost let her!"

"Oh believe me, it was a struggle to be civil. I shouldn't have looked at Mrs. Brayford. I didn't want to embarrass her. I think she was fond of me at one time, don't want to spoil another invitation."

"That's wise. Mr. Casner is to be here another week, I believe. I think he likes you."

"Likes me?" Wren's heart gave a traitorous leap of joy. "I hardly know him. And he knows nothing about me."

"Well, then. I suggest you make sure he knows you at least a button before we leave."

As if summoned by the utterance of his name, Casner strolled through the door with the other men. The small groups around the

A Pretty Game

room swelled as they dispersed. Within minutes Wren found herself partnered with Casner in a game of cards against Lyn and Gideon.

"You are dragging us down, Mr. Casner. Are you sure you don't have a three?"

"Oh good lack, I do." He picked up the card he had just laid and replaced it with the three of clubs. "I'm sorry you've been saddled with a dunce like me."

"Even an ape can pay attention. Gideon has laid four pairs already and if you left that card, he would lay another. Near the end of the game, it isn't hard to predict what is in your opponent's hand."

"Really?" he said. "Where did you learn such scheming?"

"From her brother," Gideon replied for her. "His card counting is unmatched."

Wren grinned. "*Was* unmatched. Play your six, Giddy."

"Giddy?" said Casner. "Garwick, should I be calling you Giddy?"

"No." Gideon put down his six.

"I see. A name reserved only for childhood friends. And what does an old friend call Miss Amberton?"

Gideon looked up at Wren, the corner of his mouth twitching once. Wren gave a little shake of her head.

"Wren," he said simply.

Lyn, who was new to the game, snorted in frustration. "I don't know what to play. I'm afraid his lordship is the unfortunate one in our partnership. It was so easy when there were still so many cards."

"Either card if you have what I think you do. You can't win."

"She lies," said Gideon.

"Never!"

Lyn hesitated a moment, then threw a card to the table. Wren picked it up, set down a match, and declared the win.

"Well done, Lyn," she said. "You may have lost, but that is a very respectable score."

"Don't forget I had a partner. Thank you, my lord, for being so patient."

"Oh, Gideon isn't competitive," Wren said. "He never cares whether he wins or loses."

"Is that true Garwick?" Casner asked. "I never would have known from the way you box."

"Depends on the game," replied the one in question.

"Well, I for one have had enough competition for the night," Casner said. "It is warm enough outside for a walk. Have either of you recently seen Garwick's gardens?"

The girls shook their heads in unison.

"Well, that settles it. A walk!"

Gideon glanced at his mother who was cheerfully engaged in conversation with Lord Figi and his wife.

"You are lord of this house," Casner said, reading his mind. "You don't need to get permission."

"I know," Gideon almost snapped. "But it is *her* party. I'll be right back."

The trio watched him cross the room to his mother and whisper in her ear. She smiled and patted his cheek before excusing him back to his friends. They passed through the cloakroom to retrieve coats and shawls, then hurried out into the dim light of dusk.

It wasn't as warm as Casner had thought, but Wren still found herself preferring to be outside. The gardens were in their late summer ensembles, with most shrubs donning leaves of both green and gold, and a few having al-ready phased into a brilliant red. Blankets of hardy flowers breathed into the evening air, releasing a sweet perfume onto the path. Wren wondered at the perfectly manicured lots, every spent bud snipped and not a hollow stick to be seen.

In minutes, she found herself walking alone with Casner, while Gideon stopped with Lyn to admire a clump of asters. No doubt she was looking for inspiration for her next painting.

"Do you enjoy the outdoors, Miss Amberton?"

Wren inhaled a deep breath. "Yes, I do. I think I could be happy living in a cave."

He laughed. "You surprise me. Live in a cave? I cannot imagine anything more awful."

"Awful? No. Think about it. No one to pester you. You could keep it as neat or messy as you want. And always be outside."

"That's the trouble with it. Always outside, whether rain or snow. You would not last as a cave woman."

Wren felt a little ruffled but conceded. "Maybe not. But the idea of it—living as a creature of the woods. Depending on no one and everything at the same time. It would be liberating."

"I guess so. Still, it would be hard for me to give up a soft bed and a table full of food."

She smiled not knowing what else to say.

"My uncle is the master of an extremely large estate. The Duke of Mendshire. Have you heard of him?"

"Yes, I've heard a little."

"Well, his gardens are three times this size. But they lack the touch of a woman. There hasn't been a duchess there some forty years. My mother tries to advise him, but he doesn't listen."

Wren looked around herself. "Yes, I believe Mrs. Brayford has added her own touch here. Brayford Hall's garden was always pretty, even though it was simple."

He looked up thoughtfully at the starry sky. "Not just any woman can manage a large estate. Or be the wife of a prominent man." He brought his face down and stared at her a moment, though she pretended not to notice. He paused his steps. "You know, there is not a flower in this garden to compete with you. Everything about you begs to be admired. I'm certain you have the makings of a duchess!"

Wren felt her heart skip as she met his intense eyes. When the stare felt like too much, she turned to keep walking and blurted out the first thing that entered her head. "Bortin pigs have tusks that can grow up to nine inches."

Casner caught up to her. "Really? That's…something."

"Yes, they use them to fight off predators or fight each other for mates. Quite brutal, you know." When he didn't say anything, she spouted off a few more facts about the foreign pigs, then switched to rhinoceroses. Their similarities and their differences. He listened to everything she said until Lyn and Gideon caught up with them.

"I think I've been more educated in the last five minutes than I was in all of my secondary schooling," Casner said. "Miss Amberton is a walking textbook."

"It's true," Lyn said proudly. "I have never been bored with Wren."

Casner held out his arm to Wren. "Bored? I must agree, Miss Pak. I can't see how anyone could be bored with her."

Wren bit her lip and slid her arm into his warmth. The walk proved to be a refreshing break from the crowded room inside. When music floated out the window, Gideon abruptly deemed it time to return.

As they passed through the door, both Gideon and Casner reached out to help Wren remove her shawl. Casner's hands were quicker, and Wren felt his fingers brush her back. The tingle did not fade until she closed her eyes on her own pillow two hours later.

CHAPTER TEN
Glory and Mud

When Sunday arrived again, Wren and her remaining family members attended church as usual. Seated on their pew, whispers flitted around the chapel like birds in the rafters.

"I cannot believe the transformation."

"How has she done it do you suppose?"

"I heard they sent Miss Eillie away."

"The younger one was so pretty. A shame she blossomed too early."

Wren shifted on the hard bench and fingered the lace of Eillie's peach gown.

When the sermon ended and everyone filed out of church, Wren couldn't help but notice all the staring eyes again. How the old women beamed at her as if she had done something wonderful and how the young men and boys fell over themselves to tell her good morning as if they might turn into stumps if they didn't. Wren felt like a parrot, repeating *good morning* and *how do you do?* over and over again.

"Mrs. Amberton, how do you do this fine morning?" Mrs. Starly said, hardly granting her a glance. "And Miss Amberton, no need to ask you. I am sure you are feeling well with a face like that."

Wren wasn't sure what that meant.

"We are well, thank you, Mrs. Starly. And your family?"

"Fine, fine. Miss Amberton, I am thinking of having a small card party this week. Is there a day that would suit you best?"

A Starly card party. She had never been invited to one of theirs before and wondered who else would be in attendance. "I—"

"She would be delighted to attend any evening," Mrs. Amberton replied for her.

"Wonderful! I shall plan it for Wednesday."

"Thank you. You are too kind, extending an invitation to our daughter." Mrs. Amberton curtsied graciously as though Mrs. Starly were the queen herself.

"Yes, thank you, ma'am," Wren said, feeling a little cross she had not been allowed to answer for herself.

Mr. Amberton left his conversation with an older gentleman and held out his arm to his daughter. Wren looked at it.

"Wren, take my arm," he said through his teeth. "Staring at me as if I had asked you to stick a pig."

She slipped her arm through. "Sorry, Papa. I just…" His arm had never been offered to her before. Usually, Eillie held this place.

As they turned to leave the churchyard, Wren felt a thrill in her heart to see Casner waiting by the gate. Gracious he was dashing. And Gideon was with him, of course. They politely greeted her and her family, then Casner cut to their purpose.

"Sir, we would like to take Miss Amberton out for a drive."

"Certainly," her father said, sounding pleased. "But a daughter of mine mustn't go about with only two gentlemen."

"I agree," Wren said. "Two is far too few. I am sure we could round up a few more, Papa."

A Pretty Game

He squeezed her hooked arm in a manner that told her not to speak again.

Casner suppressed a smile. "Of course we will find a chaperon or another young lady. Where is Miss Pak?"

"The Paks do not attend church," Mr. Amberton said.

"Hm." Casner tapped his chin and looked about the yard. "Garwick, what about your sister?"

"Lucy is not fond of rides."

"Well, she might like a *Sunday* ride. Let's go convince her."

"I'll not stop you," Gideon replied.

Casner dashed away and much to Gideon's evident surprise returned with the feathered Lucy. "She has agreed on the condition she not ride on the driver seat."

"And that I am not seated beside my brother," she added, cocking her head playfully to the side.

Casner grimaced, then schooled his expression and handed her into the phaeton with a most handsome smile. "As you wish it." He turned to Wren. "I am sure there is room for three."

Wren glanced at Lucy, whose stare was enough to make even the stoutest of persons vaporize into a poof. "I prefer the driver seat, if that's all right with Gideon."

"Fine with me," Gideon said. "So long as you don't mind the bumps. It's not as comfortable as the back."

In truth, Wren wanted to sit by Casner, but she would be far more comfortable away from Lucy. "I don't mind."

Gideon held out his hand. "Good." She placed her gloved hand in his and allowed him to help her up. Then in one easy movement despite his short stature, he was beside her. With a slap of the reins, the vehicle jerked into motion.

"Are you liking your break?" Wren asked him.

"I guess. There's always a list waiting for me when I come home. Truthfully, I have less to do at school than I do here."

"Don't you like being Lord of Garwick?" Wren said in her fanciest tone.

Gideon looked sideways at her. "Yes," he said slowly. "But also no. Parts of it I'd rather leave off. Not that I mean to be ungrateful or anything," he added hastily.

"No, I didn't think that," she replied. "I guess I just assumed gentlemen of your rank spent most days lounging by a pan of iced cream with a giant spoon, reading poetry while their toenails get filed and their hundreds of servants worry about everything else."

He smiled. "If only that were true. Though I wouldn't be reading poetry, Wren."

"What would you read then?"

"I don't think I would read at all."

She gasped in mock surprise. "Not read at all? Well, how would you spend your free time if you had hours of it?"

"I don't know. I've never thought much about it." He turned the cart down a little lane shrouded in golden poplar branches. "I think I should like to learn how to play the piano."

Wren almost laughed, picturing Gideon's farmer hands playing delicate tunes on the piano. But she checked herself when she realized not even his eyes were smiling. He was serious.

"I'm surprised," she said when she felt herself in control. "I had no idea you had interest in music."

He shrugged.

Suddenly Wren felt squirmish sitting up next to him. Moments ago she had been riding beside Giddy. Now? Perhaps she was sitting

A Pretty Game

beside Lord Garwick. Out of the corner of her eye, she analyzed his hands, his movements, even his boots. Searching for evidence of who he was. In the rushed seconds of her analysis, she concluded he was Gideon. Caught somewhere between the boy running through fields and the man he was destined to become. And she didn't know what it would mean when he was fully the latter.

A flowery laugh floated up from behind. "Casner, you flatter me. Do stop."

Wren looked over her shoulder and felt a flicker of jealousy. Both Casner and Lucy were all comfort and bright faces. So, he wasn't too disappointed to be sitting beside Lucy instead of her. She should have tried to squeeze in with them.

"Is this your country, too, Garwick?" he asked.

"Yes," Lucy piped up. "My brother owns both sides of town. This is the old property. Not as large as Garwick and a bit rough, but still very pretty, isn't it?"

"Let's stop for a bit, Garwick! I want to see it better."

Gideon maneuvered the phaeton to the side of the road, and each gentleman handed out his riding companion. A single file line was formed and a narrow trail was followed until they came to a large pond, glittering in the morning sun and hemmed with lily pads.

"I don't remember this pond," Lucy said.

"Oh, I do," Wren replied quickly. "We used to play pirates here. Pirate Pond we called it."

"How original," Lucy drawled.

Wren ignored her and went on. "That log over there was our ship, and the sticks from that tree made the best swords. Somewhere here is our buried treasure. And Luke used to make me jewelry and crowns with the willow vines. Do you remember, Gideon?"

He reached out and pulled a few said vines from the ancient tree. "Of course."

"Pirates?" said Casner with a wide grin. "Why Miss Amberton, I cannot picture you swinging a sword. Were you usually the damsel? A stolen princess?"

"No, we never had enough players for that. I had to be first mate. Luke was always captain, and Gideon was our henchman."

Casner laughed. "That I can picture. But Miss Amberton, you surprise me once again."

His tone was so full of affection, Wren's cheeks flushed with heat, and she turned away hoping no one had noticed.

Lucy adjusted her shawl. "Yes, well, she was always a wild thing. How many pairs of Gideon's trousers did you tear holes in? Mother had quite a time always mending them."

Wren held still under Lucy's verbal pounce, struggling to even loosen her tongue. She could feel Casner staring at her from the side. What was he thinking of her?

A sudden splash startled Lucy out of her victory.

Gideon picked up another hand-sized rock and launched it into the middle of the pond. "I think I've beaten the record," he said under his breath.

"Casner," Lucy said, pointing across the pond, "will you walk with me over there? I see some chrysanthemums I would like to pick for Mother."

Casner let an exasperated noise slip before he recovered and held out his arm, oozing compliments and good looks. Wren rocked back on her heels, letting them squish into the mud. She never would have had the nerve to ask Casner, or any young man for that matter, to walk with her.

A Pretty Game

She watched the pair move halfway around the pond before she remembered she was not alone. Gideon stood a small distance away with his hands in his pockets, his expression thoughtful. He looked so much like her friend from years ago, she couldn't help feeling a little leap of glee. Perhaps the boy who lent her pants was still in there somewhere. She would just have to make him come out.

"Where do you suppose we last buried that treasure?"

He rolled his tongue in his cheek and shrugged.

"Come on," she said, grabbing him by the arm. "Let's see if we can find it. I bet it's over by that tree."

He let her drag him over the debris and a few steps into mud before pulling her back and making her take the long way around where the ground wasn't marshy. Once they reached the tree, the search began.

The treasure was always marked with a red-painted rock. They had tried marking it with an X made of sticks once but discovered that in a blanket of twigs, two sticks carefully laid were impossible to find again. Wren still thought of the doll she had buried that time with a little wave of remorse.

"Can you even remember what is in the crate?" he asked.

Wren removed her gloves as she kicked away organic matter and ventured into softer ground. "It isn't a crate," she said, stooping to poke around in the soggy earth with her bare hands. "It's a pirate's chest. And I only remember putting in Luke's wooden horse."

"Lennox. Yes, I remember him. I was surprised Luke was willing to bury it."

"Well, he died in battle, remember? He had to be put down."

"That's right. How do you remember all this?"

"How do you forget?"

He raised his eyebrows and bobbed his head in defeat.

"Ah-ha!" she shouted. "I think I've found it. Avast!"

"Avast? You know I've since learned that doesn't mean what we thought it did."

"Of course it does. It is an exclamation of victory." Wren rolled away the sharp, red rock and began digging with her fingers.

He squatted beside her and put a strong hand into the mud. "No, it means stop."

"Oh." Wren scooped up a handful of mud and plopped it onto his boot. "Smarty pants."

He smiled and tried unsuccessfully to wipe the muck away. "These are genuine Roycen leather, you know."

"I've never known you to worry about getting a little mud on your boot."

As she put her head down to dig deeper, he scooped up a thick handful and dropped a bit in her hair.

She gasped. "Gideon! My ribbons!"

"Ribbons? So now you're worried about ribbons?"

She tried to feign a look of fury, but it gave way to mischief. Taking advantage of his precarious position, she gave his shoulder a hard shove and toppled him onto his side. His wide-eyed look of surprise sent her into a peal of laughter. Until she felt a boot loop beneath her bottom and knock her feet out from under her. She sucked in a sharp breath as cold wet seeped right through her dress and a stick jabbed her in the arm. But Gideon was laughing like she hadn't heard in years, and she certainly couldn't stop now.

Mud was slung, hair was tousled, and one mouth was partially filled. Within minutes both parties found themselves thoroughly muddied and gasping for breath through laughter.

"What the devil?!" came an exclamation overhead.

Wren, sprawled out over Gideon's middle, looked up to find Casner staring at them—half amused, half horrified. Lucy looked at her with such disdain, Wren was surprised her hair didn't catch fire.

Gideon cleared his throat and gently pushed Wren off of him. "Where did you say that treasure was, Miss Amberton?"

Wren snorted and crawled back to the red rock. "Um, I think it was here, my lord. If you please, will you dig some more."

"Garwick! Your boots. And Miss Amberton—your dress!"

Wren looked down at her sullied dress and sucked her tongue over her teeth. "Yes, I tried to tell his lordship to be careful of my ribbons, but he refused."

"You started it," Gideon muttered. A smile teased the corners of his mouth.

"Ah, avast, the treasure!" Wren pulled and wiggled the little crate loose from the muck, and Gideon pried it open with his bare hands. They peered inside.

"Wonderful!" Wren cried, pulling out a little, dirty roll. "Ribbons!"

Dearest Lyn,

Rediscovered Pirate Pond today. We found the buried treasure. Did you know mud in your ear is really hard to get out? Also, did you know Lucy Brayford wants me dead? You probably did.

Your friend,
Wren

CHAPTER ELEVEN
The Assistant

Wren's glorious return caked in mud did not go unnoticed, much to her dismay.

"What will the town think of us, letting you parade around like that?" her mother had scolded. "And spreading your hoydenish filth to Lord Garwick—I'll be surprised if his mother ever speaks to us again. Shame on you, Wren! I forbid you to go anywhere for a week so you can think of what you have done."

The punishment, though annoying, did nothing to create regret. She snickered to herself whenever she pictured Gideon flailing into the mud and was glad to have made him laugh. He had let her down out of the phaeton in such high spirits. She only felt a little chagrin when she remembered Casner's reaction.

Mrs. Starly sent a note stating the card party had been moved to the following week, which was convenient, though she was sure her mother would have made an exception in her punishment and allowed Wren to go. Lyn had come at Wren's request to help pass an afternoon and had thoroughly enjoyed hearing the full details of the mud escapade. Also, two letters had come from Eillie, one for Mrs.

A Pretty Game

Amberton and the other for Wren. After hearing in her mother's letter that Eillie had made it safely to her aunt's and was settled, Wren had set her letter aside, and there it had stayed on her desk for several long days.

Standing by her little window for the hundredth time since her imprisonment, Wren suddenly felt a pull from the little note. She *had* told Eillie she would write. With a huff, she crossed her room and dug through papers until she found it. When she broke the seal, she was surprised to see the letter so short.

My dearest sister,

Our aunt has been so kind to me—my accommodations are quite comfortable. The only thing lacking is someone to make me laugh. I wish you were here.

I have not really felt much like writing, and Aunt has kept me busy going to parties and to the Springs for daily walks. At first, I had hoped the sea air would somehow restore my complexion or do something for my now lank hair, but I'm afraid there hasn't been much improvement in either. It's strange, Wren. Almost overnight I seemed to have changed so much. I feel like a different person. I am treated so differently. Where once rooms would be still to hear me speak or play the piano, now things seem to carry on without me. No one stops to watch me dance. I feel a change in me that I can't explain.

I hope you are staying out of trouble and not giving Mum fits. Give Charley a kiss for me. Please write soon. I haven't written anyone in town. I don't care if I never talk to any of them again.

Eillie

Wren stuffed the letter back into the envelope and scratched her head. Poor Eillie. Her life had changed very suddenly. And, for good or bad, she didn't even seem to suspect Wren of anything. Eillie was far away and depressed and here Wren was enjoying the fruits of a beauty's life.

She sat down at her desk and took out a sheet of stationery. In her messy, quick hand, she wrote out her mudslinging with Gideon and a few other little notes about some of Eillie's friends in town. It was strange she didn't want to write any of them. She had always had so many friends, one would think they would be a comfort in a time like this.

She closed the note, sealed it up, and went down to find Plucky to ask her to post it. Voices in the sitting room gave her pause before pulling her through the door.

"Casner! Gideon! What are you doing here?"

Both young men stood, and Mrs. Amberton cleared her throat. "They have come to call, of course. And received a proper greeting until now."

"Oh." Wren bobbed into a curtsy. "Mr. Casner. My lord. How nice to see you."

"We've just come to say goodbye," Casner said regretfully.

"Goodbye?"

"Yes, my mother has requested we come stay with her for the last few days before going back to university. Garwick is too kind to tell her no, though I think I could have easily fobbed her off."

Gideon's ears turned red, and he mumbled a response, though no one but him knew what it was.

Wren smiled to reassure him and said to Casner, "Well, I'm sorry you are going, but I bet your mum will be so happy to have you."

A Pretty Game

"Oh, I'm sure she will. I have the luxury of being her only son, and therefore, unfortunately, I often get whatever I want."

He flashed his rueful smile, and Wren felt her heart skip. It wasn't fair for a boy to look like he did.

"Will you be here for Hollyfest, Wren—er, Miss Amberton?" Gideon asked, looking from daughter to mother then back again.

"Yes, I believe so. Will you come home for all of your break?"

"I plan to."

"And I plan to come as well," Casner interjected. "If Garwick can stomach me that long. I wouldn't miss any chance to be near you, Miss Amberton."

Wren cursed her face when she felt a rosy blush.

The young men departed, one with a flourishing kiss of Wren's hand, the other with a curt bow, and Mrs. Amberton waved and blew kisses to them their entire ride to the hedge gate.

"What delightful boys," she said, shutting the door with a sigh. "So polite. So polished. And dearest, I think Mr. Casner is very fond of you. It is important to not appear too anxious for his attentions but really you could encourage him a little more."

"Mum!" Did her mother really want her to flirt harder?

"I know you haven't had much experience with gentlemen, but Mr. Casner is perfect to practice with. Try to smile more. Be excited to be in his presence. And you really should laugh at his jokes."

"He didn't say any."

"Oh, maybe not directly, but young men like to be flattered into thinking they are funny. They want to please and amuse. A little giggle now and then wouldn't hurt anything."

Wren was flummoxed. She could not *giggle* at something that wasn't funny. Mrs. Amberton widened her eyes in expectation. To appease her, Wren thought of Eillie's laugh and let out a shrill little chortle. "Like that?"

"Yes!" Mrs. Amberton beamed. "Just like that. That is what the young men want to hear. You practice. And next time, don't forget to tilt your head a little when you speak. It's more inviting."

Wren left her mother in favor of her bedroom window again. She wished she could see the road to watch her friends go. She had known the time for them to leave was coming, but she was still disappointed. She had wanted Lyn to go out for a picnic with them. It would have been so much more fun than an outing with Lucy.

Wren began to pace. It was day four of confinement, and she was two days past feeling like a trapped animal. She thought of the little cottage down the road. Maybe…

She tied on her bonnet, grabbed her jacket, then hurried down the stairs to knock on her father's study.

"Come in," he said impatiently.

Slowly, Wren opened the door, just in case he hadn't really told her to come in. "Papa?"

"Yes! I said come in! What is it?"

"I was wondering, since I have stayed inside for four days now, I was wondering if I might go see the Adleys? I am sure they have been expecting me, and since you asked me to go…"

He leaned back in his chair and thrummed his fingers on the desktop. "Yes, I suppose you've been away from them long enough. How is the mad woman, anyway? Is she nearing the end?"

Wren stiffened. "No. I mean, I don't think so. And she really isn't—"

"Fine, fine. Never mind it. Just go." He leaned forward again over his ledger. "I said out!"

A Pretty Game

Wren jumped at his sudden shout and ducked back into the hall, careful to close the door tightly. She shrugged off the startled feeling and hurried to the door. Before anyone could stop her, she was across the yard and out the hedge gate. Five paces down the road, there was a rustling in the bushes.

Charley leaped out in front of her. "Avast, you sister! Where are you going with your rebellious feet? You're supposed to be inside."

"Move," she said, shoving him aside, annoyed he already knew the correct usage of the word *avast*. "I'm going to see the Adleys."

He fell into step with her. "But mum said—"

"Papa said I may go. I asked."

"Oh. Are you going to come back covered in mud? I liked it when you did."

"Maybe. Sometimes Mr. Adley has me help bury the bodies."

Charley halted with a gasp. "Bodies?" he whispered. "I knew it."

"Knew what?"

"I heard Papa call Mrs. Adley mad. She really is then? And she—"

Wren turned and grabbed him up sharply by the arm. "Stop that! I didn't mean it. There aren't any bodies. I shouldn't have said that. Just forget it."

He pulled away and looked up defiantly. "But Mrs. Adley really is mad, isn't she!"

"Mrs. Adley is unwell. She is a good, sweet lady. You shouldn't talk about her that way, Charley. Don't let me hear you call her that again, understand?"

He nodded and kicked at the ground. "I don't know why it matters."

"You of all people should know the importance of words, Mr. Playwright." Wren turned on her heels and marched away feeling more ruffled than when her father had yelled at her. It shouldn't really matter what word was applied to Mrs. Adley, should it? She didn't know why, but for some reason it did.

She arrived at the cottage to find Mrs. Adley pacing in the open doorway. "Hello, Mrs. Adley, how are you?"

The woman muttered words Wren couldn't catch and shook her head with a frown.

"May I come in?"

Mrs. Adley narrowed her eyes and began to close the door.

"Mrs. Adley. It's me. Wren Amberton." Remembering how much the woman loved flowers, she snatched a cosmos bloom from the flower bed beside her and held it out. "I've come to visit you."

Mrs. Adley smiled at the little offering, took it, then turned away and went into the sitting room. Wren crossed the threshold and shut the door behind her. "Mr. Adley? Mr. Adley, are you here?"

"He left," said Mrs. Adley. "I think he might, when he does, but he isn't here. You know. He's not coming."

Wren heard the fear in the woman's voice and hurried into the sitting room to sit beside her. The flower she had just given to Mrs. Adley was crushed tightly in her hand, and she began to rock with little tears streaming down her cheeks.

"Where is he, where is he? I know, you know that thing. We could do it, you know. But he's left. I've got to feed the cat."

Wren took up the woman's empty hand and gave it a reassuring squeeze. "How long has he been gone?" She looked about the room for signs of her friend. A pile of peanut shells lay on the table beside a lukewarm pot of tea.

She looked Mrs. Adley over. Her dress was clean, and her hair was neatly combed and pulled into a bun. Wren knew she could not do her own hair or prepare tea. Mr. Adley must have been home earlier. "Did he go into the woods?"

Mrs. Adley shrugged. "I don't know. I mean I'm not sure. We could, though." A fresh wave of tears began.

Wren nodded and tried to think of a way to calm her friend. A small book lay on the table near the peanut shells. She picked it up and read the title. *Poetry of Summer: A Compilation.*

"Would you like me to read to you?"

"I like music, but we could—if you don't think they'd like it," came the reply with more tears. Mrs. Adley dropped the crushed flower onto the floor and rubbed her head.

"Music. Right." Wren opened the book to where a little slip of paper had been placed. She didn't really have the voice for reading or singing for the enjoyment of others, but she was willing to try if it would keep Mrs. Adley from crying. Of course, there was the chance it might make matters worse.

She cleared her throat anyway and picked a tune from her memory. It was one Plucky used to sing in the nursery, when she did her mending and watched Wren and Eillie play with their dolls. It was a happy tune, and Wren had always found it soothing.

She hummed it for a minute, then set the words of the poem to the melody, letting them flow out despite her occasional voice cracks at the high notes and misses in the rhythm. Mrs. Adley closed her eyes and listened, still rubbing her hand across her forehead. Wren felt the other hand slowly cease to tremble in hers. When the words of the selected poem ran out, Wren decided just to hum. It took much less effort than trying to squeeze phrases into notes.

And without words clogging up her thinking, Wren was able to observe and ponder the woman seated beside her. Through the gray streaks and the fine wrinkles, Wren could clearly see the handsome features the woman had once possessed—no, still possessed. Her high cheekbones. Her straight nose and bright eyes. But there was something else. There was something more to Mrs. Adley that Wren could see but not yet define.

The tears stopped, but Wren continued to hum, watching for the worry lines to soften. What was that something more? What was it about Mrs. Adley that drew Wren in?

She looked down at their clasped hands. Mrs. Adley's hands were small, much like the rest of her body. What had these little hands accomplished in their lifetime? Wren wished she could have known Mrs. Adley before she had fallen ill. When she had been able to form sentences and follow conversation. When she had run her household and busied herself with her study, seeking cures and refinement of imperfect substances—her sure hands mixing chemicals and taking notes. How sad, it seemed, that all that should be taken away.

The creak of the front door alerted Wren to Mr. Adley's entrance into the house. His quick tread brought him to the sitting room in an instant, and he smiled broadly when he saw Wren sitting beside his wife.

"Why, Miss Wren. Finally come to us again, have you?"

Mrs. Adley's eyes flew open, and she fairly jumped from her seat and rushed to him, exclaiming unintelligible words. He took her by the hand and looked back at Wren, waiting for her response.

"I'm sorry didn't come sooner. I…had to stay home for a while."

"Well," he said, leading his wife to her chair, "that's all right. You're with us now. Been here long? I'm so glad you've come to keep her company. I was gone much longer than I expected."

Wren thought of the time she had come before and found Mrs.

Adley wandering in the yard. And today she had been nearly out the door. "Mr. Adley…do you really think you ought to leave her here? Alone?" He looked taken aback for a moment, and Wren wished she hadn't spoken at all. "I mean—sorry. Never mind."

"Bup, bup, bup." He thought for a moment and nodded. "I suppose you may be right. She used to like it when I left her alone now and then. She could get more work done without me, you know. So I keep thinking she still likes it, but I've noticed she seems anxious when I return. I thought maybe she was just worried about me. Do you suppose she's really frightened to be here alone?"

Wren recalled the face she had seen peering out the door when she arrived. "Yes. I think so. And she was almost out the door when I came. I'm afraid she might get lost trying to go after you."

"Yes," he said looking down at his clasped hands. "I think you are right." He sighed and walked over to the window. "I'm glad you have come to us, though I'm sorry to trouble such a young thing with our burdens. Growing old isn't exactly as I pictured it. And it's hard to let go of a picture your mind has made up. If I could just get the right formula! Then all of this could go away and leave us in peace."

Wren glanced at Mrs. Adley who had put her head back in her hand. She felt silly for bringing half loaves of bread and doing not much more than talking when she came. There had to be something more helpful. "Mr. Adley? What if…could I be your assistant?"

"What's that?" he said, turning from the window and from deep thought. "Assistant? What kind of assistant do you mean?"

"I mean an assistant. I'd be happy to get things for you in town and take notes if you need and—and sit with Mrs. Adley when you go out. I could come more regularly and at specific times. I'd be happy to help."

A slow smile spread across his face. "An assistant. Yes, I could use one of those, I suppose. We could work out a sum to pay you. How about a weekly wage? Say two pounds a week? Is that enough?"

Wren shook her head. "No, I don't think my father would like me to be earning a wage. And I don't want one anyway. I would like to just come. Being here makes me happy."

Mr. Adley nodded thoughtfully. "Of course, yes, I think you're right. I don't think Mrs. Adley would think a wage proper either. But I like this idea, Miss Wren. I like it excessively. I will write to your father and ask if you may come to us three times a week. I shall tell him you are to sit with Mrs. Adley, we'll leave off the helping with experiments and studies, hm? In a situation like this, I think it appropriate to leave out a few details. Just mucks everything up, don't you agree?"

"Yes," she said readily.

"Splendid." His mouth turned up in a wide, brown-flecked smile. "Do you hear this, my love? Miss Wren is to be our assistant! No longer will you sit here alone. You shall at all times be with me or Miss Wren. How does that sound?"

Mrs. Adley matched his smile and nodded, though Wren was not convinced she knew the whole of what he was saying.

"She likes it! She likes the idea. Wonderful, wonderful. She is so fond of you, Miss Wren. So fond. I think this calls for a celebration, don't you? Why don't you go get the tea things, love? This here is cold and thin. A new pot! And bring in the sugar biscuits, too."

Mrs. Adley nodded but remained seated.

"Well, go on. Go get them. You always fix up such a nice tray. Have you seen that, Miss Wren? Doesn't she fix a lovely tray?"

Wren actually had not seen that. Whenever Mr. Adley insisted his wife get the tea things, she was thrown into a fit of confusion, and he either got the things himself or Wren took her leave.

"I'll help you," Wren said, rising to her feet. "Might as well start."

Mr. Adley beamed when Wren took Mrs. Adley by the hand and pulled her out of the room. In the kitchen, she put the kettle on and began setting up a tray while Mrs. Adley moved about the kitchen, rearranging saucers in the cupboard and moving a folded towel to four different places in between.

Wren hoped she could manage what she had promised. And that she could atone for her misdeeds.

Wonderful Lyn,

I have taken on a profession! Kind of. I am not collecting a wage, of course, but I am to be an assistant to Mr. Adley, the cousin I told you about. He will be sharing his lectures with me and giving a boost to my anti-boredom conversation you seem to appreciate. And also, we will eat a lot of peanuts.

Yours,

Wren

CHAPTER TWELVE
Coming Out of the Clouds

"Your turn, Miss Amberton."

Starly gently bumped his elbow into Wren's arm and gave her an encouraging smile. It was her third card party at the Starly's, and she was afraid they were becoming a regular thing.

The unusually mild autumn season had been replete with parties (Mrs. Amberton accepted every invitation), callers (Wren struggled to put a face to every pretty bouquet), escapes (sneaking skills foiled most unwanted encounters), and visits to neighbors and Lyn (what kept her from running away).

"Oh, um…" Wren looked over her cards and settled on the one that would end the game the quickest.

Lyn squinted one eye at her.

Starly gave a playful gasp. "That settles it!" He picked up the card and laid down his set. "A shamshickle blow, Miss Amberton. I'm afraid Miss Pak and I have taken the hog home. Again."

"Oh!" Wren said, feigning discontent. "What a shame. I'm sorry I've been such a poor partner, Mr. Toone. Tonight is not my night."

"That's all right," he replied brightly. "It's been a rare pleasure."

A Pretty Game

"Thank you." Wren looked around the room as if she were suddenly aware of the other people, though she really had been bored stiff and people watching the entire hour she sat at the table. "Oh, it looks like Miss Rollings and her friend, Miss Smith, are waiting to play. We'll send them this way."

Despite the quiet protests from the young gentlemen, Wren signaled across the room to inform the girls Starly and Toone were waiting to play. Not one to display bad manners, Starly politely sank back into his chair as the girls took their seats. Wren dragged Lyn to the refreshment table.

"I saw your cards," Lyn whispered. "You had a five and a queen. Why didn't you play one of them?"

"Because then the game would have gone on another round! It was like playing with Charley but worse. I've tried—really I have—but I would rather be swallowed to my toes in a conversation about Parliament's latest decision regarding taxes on peas than sit there any longer."

"You hate politics."

"I know." Wren glanced over her shoulder at the card table they had just escaped. "But it would be better than *that*. Starly and his trips to Ferriton—ugh."

"I thought you liked him," Lyn said confused and amused.

"I did. But I've changed my mind."

"I see. And you changing your mind wouldn't have anything to do with a tall gentleman whose name starts with a C, would it?"

Wren bit her lip. "It might." She glanced across the room and locked eyes with Starly again, who smiled and flicked his nose in the air. She smiled politely and turned her back to him. "I had no idea he was interested in so little. It seems like he only knows how to talk about town parties and his tailor. And his interest in me doesn't go past my face. I doubt he even cares I have a brain behind it! So despite the entrance of Mr. C, I think I would be quite safe from my previous raptures anyway."

"Well, you really had never talked to him. I'm glad you have been cured of him. I never thought he was a good match for you."

Wren looked at her friend in surprise. "You didn't? Why didn't you tell me?"

"Because you seemed to like him so much. And he's not the bad sort—just sort of a fop. So I decided not to ruin anything for you and let you daydream picnics and proposals."

Wren grabbed her arm. "Lyn, I did nothing of the kind!" she said indignantly, even though she very well knew she had and had taken much enjoyment in doing so. Best strawberry cakes and rowboat ride she had never really had.

Lyn laughed. "What did you serve him? Cakes and lemonade? I'm sure Starly—"

"Hush! He'll hear you." Wren looked across the room again to see an agitated Starly craning his neck as if the few inches gained would allow him to hear their conversation. "I don't want to encourage him. At all. Kind of ironic since now he would actually notice my encouragement." She looked around the room again, taking in all the feathers, breeches, and pearls. She sighed. "I wish Casner and Gideon were here."

Lyn smirked and bounced her eyebrows.

"Admit it, you do, too. It was actually a challenge to play them in cards. And I could really go for a walk."

"I'm sure if I mention to my father we are ready to go, he'd be happy to call for the carriage."

A Pretty Game

Wren had come with the Paks as her own mother had come down with a cold. She looked at Mrs. Pak who was visiting with her circle of close friends. She looked so happy. "No, I don't want to take your mum away before it's over. It shouldn't last more than an hour, should it?"

Lyn glanced at the mantel clock. "No, it's after ten."

"Well. Surely we can entertain ourselves until then. Looks like Mrs. Harper and Miss Nelly's table just opened." Wren would be delighted to listen to Miss Nelly prattle away for four days if she could be spared another hour of dandy talk. She grabbed Lyn's hand and once again dragged her across the room hoping to join the women's table before Starly finished his game.

Too late. Five strides from sanctuary, they were intercepted by a handsome face on long legs.

"One more go around the stables, Miss Amberton?" Starly asked with certain eyes. Behind him, two forgotten young ladies scowled darkly at Wren. "I'm afraid Miss Smith was not up to the chop block and made for a short time. I've got a wolf in my stomach, but I have not played with you as my partner yet. If I skip refreshment, I'm sure we will take the baby with the horseshoe and still have time for another."

Wren glanced at Mrs. Starly who was peering at her in such a way she could not refuse the son. She might not be invited again if she snubbed him. Yet two minutes from the time she conceded she decided it would have been worth the sacrifice.

"That necklace around your throat reminds me of something in Ferriton, Miss Pak." He turned to Wren. "I once attended a party where the Duchess of Herbwood was."

"Really?" Wren humored him.

"While I didn't get to stand up with her when an impromptu dance was struck up—though I'm sure she would have taken my hand in an instant if time had permitted—I was seated near her during dinner. And I tell you she hardly took her eyes off me."

"Maybe it was the way you comb your hair."

He reached up and touched his head. "Why? But yes, I have had many girls compliment my coif. Don't you like it?"

"I've not thought much about it," Wren said, hoping to take him down a notch.

He swallowed and looked down at his cards. "Well, someday I shall take you to a party with the duchess. Then all shall see that beauty can outshine rank any day."

"Yes, but can it outshine conceit?"

He laughed. "I'm afraid I don't understand you."

Wren squirmed in her seat. "I think you should know, Mr. Starly, that I do not plan to ever go to Ferriton."

"Not go—why you must! If you skallied into a party on my arm, we would be the tick-tock of the evening. I'm sure your mother intends for you to have a season there."

It was Wren's turn to look down at her cards. She felt quite certain that her mother had no such plan. Though Mrs. Amberton would surely sell her off in a heartbeat in town, there wasn't the money for it. Mrs. Amberton had been counting on word of mouth to make a good match for Eillie. And now that lot had fallen to Wren. "I have no plan to go, sir."

Lyn was the only thing that saved Wren's sanity that last hour. Even Toone made her want to crawl under the table with his overreaching compliments and his obvious intention to rival Starly. Wren was tempted to knock their two heads together and scream, 'Curse your mothers for reproducing!' But instead, she allowed their little competition and slapped cards onto the table.

When she was handed into the carriage with Starly and Toone on either side of her, she was never more glad to be going home.

Wren smiled when Ebdor Cottage came into view. It was the kind of place one could not help smiling when looking at it. Offering herself as assistant to Mr. Adley had become one of the best things she had ever done. Winter would all too soon be upon them, and visits would become more difficult. Perhaps her father would allow her to take one of their horses.

A sudden boom sounded from within the house, and Wren's smile died. Smoke rolled from a window.

"Mr. Adley!" she called as she bolted up the walk. "Mrs. Adley!" She burst through the door and found the couple standing in the hallway, both coughing and hacking terribly. "Are you all right? What has happened?"

"Another…" Mr. Adley wheezed. "Another one gone wrong."

"Another?" Then Wren realized which door the strange smoke still wafted from. The smell of it was sour and unnatural. "Oh, I'm sorry Mr. Adley."

He rubbed his eyebrows, crumbling little singed hairs. "It's all right. We just need to let the place air out. I've opened the window, but perhaps we should take a walk outside." He hurried to the coat rack for his hat and his wife's heavy shawl. "I don't know what went wrong. I thought we had it. And then—kaboom! Did you hear it?"

Wren nodded and helped Mrs. Adley straighten the shawl her husband had haphazardly thrown about her shoulders.

"Thank you," the woman said, looking into Wren's eyes. And for a moment she was back. The same woman Wren had glimpsed before—poised and discerning. Then, as quick as she had come, she dissolved into a frightened face, stuttering nonsense.

The three of them walked about the yard only a moment before Mr. Adley announced he was going into the woods.

"I need to get more hogswollop," he said while wringing his hands. "I'm sure we almost had it! It will work, I know it. Will you stay while I'm out, Wren?"

"Of course. I've only just arrived. And I brought the things you ordered from the apothecary."

"Wonderful. We'll sort them later." He rushed away before abruptly returning. "And no funny business. Do not go into the lab. Understand?"

Wren nodded quickly. "I promise."

"That's a good girl. I'll be back in about a quarter of an hour. Maybe an hour. Or thirty minutes. Or…I'll just be back."

Wren watched him disappear into the trees, then turned to find Mrs. Adley no longer by her side. "Mrs. Adley? Where—?"

She spotted the woman crouched over a little bed of herbs, picking rocks from the dirt and brushing her hands over the wilted flowers. Wren's heart strings tugged. In such a short time, Mrs. Adley had become such a dear friend. When they were left alone, Wren found it easy to let thoughts fall out of her head—from Casner to Starly and the weather to her future hopes. Mrs. Adley always listened with an innocent smile and occasionally interrupted with endearing nonsensical statements. Wren usually didn't think much about what they discussed.

But today she had something specific on her mind.

"Mrs. Adley," she began, lowering herself to the same level. "I know you probably won't understand much of what I say, but…" Wren reached up and stopped her from putting a rock into her mouth. "But I want to apologize. To you. For borrowing your bottles and things. I know I asked you, but I asked knowing you could not refuse. Knowing you didn't really know what I was doing. And I'm so sorry."

Mrs. Adley mumbled something about stars and her mother coming to visit. Wren felt a little weight lift off her heart. It was easy to talk to Mrs. Adley.

"I haven't told you much about my sister, have I. *Eilliana.* She is the lucky one. I think any beauty my mother had to give was saved for her—which I still don't understand how so many perfect genes could go into one person when Mr. Adley says there are hundreds, maybe thousands, of combinations and—" she inhaled a deep breath, "—never mind. How isn't important. And she doesn't have them anymore, anyway. Though she has always been vain, I don't think it is a malicious vanity. Not like Lucy Brayford. I'm glad to not have *her* for a sister!"

Wren watched Mrs. Adley snap a dried thyme sprig and taste it. She scooted closer to the woman and helped pull the few sage leaves left untouched by autumn frost.

"It is strange to love someone and to hate them at the same time. Have you ever felt that? I don't want Eillie hurt, but I don't think it's fair that she should have everything. Maybe if you could have seen her before you would understand my feelings better. No one ever looked at me when she was in the room, much less spoke to me. I suppose hate is not the right word. But I don't know what I feel. I really am a wicked soul, aren't I?" She sighed.

Mrs. Adley sat back on her heels and took Wren by the hand. "It isn't…if you do—they certainly ought to. For you." She squeezed Wren's hand harder and nodded with faint tears in her eyes.

Wren smiled and patted her hand. "It's all right. I didn't really expect you to understand."

There was a flash in the woman's eyes, and she went back to her dirt, mumbling, "Oh, I don't know. I don't know."

Having given word to the thoughts that had so beset her mind as of late, Wren talked on, letting the conversation wander to less weightier subjects, like poverty and epidemics, with Mrs. Adley frequently whispering to herself, "Be brave, brave. Be brave," until Mr. Adley returned an hour later.

The house had sufficiently aired, and Mr. Adley led them into the laboratory to shelve the compounds Wren had brought. "I've been thinking, Miss Wren," Mr. Adley said, arranging bottles on the highest shelf. "You walk here alone. Have you ever worried about your safety?"

Wren chewed her lip for a moment while she swept broken pieces of glass and blue fluid from the desk. "No. I've never been bothered before, so I guess I don't think about it. I like walking alone."

"I thought you might say that," he said. He stepped down from his stool. "I've been thinking. If you are to come to us so often, I'd like you to have some kind of defense. Just in case." He took three little vials—corked and full of clear fluid—out from a drawer. "I mixed these up for you to carry on your person. Spark Juice, Mrs. Adley called it. Or sometimes Swine Juice if she was in a temper."

"How does it work?" Wren asked, feeling very curious about the unassuming little bottles.

"Just uncork and splash it onto your attacker. When it meets the open air, it sparks and fizzles. Quite a show. Harmless of course, aside

A Pretty Game

from a good fright. But I'll give you these, too." He handed her three little packets. "Now if you really want a show—or need to alert others to your location or something—just pour the powder into the fluid. And BOOM!" He smiled gleefully. "Make sure you give plenty of room for that. Mrs. Adley created them for defense purposes, but she did once use them at a party. Quite an impressive display. Almost magic."

Wren put one packet and one vial into her pocket and the other items into her basket. "Thank you. I hope to never need them."

"Oh, I hope that, too. But Mrs. Adley believed in planning. No need to take unnecessary risks, my dear cousin." He strode over to the desk. "Made some changes to that one formula we worked on a few visits ago. Look it over and see what you think. And cross out the one point five grams foxlanin. I think that's where it went wrong earlier. Let's halve it."

Wren took the notebook from his hand and examined the most recent entry, an adapted formula from Mrs. Adley's Fog Clearer. Shaky notes at the bottom of the original indicated it created a foul smell and caused a stomachache but did clear her mind for a short while. Wren had gone through and found another similar recipe, and she and Mr. Adley had tried to combine the two. The result was an odorless substance that severely burned Wren's tongue when she had tapped a dab to it.

"Looks promising," she said. "Maybe taking out the carconium and heston extract will eliminate the burn."

"That's what I thought. Fladimum is similar to the carconium in properties, from what her notes say, so I thought it would suit. And I kept the hogswollop and gartik root. I think they are key."

Wren got out a burner and the necessary vessels while Mr. Adley gathered the substitutes. Using the scale, everything was measured and placed into several little bowls.

Mr. Adley held up two bottles and asked his wife, "Does this note here mean we should mix them before adding them to the pot?"

"You can go," she replied. "Or we could." She covered her eyes with one hand.

Mrs. Adley's later notes were not as clear as the notes found at the front of her book, and often Mr. Adley tried to consult his wife, which always ended with her in tears. Wren could usually discern the instructions well enough, and frequently grew impatient that he would not just consult her from the start. But she could see how badly he wanted Mrs. Adley to answer his questions and never censured him for it.

"I think it means to mix them in last," Wren said. "And the fladimum should first be dissolved in the water. Didn't we read something about how to do that?"

"How to do it. My child, you just put it in." Mr. Adley picked up the bowl of fladimum and dumped the contents into the water, which instantly began to bubble.

"I think you are supposed to slowly add the powder to the water or it will..."

The water boiled over the lip of the glass cylinder and a spurt of heavy steam erupted. Wren jumped back before it scalded her face. Mr. Adley pinched his lips together and eyed the cylinder as the water settled.

"Seems fine. Let's proceed."

Wren placed the drip cup on a stand over the burner pot and poured in the fladimum water. Four bowls were emptied into the burner pot, and Mr. Adley turned the screw beneath the cup to allow an even drip. With a long, forked rod, Wren stirred the pot contents, breaking up clumps as they formed. When the drip cup was empty, the cotton wick of the burner was lit.

The reduced amount of foxlanin was combined with a previously concocted solution in a large, lidded beaker, and the remaining bowls were emptied into a special device Mrs. Adley referred to as "the emulsifier." It required winding, and when released, cogs turned, somehow shaking the container rapidly back and forth.

The locking lid was secured, and with long, curled glass tubes tipped with rubber, Wren connected the burner pot, the beaker, and the emulsifier canister. When the pot mixture reached boiling point, orange liquid sucked up into the tube and swirled its way to the beaker before coming to rest in the emulsifier.

"Here's where the last one blew up," Mr. Adley said matter-of-factly.

"What?" Wren gulped and took a step back.

"I'm certain it will be fine." He clasped his hands and complacently tapped his forefingers together. The second tube gave a little shake. "But we could give it some room," he said, backing away.

Mrs. Adley laughed from her corner chair and rubbed her head.

The tube shook again as the last of the liquid spun through and a hissing sound came from within the emulsifier. There was a slight hesitation before either amateur alchemist moved.

"Ah, good. We'll wind it up and see what we get." Mr. Adley hastily wound the contraption, grinning to himself. "There. And now—"

"Wait!" Wren shouted. "The tube." She reached out and disconnected the glass, replacing it with the stopper.

"Bup. Yes, of course, of course. There's a good assistant. We're running low on those tubes. Thank you. All set?"

He released his hold, and the contraption whirred into motion.

Wren considered Mr. Adley while they waited for the emulsifier to run its course. His wiry, singed eyebrows were raised, and his mouth twitched as he whispered to himself. He appeared almost crazed. She swallowed hard.

"Done!" he proclaimed when the cogs slowed. "Now, let's see what we have." He eagerly unfastened the clamps and removed the lid, releasing dark green steam into the air. They both peered inside.

"Should it be that color?" Wren asked.

Each failed attempt had made her more and more leery of strange colors. Burned tongue. Splotchy rash. Headache. It seemed the more off the color, the worse the effect.

"Well, how should I know what it should look like? My love, is this right?"

Mrs. Adley smiled blankly in response.

He bobbed his head. "Let's give it a try, shall we?"

Wren performed the only test Mr. Adley would allow her to do. She dipped her finger into the goop and dabbed it onto her tongue. She rubbed it around in her mouth and shuddered at the horrific taste.

"Fine," she coughed. "It doesn't burn. But it sure is awful."

Mr. Adley grabbed up a spoon and put a heap into his mouth, convulsing once as he swallowed. He smacked his lips a few times and pressed his eyes shut, wrinkles creasing the corners. Then the room was silent. Wren studied him carefully, waiting for a third arm to pop out of his chest.

"Are you all right?" she ventured after several minutes.

His eyes opened, and he smiled. "Why, Miss Wren. You're early."

Wren's shoulders sagged.

He spotted the notebook in her hand. "Oh yes, you've found it. I worked that out last night. Shall we have breakfast before we get to work?"

"Mr. Adley," she said slowly. "We've just done it."

He pinched his brows together. "Have we? Did it work?"

"No. Quite the opposite it seems."

He glanced at Mrs. Adley, who had gone to sleep in her chair. "Oh. Yes. Well, next time." He shut off the burner and stared at the messy desk a moment. "Next time we'll get it. I'm rather tired now. I...I think I'll go rest."

Later that night as Wren lay tucked in bed, she thought of her poor friends. She had stayed long enough to ensure Mr. Adley was all right, though his memory of the morning never returned. It had been hard to leave him looking so discouraged, his usual optimism snuffed out. How he must miss the woman his wife used to be.

Wren rolled over and stared at the little gladiolus bulb sitting on her nightstand. As Wren made ready to leave the cottage, Mrs. Adley had pressed it into her hand saying, "It is still there. You. And the trees."

How had such a mind fallen so far?

In health, Mrs. Adley obviously had been an indomitable woman, full of ideas and wisdom and wit. Her admiring husband had said as much, but there was also something about her person that added proof to his claim. Though nothing she said ever made sense and she jumped unaccountably from emotion to emotion, there was always that certain something—an underlying current. The very core of who Mrs. Adley was.

The flash Wren had seen in Mrs. Adley's eyes emerged from her memory. Maybe she had understood Wren's words after all. Maybe her mind was not as fallen as everyone supposed. Maybe the real Mrs. Adley was still there, tirelessly fighting a torrent of broken connections for a chance to emerge and show who she really was.

Wren wondered. Did *she* have such a core?

CHAPTER THIRTEEN
Fancy Games

Dearest Lyn,

I was just thinking. When we become mistresses of our own mansions, do you think we'll be able to turn out unwanted guests with more ease or will it become more difficult? I bet it wouldn't be hard if one made up the right menu. A boiled egg. Every meal. That's it. With maybe a little bit of gruel in a cup to chase it down. Remind me of this idea if the need ever arises.

Thanks,
Wren

On a clear and crisp late autumn morning, Wren awakened with such a feeling of dread in her stomach. Just thinking of going downstairs and eating another boiled egg filled her with a desire to meld herself with her bed. When Plucky came to check on her and was informed of her former charge's ailment, she promptly returned with a tray of buttered scones, bacon, fresh milk, and tea.

"Now not a word of this to my mistress," Plucky breathed, setting the tray on the bed. "I told her you weren't feeling quite the thing this morning. But I have long thought a boiled egg deficient in providing a growing girl with all the nourishment she needs. I told her so once when she started the same diet for poor Miss Eillie and such treatment I got. Ripped me in two, then didn't speak to me for nearly four days. So I don't say a word. But we both know how Miss Eillie's health has gone. So mind you, now that I know you are practically wasting away, there's always a real breakfast for you in the kitchen. Such a feather-headed notion. A single boiled egg."

She continued to mutter as she shut the door tightly behind her. Wren gaped at her tray.

A whole breakfast!

She wanted to eat it slowly and savor the salty, buttery meal, but a fear that her mother would walk in at any moment pushed her into a two-handed attack that stripped the tray in minutes.

Completely satiated, she decided to linger in her room drawing for the rest of the morning to give backing to Plucky's claim she wasn't feeling well. It was lunchtime when she finished, and after pitifully washing the ink from her hand, she went down to join her mum and brother in the dining room.

"Wren," Mrs. Amberton said, looking her daughter up and down. "Isn't it the twenty-fourth? Why are you not ready?"

"Ready for what?"

"For your visit to Garwick, of course! I told you days ago that Miss Brayford had sent a note requesting you to join her for a luncheon. I sent an acceptance."

"You didn't tell me!" An image of Lucy's cold smirk flashed in Wren's mind. "What if I don't want to go?"

"You were out, and I had to give a reply."

"But—"

"And why shouldn't you want to go? Quick, go change into that blue gown. The carriage will be here any minute to collect you."

A rap at the front door echoed through the hall. An exchange between Plucky and an unknown man was heard, then the housekeeper appeared behind Wren.

"The Garwick Carriage is here, Ma'am."

Mrs. Amberton let out a strangled cry. "Go! No! Not that way. I meant go fix yourself."

"But I shouldn't make him wait, Mum. Aren't I fine as I am? I'm sure Mrs. Brayford won't mind."

Mrs. Amberton flapped her hands. "Oh, you're wasting time. Such stubbornness. You are going to Garwick. What will they think if you show up in that frock?"

Wren looked down at her muslin dress. It was simple, it was true, but it was clean and well cared for. Lucy would surely be dressed in her finest with feathers and lace and beads. Another flash of the girl's calculating eyes, and Wren felt an anchor of retaliation set its hook. The Brayfords knew her well enough not to expect her to show up in a ball gown. "I shall go like this, Mum. There is nothing disrespectful in it. I just need my jacket and bonnet. It will be fine, I'm sure."

"But—"

Before another argument could be flung at her, Wren dashed to the hall closet, where she had picked up the habit of leaving half of her going-out things, and was out the door. And before realizing she had done so, Wren decided if Mrs. Amberton was going to accept invitations on her behalf, she would just have to accept her going as she pleased.

The carriage made one stop to gather Mrs. Harper and would have been on its way in seconds if Miss Nelly had not come out to see her sister off and spied Wren looking out the carriage window.

"Why Miss Wren, hello. Hello there! So you are on your way to *Garwick*, too. My, my, someday I shall be as brave as you. But I think you've been there before, so it's not quite as frightful to you as it is to me, who has never even stepped foot in a house half its size."

"We must be going now, Nelly," Mrs. Harper said curtly.

"Oh yes, of course. But there now, look at you Miss Wren, just like a rose. Isn't she, sister? A rose. But you've always been a good girl, it's just what's inside coming out, that's what I say. Oh, I see my sister giving me looks, aren't you, Cordelia? I shouldn't keep the Garwick carriage. I'm sure their mistress has the table all laid out. I'm so anxious to hear what kind of delicacies she presents today, but oh! The horses are getting restless, I best step away. I say! You men are doing so well. Just fine trimmings you wear—and oh! Yes, your shoes are so clean. Look at them when you get out sister."

"Nelly—"

"My how do they keep such clean shoes driving these roads. That's what I always worry about going into Garwick, you know. Dirty shoes. But there, the carriage is starting to roll now, so I'll just step away. I'll be here when you return, Sister. Goodbye, Miss Wren. Such a pretty little dress you have on, you'll…."

And the carriage drove off before Wren could hear the rest of her praise from the sweet chatterbox who was left behind. Wren leaned out the window and waved and was rewarded with an exuberant return wave. When she pulled back in, she was subjected to a lecture from Mrs. Harper about the importance of moderating one's speech for the duration of the drive.

When they arrived at the mansion, Wren shrunk a little in her new convictions of bravery in the face of criticism. The formidable high gables and sharp corners looming overhead. The dozens of haunting dark windows with who knows what lurking behind them. Somehow the house seemed terribly uninviting knowing Gideon was not inside. She gripped her skirts and followed the nimble butler to the drawing room where the glamorous Lucy was waiting with her mother and younger sister, Miss Carly, along with a vaguely familiar woman in a simple dress and two very fine ladies Wren did not know at all—a mother and daughter no doubt.

"Mrs. Harper. Miss Amberton!" Mrs. Brayford exclaimed from her velvet settee. "We are so delighted you both could come. May I introduce my good friend Lady Tounscend, of Colton, and her daughter, Lady Julia."

Wren curtsied, and Lady Tounscend smiled widely at her, hardly sparing a glance for Mrs. Harper. "You spoke truth, Mary. Yes, a very pretty little thing. Amberton. I have not heard the name. Has your family long resided in Tremdor?"

Wren absently smoothed the wrinkled fabric where her clammy hands had been. "Yes, ma'am. Several generations. My great-grandfather built our home late in his life."

"Very quaint. I feel I shall enjoy getting to know you, child."

Wren bobbed her head and noticed Lady Julia eying her with the same contempt many of the girls in town often did. She wished keenly for Lyn to be at her side.

Mrs. Brayford invited her to sit beside Miss Carly and Miss Lostmyer, who Wren now remembered was the governess. At thirteen years old, Miss Carly was already stately in appearance but with softer features than her brother and sister, more resembling their mother than father. Wren did not know her well but was gratified by the genuine smile the girl bestowed upon her.

"Miss Amberton," she said quietly as the chatter struck up around them, "I'm so happy you could join us." She gave a furtive glance at her governess who was obviously listening but trying to appear she wasn't. "Mrs. Harper says you are a good friend to her and her sister, so I know she is glad you are here as well. This is my first time being invited to one of Mum's luncheons. I don't even know what we're having. I hope it's not wild goose. We had that almost four weeks straight when my brother was home last, and I'm sick of it. I—"

Miss Lostmyer cleared her throat.

Carly straightened her back. "But I'm sure whatever is presented will be a pleasure to eat."

"I'm sure it will," Wren agreed. "As long as it's not boiled eggs, I think I'll be fine, too." She leaned in and whispered, "I'm sick of them."

Carly beamed. "I don't think Mum would serve *only* that. She is very good at making up the menu. She knows just what each of us likes and tries to please us. Especially Gideon. Which is why we had so much goose."

The luncheon was announced, and the group was escorted to a sunny, tastefully furnished dining parlor. The round marble-topped table was set beautifully though simply, especially compared to the one laid out for the dinner party months ago. Blue porcelain this time, with dainty, sparkling glasses and ornate silverware. When the salver lids lifted, an assortment of salads and petite sandwiches were revealed to tempt the diners. Wren looked at Carly and then at the egg salad and made a face. The girl followed her gaze and covered her mouth with her hand to hide a snicker.

Wren carefully placed several sandwiches on her plate and a few scoops of autumn fruit salad. She and the rest of the table listened to Mrs. Harper, Mrs. Brayford, and Lady Tounscend discuss a trial for an established banker in Ferriton, with Miss Lostmyer occasionally contributing. When that topic ran out of material, Mrs. Brayford turned to Wren.

"Wren, how is your sister? Is she enjoying Forthshire?"

Wren lowered her pear-loaded fork and smiled to mask her uncertainty. No more letters had come from Eillie, and Wren had learned not to give her sister much thought. "Yes, she seems to be. She doesn't write much. Busy with…stuff."

Lady Julia took a sip from her glass. "Have you ever been to Forthshire, Miss Amberton?"

"No, I haven't."

"What a shame. It is such a relaxing place, yet so full of things to do. That's where Lucy and I first met, isn't it? Was that only a year ago? It seems like ages we've been friends."

"I know," Lucy said, glancing discreetly at Wren. "I think our kind are simply destined to find one another. And I know Gideon was very delighted to make your acquaintance then. I think he was hoping for it when he found out you were in town."

"Was he really? I felt the same!" Lady Julia gushed.

"And such an exceptional young man he has grown into," Lady Tounscend said. "You know, I don't believe I have told you this, Mary, but a month ago I heard quite the praise for your son. Lord Crackwell—who you know was the headmaster of his secondary school—said that Parliament is anxiously awaiting him to finish university and come of age. What did he say, Julia? 'A pretense-less, steady lad such as that one gives us hope for the future of Langley.' There now, have you ever heard anything more flattering for a young man?"

"Indeed, that does him right," Mrs. Brayford agreed, obviously very pleased. "Though I worry he has grown too serious for his age. He'll be just nineteen next month. But he is determined to manage everything. Why, I hardly have a hand in anything anymore—bless him, so aware how business burdens me."

"Yes, a very in-tune young man."

"That he is. And he just seems to have the knack. Brayford Farms is on the rise again, I think. His father would be very proud of him."

"Well, we certainly share in that pride," Lady Tounscend said fervently. "Don't we Julia? We claim your family quite as our own, you know."

Wren adjusted the napkin on her lap. She wanted to add that she did, too, but Julia was quicker.

"We really do."

"And," Lady Tounscend continued, "we hope to always be on dear terms."

Me too, thought Wren, but again Julia beat her to the punch.

"Yes, we do. I would be quite lost without Lucy. Or Gideon. I long for the next few days to disappear so he can arrive sooner."

Wren felt herself suddenly on guard. Lady Julia use his given name—well!

"Gideon used to lend me his trousers!" she blurted out, much louder than necessary.

All eyes turned toward her. An excruciating pause followed.

"Did he?" Lady Tounscend finally replied. She glanced at her daughter who looked positively scandalized.

Mrs. Brayford took a teeny bite of sandwich and laughed under her breath. "He did indeed. Gideon has been friends with Wren's brother, Luke, almost since he was breeched," she explained. "And by default, with Wren—because the little imp refused to be left behind. How

A Pretty Game

many holes I repaired before I realized his trousers were pulling double duty I do not know. But I am sure Miss Amberton has long given up her habit of borrowing his pants."

Wren blushed scarlet and squeaked out confirmation before shoving an entire lox sandwich into her mouth.

"Well, I don't know when I'll make it back to Forthshire," Mrs. Brayford continued smoothly. "I've been very busy here trying to redesign the garden and my linens are in such a state. I…"

She talked on, summoning the attention of everyone at the table except Carly's. She leaned over to Wren, "I wish there were plain olives on this table. I like them best. These green ones stuffed with fish make me cringe."

Despite her burning cheeks, Wren smiled, grateful for the subject to move on entirely. "I prefer them stuffed with cheese."

"So does my brother. If he were here the table would surely have them. Mother says most ladies don't like cheese." She stealthily pointed to Lady Tounscend and made a snobbish face—her nose stuck up in the air.

Miss Lostmyer cleared her throat again, and Miss Carly fell silent, nibbling at her sandwich with her little finger in the air. As Wren listened to the conversation turn toward the latest news regarding the popular families in Ferriton—sounding almost like a foreign language in her ears—she couldn't help feeling like this was the sole purpose for Lucy's invitation. To wave fancy friends and fancy conversation in Wren's face. Lucy's occasional smooth, victorious glances furthered her suspicion.

Determined not to show her discomfiture after the third or fourth look, Wren rolled her shoulders and put a pleasant smile on her lips, pretending to listen with great interest, nodding and 'm-hm'-ing in agreement or gasping in absolute disgust when appropriate. When she saw Lucy shift in her seat, it became a new game. Wren called it *How Well Can Wren Fit In With The Fancies?*

At her first opportunity, she broke into the conversation with the only bit she had. "I read in the paper that the engagement between a Mr. A. Firth and Miss B. B. is off. Is that the same Mr. Firth?"

"It must be." Lady Tounscend replied. "He was engaged to a Miss Border last I heard. She is quite unknown. From somewhere up north, I understand."

"Well, I am sure there are many happy young ladies then," Wren replied, setting down her teacup with a soft clank. "He sounds like a very popular gentleman."

"Oh yes," Lady Julia agreed. "Though I never saw much in him. He likes to wear an orange waistcoat, and I just can't bear the color orange."

"Oh, I quite agree," Wren said solemnly. "It's too bold. The signature of a fop to be sure."

Julia laughed sweetly (Wren awarded herself one point). "Yes, that's exactly what I think! I do wonder about this Miss Border, though. I've never seen her, but I bet she is lovely. He wouldn't have engaged himself to her if she weren't."

"But what of wealth?" Wren said, rubbing her fingers together. "I think money can easily supersede a face, don't you?"

"That's the truth of it, Julia," Lady Tounscend chimed in. "Miss Amberton has hit upon it."

"But we have never heard of the Border family. They cannot be of great wealth, can they? No, I'm sure she is a pretty face. A pretty face will charm any man out of marrying for money or status."

"It's dreadful, isn't it?" Lucy said coolly. "How—no matter how vulgar she may be—a pretty face makes men lose their heads. Miss Amberton has lately experienced more than her fair share of that."

Rot. A point for Lucy.

"Have you?" Julia asked, intrigued—possibly a little jealous.

"Oh, I suppose a little," Wren conceded, poking her fork into a blueberry. "But despite my best efforts, I have yet to see any heads actually roll."

The table was quiet for a few breaths before Julia broke into a fit of pretty laughter. "Heads roll. Yes, I should like to see that!" Her mother and the others seated round the table shared in the amusement. All except Lucy. Another point for Wren.

Wren daintily dabbed her mouth with her napkin. "I think a gentleman really ought to know more about a woman than her features before he signs away his heart. Many a unhappy marriages have been formed based on a woman's nose. Only fancy, waking up one day and the little button is swollen into a turnip. Then what do they have to go on? One can only hope she has spectacular hair."

Julia was greatly amused. "Miss Amberton, you are so funny. Lucy," she said in a mock-scolding tone, "you did not tell me she was such fun."

Lucy forced a smile, and Wren grinned.

Point!

Wren relaxed a little, feeling pleased she could hold her own at this table. She let the others lead the conversation again and chimed in every so often, when she thought she had something clever to add. By the time they had finished and removed to Mrs. Brayford's favorite sitting room, Wren felt secure in her four-point lead over Lucy.

"Mum," Carly said blithely, looking out the pristine windows. "Since it's sunny out, may I go for a walk in the gardens?"

Mrs. Brayford readily consented, and Miss Lostmyer whispered something to the girl.

"Oh, right. Good thinking. Would anyone like to join me?"

For half a moment Wren planned to remain and continue the game, but in the end decided to quit while she was ahead and claim the win. "A walk sounds glorious," she said with a sigh and pranced out the double glass doors with Carly on her arm.

Outside, the air was crisp and fresh. For a late autumn day, it almost felt too warm. The fountain had been drained and lined for the season but was obviously swept and cleaned regularly to keep from appearing unkempt. Despite the lack of lush color, the park was still enjoyable, with tastefully placed statues and benches, clean gravel paths, and various evergreen shrubs dutifully holding onto their color.

"I wish winter would never come," Carly said heavily. "Mum doesn't let me walk if there's snow or wet on the ground. Or if the wind is blowing. She is nervous I might catch a chill."

Wren recalled Squire Brayford's sudden demise and nodded in understanding.

"Usually I have to walk with Miss Lostmyer," the girl continued. "She makes me keep my back straight and my feet out of the mud. Which I guess is all right. I do want to be a proper lady someday." She guffawed. "Then maybe I can make a head roll, too!"

"Just one head?" Wren asked.

A little blush touched Carly's cheeks. "Well, I shouldn't like to be greedy. Or maybe there is one particular boy. But I've only met him twice. But he's so nice."

"I'm glad to hear it. Nice is a good trait in a boy."

"Is there anyone you've got your eye on, Miss Amberton? You're so pretty, I bet you can have your pick of any gentleman in Langley!"

"Oh, I don't think I could have my pick of all of them. A blind man wouldn't be duped by my face. He'd see me only by what I say and do. And that might be enough to scare any man away."

Carly laughed. "But you are so funny. And I'm sure you are good. Gideon would not think so well of you if you were a leech. And I know Mr. Casner was impressed by you."

"Was he?" Wren caught the girl's sly look, but she took the bait anyway. "What did he say?"

"Oh, I can't remember for sure. Something about you being the most beautiful creature he'd ever seen. I always think it's weird for boys to call girls creatures. I guess we are in a way, but it's a strange word." She hunched her back and raked her fingers through the air. "Makes me feel like a creeping thing. Anyway, he lit up any time he heard your name. He usually likes blondes, he once said, but that you might change his mind."

"Really?" Wren felt a tickle of glee. "What else do you know about him?"

"Let me think." Carly tapped a finger on her chin. "Gideon says he is very smart. He does well in school, though not so well as Gideon, I bet. Mr. Casner likes to play. He was forever trying to get Gideon to go and ride or shoot when my brother had business. What else? His uncle is a duke, can't remember which one though. He likes to spend time up there on that estate, though I heard him tell Mum he is getting to prefer here over almost any other place. If it weren't for Lucy, I bet Garwick would be top of his list."

It was wicked, but Wren couldn't let the opportunity slip away. "What makes you say that?"

Carly smiled broadly. "I once saw him turn around halfway down the stairs and scramble into the upper hall closet at the sight of her coming out of the library. He didn't see me, but I saw him. His face—almost complete fright! It's no wonder though, she hardly lets him alone. Boys don't like to be smothered, do they?"

"Nope. I don't think so. But me giving advice about boys is as helpful as a slug giving hunting advice to a tiger." They walked a small distance before turning back toward the house. "So do you know when Mr. Casner will be coming back?"

Carly smacked her lips. "Well, I did hear Mum tell Lucy that he might be coming next week with Gideon for their winter break. His mum is kind of bossy though, so I don't know whether he'll be able to get away or not. But I can write Gideon to say you'd really like him to bring Casner with him when—"

"No! No, please. Don't do that. I was just curious."

They entered the house and rejoined the group for another half an hour until Mrs. Harper deemed it time she and Wren took their leave. Julia bid farewell to Wren with a clasp of her hand and a wish to see her again soon. Wren uttered a brief return of the sentiment, though for some reason she couldn't bring herself to wholly mean it.

As soon as Wren's foot stepped across the worn threshold of her own home, Mrs. Amberton's excited call bounced out of the sitting room.

"Wren! Wren, is that you?" She fairly flew into the hall. "How was your afternoon? Oh, never mind. Your Papa has brought back two parcels for you from the post office. Come quick so I may see what they hold."

Parcels? Wren dropped her bonnet and jacket and followed her mother back into the sitting room. "Who are they from?"

"This one is from..." Her mother leaned away from the package and squinted at the letters. "I still can't make it out, the writing is so scratched. You'll just have to open it. But *this* one," she said holding up the other package like a sacred relic, "is from Mr. Casner."

Casner! What could he have sent her? Wren took the packages from her mother and sat down in her chair, examining the heavier, mystery package. She thought she could make out a G and a k in the return address. Gideon, perhaps?

She decided to open Casner's first and pulled the parcel string.

"Gently, dearest. It's not the wash. A lady never tears the paper."

It was light, whatever it was. Through folds and folds of tissue paper, she found the gift. A set of hair combs, heavily embellished with pink pearls and silvery rhinestones.

Mrs. Amberton gasped. "What taste he shows. They are lovely, Wren. Such a compliment to you. You don't have an understanding with him, do you?"

"No!" Wren said with a startled laugh. "No, Mum. I hardly know him. But they are lovely."

"You must wear them the next time you see him, to be sure."

A note had been tucked underneath the accessories.

My uncle obtained these on his last trip to Royce. I have told him of your loveliness, and we both wished you to have them. He entrusted me to send them to you. I am anxious for the day I see you again. Perhaps Hollyfest?

Yours ever,
Casner

Wren pressed her lips tightly to refrain from smiling too wide. She set the combs and paper aside and turned to the other package. As soon as the paper was off, she knew for sure it was from Gideon. It was a thick book titled *A Deeper Look into the Wild World*. Wren was astonished to note one of the authors was a Mr. Wilfred Adley.

"A book?" Mrs. Amberton whispered disappointedly.

Ignoring her mother, Wren flipped through the pages, and as she hoped, a loose slip of paper revealed itself. It was dated several weeks prior, shortly after the university term had begun.

"It must have gotten lost," Wren said. "Gideon dated the paper quite some time ago."

"Giddy sent this? Well, I am not so surprised then. And it's no wonder it got lost, the way he scratched out his letters. You'd think a boy who had been to the finest secondary school in Langley could write properly. But I'd be the last person to criticize our Lord Garwick. I suppose it is a good gift for you. Not very romantic but—"

"Romantic?" Wren said with a laugh. "Of course not. I should never expect something like that from *him*." Wren squinted at the note and slowly made out the words.

Wren,

I received my class list for the coming terms and collected my books. After I read through a little of this one, I went back and purchased another. It has some good artwork, and some pages were even printed with color. I think you'll like it. Hope you and your family are well.

Gideon

Wren tucked the note back between pages and flipped through the book again. It did, indeed, have pictures she thoroughly liked, even with only one glance. And that it was part-authored by her cousin was a delightful coincidence.

Collecting her new things, Wren returned to her room. She carefully wrapped the combs in one of her dabbing cloths and placed them in the top drawer of her desk. Pulling out a new sheet of paper, she found a chapter written by Mr. Adley in Gideon's book and selected one of the drawings to copy.

CHAPTER FOURTEEN
In Need of a Dark Horse

In a matter of days, the air turned from crisp to frigid, and suddenly winter was upon Tremdor Valley. When the first snow fell before November came to an end, Wren found herself trapped indoors, unable to go on her visits. The thick icing of white was beautiful, though, and she was hopeful the winter would be more typical than the fall had been and the snow would thaw within a month, leaving her to battle only several months of rain.

"I am certain I should feel quite out of touch with the world if it were not for Mrs. Thorte's letters," said Mrs. Amberton over her dinner plate one December evening. "No one lingers after church to gab, you know. Not when the air bites so. She is so fortunate to live in town—always hears the best tidbits. She informed me just today Miss Smith has become engaged to that young Mr. Thovas from Rembly. I guarantee you he hasn't seen our Wren, Mr. Amberton. I'm sure any young man who has will not engage himself until she has been secured by another and made out of reach."

Wren winced. These constant little pebbles of flattery flung her way were beginning to feel like stones.

A Pretty Game

"And," Mrs. Amberton went on after a sip from her glass, "she also said Mrs. Trunce has finally passed away. Winter does that, you know. The old and ailing start to drop off when the snow falls. She's the second passing in our valley that I've heard of. Though she left no young ones like Mrs. Clamp."

Wren choked. "Mrs. Clamp?"

Mrs. Amberton set down her cup and returned to working on her pork chop. "Yes. A sad situation there. Galloping consumption. To think of all those children. Mr. Clamp certainly has his hands full. Lucky the eldest is a responsible girl and can care for the baby when he goes back to work in the spring. And such luck he is employed under our Giddy. He'll not turn him out if he gets behind on rent."

"When did this happen?" Wren asked when her breath recovered.

"Oh, it's been almost a week. I am sure they've recovered a great deal by now. Mr. Amberton, how is your squash tonight? Didn't Plucky do a fine job?"

A half-hour later, Wren sat on her bed, still stunned by the news. Mrs. Clamp had died. So sudden! The last time she had been to the little home—less than a month ago—the woman *had* seemed weak. And her cough had been much worse than it ever had been before. But dead? Mrs. Clamp had been dying while Wren swept the floors.

She just couldn't believe it. She shook her head and went to the window. The winter sun was setting, igniting a blush from the sky and casting long shadows across the snow. The little Clamp children were so small, and though with little resources, their mother had done for them all she could. And now she could do no more. There had to be something to be done.

Wren went to her wardrobe and pulled out Luke's old great coat. As she tied her boots a hasty plan began to form. Slowly, she pulled open her door. The hallway was empty. She crept to her parents' room, not a board squeaking underfoot, and found it empty as well. Scurrying to her father's wardrobe she tripped over a turned up corner of the rug and stumbled loudly before catching herself upright and freezing deathly still.

No sound came from the stairway for several minutes, so she resumed her mission. A large, purple robe was taken from its hook, and under her parents' bed, she searched among hat boxes for just the right thing. In the furthest box she discovered an old, feathered turban she had never seen in her life. It was green satin with a pitiful peacock feather drooping to the side. Perfect. She tucked the lucky find under her arm and silently made her way back to her room.

After stuffing her contraband into a burlap bag, then snatching two vials and powders from her desk drawer and tucking them into her coat pocket, she was ready for phase two.

She couldn't get to the kitchen by way of the stairs, as she would surely be seen and questioned. So there was only one alternative. She threw open the window and stuck her head out into the chilled evening. She frowned. Her father had instructed Mr. Forner to take down the trellis after one of Starly's visits. Wren had laughed at the time but now was annoyed. Only the hooks on which the trellis had hung remained. They looked big enough to be footholds, and probably sturdy enough for her weight. It was worth the chance.

She tossed the bag down into the snow, then threw her backside over the ledge. Her legs dangled for a moment before her right foot found the first hook. Bouncing a little, she found it solid and maneuvered her other foot to the next, while lowering herself with her arms. She was hoping to move like an experienced cat but found herself moving more like an uncoordinated kitten, stretching herself in timid movements and practically flopping against the bricks, sweating and shaking.

A little sound escaped her throat that sounded much like a *mew*.

When her foot touched the sixth hook with growing confidence, it was rudely betrayed. The hook broke loose from the wall and her other foot slipped from its perch. The brick scraped her cheek as she slid against it with an *oof*. She hung precariously for a brief second until her arms, overstretched as they were, convinced her fingers to let go. She plummeted into the snow, landing clumsily on her feet before crumpling to her backside.

After a quick assessment—wiggling her toes and feeling about her head, she assured herself she was still whole. Now she moved like a cat, gracefully hopping to her feet on solid ground. She brushed the snow from her coat, scooped up her bag, and slunk to the little window in the kitchen door. The room was empty.

Lifting the latch and pulling up to ease the weight on the old, creaky hinges, she silently opened the door. Warmth and the smell of cinnamon and fresh bread greeted her. She hurried to the pantry and opened it, startling at the two wide eyes staring back.

"Charley!" she whispered.

The boy opened his hand and let the half-eaten sugar biscuit fall to the floor. "I was just checking to make sure we had some."

Wren put her hands on her hips, doing her best impression of Plucky. "Bunch of rot," she said still in a whisper. "But I tell you what. I won't breathe a word of this to Plucky or Mum if you forget to mention you saw me."

"Why are you whispering?"

"Because I don't want *you* to be caught."

"Oh! Thanks." He squinted one eye. "But why are *you* here?"

"Never mind. Just pretend I'm not."

"All right," he said with a one-shoulder shrug. He picked up his biscuit and shoved it into his mouth before attacking another.

Wren grabbed an empty tin and proceeded to fill it with nine sugar biscuits and a handful of Plucky's caramels, then snagged a small wheel of cheese. She lifted her finger to her lips and backed out of the pantry while Charley continued to fill his cheeks, not even looking up at her once. She closed the door and slipped back outside. Dropping the tin and cheese into the bag, she slung it over her shoulder and scampered through the deep snow to the corner of the yard.

The hole in the hedge was partially obstructed with a drift, but still open enough to push the bag and herself through. Once on the other side, Wren inhaled a burning breath. Success. Her way was clear now.

A few steps from the hedge, the sound of horse nicker broke the cold hush. She sucked in a breath and tucked back against the spiny hedge with her eyes closed, hoping that whoever was about to come around the bend would be anxiously focused on the road before him. When she heard soft hoof steps in the snow, she risked a peek. Through one eye in the dim light of dusk, she saw the familiar black thoroughbred with its dark-haired rider. Wren allowed her other eye to open but remained pressed against the hedge to watch him come.

Gideon had not noticed her and was indeed very focused on the road before him. As he neared, she could see his thick brows were pinched together and his eyes edged with fatigue. She again had the feeling she was not watching her friend Giddy—a boy who liked to swim and box and ride—but a man. A viscount. With responsibility toward respectability and weights of duty heaped onto his shoulders.

He looked up from the road before him and over her head at the house behind her. A thought—a flicker of something behind his eyes—altered the expression for just a moment. Like the flashes that revealed the real Mrs. Adley, the real Gideon rode toward her.

She stepped out from the shadow of the hedge into the path of his horse and felt a sense of delight in the surprise that overtook his face before he recovered it with his mask of gloom.

"Giddy, where have you come from? That is the wrong way."

He cleared his throat. "I've been to Brayford Hall to see my steward on business," he said flatly. He glanced down at her bag and changed his grip on the reins. "Where are you going? It's near dark."

"I need your horse."

"No."

"Yes, I need to borrow your horse."

"Last time you borrowed my horse, it came back green."

"Well, then I was ten. And it wasn't all green, just the flanks. I ran out of paint. And that one was white. I won't be able to bring a black horse back green now, will I?"

"No. One reason I selected him."

They stood there a moment staring at each other, he still waiting for her to answer his question and she waiting for him to hand her the reins.

When he didn't move, Wren adjusted the bag on her shoulder and strode past his horse in the direction he had ridden from.

"Well, I better be off then. If you won't give me your horse, it will be quite a walk."

From behind, she had the satisfaction of hearing him sigh before there was a sliding of leather and a soft *shump* of his boots diving into the snow.

"Here," he said in resignation, bumping her shoulder with his fistful of leather strap. "But just tell me. Where are you going?"

"We. Where are we going. It is a surprise."

"I don't want a surprise."

"Hold this." She dumped her bag into his arms and clambered up onto his horse, tucking her skirts awkwardly around her legs. "There now, pass it up."

He handed her the bag. "Just take the horse."

She smiled. "All right, but if he loses a leg…I can't very well help where traps are laid in the woods."

He shook his head and waited until she pulled her foot from the stirrup, then slid up behind her, reaching around her to grab hold of the reins. A sudden breeze stirred the snow, seeking any heat it could whisk away, and Wren was glad to have his extra warmth against her back. They rode in silence until the snow began to crunch beneath the horse's hooves and the little Clamp cottage came into view. Bless them, it wasn't even a cottage. Merely a shack held together with who knows what. Wren's heart ached for the little family and wished she could do more.

She pulled the horse to a stop. "Let's get off here."

Without a word, Gideon obeyed, then reached up to help her down. Though his hands dropped from her waist immediately, he didn't step away, and for a moment she was pinned between him and the horse, which kept bumping her forward. She looked into Gideon's stony face and smiled, hoping he would move. But he just stood there staring at her with a mysterious glint in his eyes and words seemingly on the tip of his tongue.

Her heart gave an unfamiliar thump. "Right. Well," she gave his shoulder a little shove and forced herself to swallow as she pushed past him. "Here we are." She reached into her bag and produced the purple robe. "Put this on."

A Pretty Game

"No."

She removed his hat and plopped her mother's turban onto his head. "You must be dressed up or you'll have to hide in the bushes."

He moved for the overgrown brush, but she caught his hand and began working his arm into the robe sleeve.

"Don't be a mule. Think of the children."

"What children?"

"The Clamp children. They have just lost their mother. Imagine how they hurt. They live on *your* land. This is your duty. There!"

He stood before her, the purple robe giving him the look of a haggard bear, and the shabby, nearly too small turban with its peacock feather hanging in his face—perfection. She didn't try to stifle her laughter.

"You have no heart," he said miserably.

"And you are a coxcomb. Come, you aren't too fancy for fun, are you?"

He didn't smile, so she waved him off and rummaged in her pockets for Mrs. Adley's Spark Juice.

"Here, hold these," she said as she handed him the two vials. "Don't mix them until I say." She dropped the powder packets into his robe pocket.

"Wren, what the deuce are we doing?"

"Spreading cheer, my friend. Spreading cheer."

The sun was completely gone by this time, making the lighting just right. They walked up the short drive and knocked at the door.

"Oh, did you tie your horse securely?"

"Why?"

"Because I don't want to walk home."

Just then the door opened, and Mr. Clamp stared out from the dim home. Seven little faces gathered around his legs before anyone could speak.

"Good evening, Mr. Clamp." For a moment words failed Wren. Seeing the motherless children proved to be more difficult than she expected. It felt awkward to acknowledge the loss, yet wrong not to. She looked at the children's faces again and gathered courage. "We have come bearing gifts," she said as merrily as she could.

The smallest of them smiled, but the rest still stared. She opened her bag and handed over the tin and cheese. The faces lit some at the sight of sweets.

"Thank you, Miss Amberton," Mr. Clamp said quietly.

"You're welcome. I'm sorry it isn't more, and I'm so sorry..." She looked at the children again and remembered her surprise especially for them. "And that is not all. Tonight, I have a treat for the eyes. I have brought with me a *magician*."

Gideon cleared his throat. "I'm not really—"

"Oh yes," Wren cut in covering his mouth. "Oh yes, he is. And he has prepared a show just for you."

She motioned for Gideon to put the two bottles in the snow a distance behind them, but he didn't understand her gestures.

"I shall assist!" she said and dragged poor Gideon by the arm a safe distance before placing the vials herself. Then she pulled the compounds from the robe pocket and whispered, "Put one in each bottle and run back to the house."

"But—"

"Just do it. Quick!"

She hurried away and turned just in time to see Gideon shake the powders into the vials. He stood a moment watching them fizz and bubble. Small snaps sparked inches from the rims.

A Pretty Game

"Gideon, I said run!"

The first red burst erupted from the bottle, and he jolted from his trance. The feather bounced with each step, and he really did look like a bird then, running through the deep snow with high knees. Wren and the children laughed at him but stopped when the show stole their attention.

Bursts of yellow and red, green and blue lit the evening. They crackled and glittered, swirled and whistled. It was magic, just like Mr. Adley said it would be. The whole lot of them stood in stunned silence, mesmerized by the spectacle.

Beside her, Gideon inched closer until his robed arm touched hers. He held still just a moment before he reached for her hand. The brush of his skin unleashed a hundred childhood memories. Many times had he taken her hand, over logs and out of ditches. It had always been safe. She allowed him to take it again and glanced at his face. He returned her gaze.

And suddenly his touch was not a memory. It was new. Sparking a response that flashed through her. Abruptly, she made the excuse of needing to tighten her coat around herself and withdrew her hand from his grasp.

When the show finished, the children whooped and clapped for the humble magician who stood stiffly by her side. Wren bid each child goodbye with a hug and kissed the baby before Mr. Clamp gently caught her hand.

"Thank you, Miss Amberton. Lord Garwick," he whispered.

Wren looked away from the tears in his eyes and muttered some sort of response. Gideon shook his hand. They left the shack only to find their horse had not been tightly tied. With no other choice, they set off on foot to find him or home, whichever came first.

Wren flicked her fingernails over her palm and glanced at her companion. He was even more stoic than when she had found him on the road. She began to worry she had insulted him by taking back her hand. But what could he have been thinking? They weren't playmates anymore.

She didn't like the silence. "I...this snow is really crunchy."

He nodded but didn't say anything.

"The almanac says it is to be a short winter. I wonder when the snow will turn to rain."

Still, he didn't speak.

"I think they liked your magic."

"Hm?" he looked up from their path. "Oh, yeah. I think so. How did you come by such a display?"

She smiled. "Magic is a secret not meant for all to know."

One corner of his mouth tugged upward. "But I am the magician. Shouldn't a magician know his own secrets?"

"Not if he enjoys the magic just as much as his audience." She looked at him, still wearing the peacock hat, the feather waving with each step. "I got it from a friend. That's all I will say."

They reached the road, and Wren was glad the snow was packed enough to only reach her ankles. She tried not to think about how much further they might have to walk. Gideon noticed her shiver and slid out of the robe to place it over her shoulders.

"Do you think your ride has gone all the way back to Garwick?" she asked, raising her shoulders to brace against the chilled breeze.

"Not sure."

"Well, you can take one of Papa's if we don't find it before my house. He won't notice, and if he does, he won't mind once I tell him you are the thief."

"No? I didn't know he liked me."

"He doesn't like *you*," she said shamelessly. "He just likes the Viscount of Garwick, who happens to be you at the moment."

He stopped walking, but Wren kept marching, a wicked smile stuck on her face. Suddenly something thumped against her back and a spray of snow shrouded her head. She stopped and shook her head slightly, the grin deepening. She turned on her heels and bent to scoop up two hands worth of snow just as another ball of snow pelted her face. She staggered back, trying to blink away the icy dust.

"Wren!" Gideon said, a laugh just under his breath. He jogged toward her. "Are you all right? I wasn't expecting you to turn—"

Before he could finish, her handful of snow was smothered in his face, and the fight began. She fled, snowballs flying in bursts around her, and ducked behind a tree in time to save herself from the largest missile yet. Panting, she dropped to her knees to make several balls and leaned around the rough bark to retaliate against her foe. The first two missed, but the third struck his leg.

His laugh rang through the woods as he returned fire. She bent over to arm herself once more and looked round to find him running at her again. She took off heading back toward the road but was cut short when a strong hand gripped her arm the same time a root caught her foot, and both she and Gideon tumbled to the frozen ground.

"You can't…" she wheezed with laughter, "tackle…someone…in a snowball fight!"

"You ran away. I had to." He sat up on his knees with his hands behind his head. His hair was mussed, the turban having met its long overdue demise somewhere back in the trees.

"I wouldn't have run if you hadn't come barreling at me. My heart went to my throat!"

He grinned boyishly for a few breaths, then got to his feet and held out a hand. She threw hers up into his, and he pulled her up.

They tromped the rest of the way back, discussing what they had learned from the textbook he had sent, the success of his farm's last harvest, then their plans for the holiday. Wren was disappointed to hear Casner wouldn't be coming after all. His mother had begged him to attend her on a visit to the Duke of Mendshire, and he couldn't refuse.

"He asked me to give you his regrets," Gideon said, watching her.

"Why should he send his regrets to me?" Wren replied, a warm blush thawing her cheeks. "It'll be a quiet holiday this year, without his visit. And Eillie or Luke."

"Have you heard when he'll be on leave?"

"I haven't, but Papa expects in the spring. Maybe May?"

"Good. That would be during my longest break from university. I hope we line up. I should like to forget my responsibilities for a while."

Wren laughed. "Yes, Luke is good at that. I was shocked when he said he was going into the King's Navy. I said, 'You do realize you'll have to work, don't you?' The look he gave me!"

Gideon smiled. "I asked him the same thing."

The Amberton property was nearly in view. Wren could hardly feel her toes, but somehow, she didn't want to go in just yet. They rounded the bend, and the dark house appeared, half-hidden behind the blanketed hedge.

"Your horse, Giddy." Wren glanced around. "I hope he's all right."

"I thought we'd come to him by now. I don't think he'd run all the way back to Brayford Hall but can't be sure. There are so many tracks on the road."

"Maybe I'll walk with you a little further—just to see if we can find him. If not, you really should take one of ours."

They marched on, seeming to have run out of words. But Wren felt comfortable in *this* silence. Peace between them, there was no need to scramble for something to say. After passing the far corner hedge, a large black shadow was spotted a little further down the road, stamping its foot in agitation.

"Ah, Aetius. There you are." Gideon turned to face Wren. "You don't have to walk me the rest of the way. I bet your feet are frozen."

Wren tried to wiggle her stiff toes. "Maybe. I can't really feel them anymore. But I'm glad you came down the road. Thank you for going with me."

He gave her a crooked grin. "You didn't really give me a choice. You're crazy, Wren. And I'm sure you would have ended up buried in the snow and lost your toes."

"Then I'd be able to fit into my favorite pair of shoes again," she retorted.

He shook his head as he took a step back. "Good night."

"Good night, Gideon."

Dearest Lyn,

Is there anything more romantic than a walk with your lover on a warm summer's evening? I don't know, really, as I've never been on a walk with a lover on a warm summer's evening. Only a trudge through the snow with Gideon on a freezing winter's night. Not quite the same thing, I'm afraid.

Wren

CHAPTER FIFTEEN
Lessons

Though it long outstayed its welcome, the snow finally gave way to slush, then puddles. By mid-February, Wren was out walking regularly again, despite her mother's fretting.

"You'll catch a chill," she cried one Thursday morning. "I know it. Then I shall suffer the loss of two lovely daughters."

"Mum, Eillie is very much still living and breathing."

"Of course I know that. I only meant…never mind. I do not like thinking about it. But why you have the desire to scamper about the country, getting mud up to your knees, I'll never understand."

"But I receive great benefit from walking. It helps me maintain my *glow*."

Her mother gave her a sidelong glance and puckered her lips. "It does nothing of the sort. I cannot see why you shouldn't listen to reason. One would think I've raised a mule."

"Only a prancing pony, Mum," Wren said, giving her mother's forehead an affectionate peck. "You've raised a prancing pony. Now may I be excused? The Adleys are expecting me."

Mrs. Amberton waved her hand. "I suppose. If you are expected."

A Pretty Game

Walking along the edge of the road to avoid as much mud as she could, Wren pondered the coming months—sharpening her social plan. Now that the snow was gone and the air beginning to warm, suiters loomed in the shadows of spring. One consolation over the winter isolation had simply been the silence of her own front door. No bouquets. No dandies. She had received a handful of letters from Starly, Toone, and several other young gentlemen through the post and the kitchen door. But those were easily burned.

Now that spring was coming, the regular parties would start up again. The only method she could come up with to selectively send acceptances would be to stay home and catch every invitation that came through the door before her mother did. But she wasn't yet resigned to that!

The waking birds chirped from their nests, and Wren inhaled a deep breath. If only Gideon and Casner would come. Then maybe she could be kept busy with Garwick parties and lunches—events she actually wanted to attend.

Gideon had stopped by several times over his winter break, when traveling between his two estates. He had chatted politely with her mother and on one of the visits had even talked over recent political issues with her father. She smiled remembering how he had thrown snowballs at Charley's window when the little boy had made faces at him through the glass.

The sound of a horse approaching from behind caused her to turn and sigh mournfully. Starly bounced her way, a victorious smile on his face.

"Miss Amberton!" he called. "Good morning! I'm so glad I've caught you. Your mother said you would be walking this way and that I should escort you."

He pulled up beside her and looked at the muddy road, a slight wrinkle creasing his nose. After a long hesitation, he slid from his saddle.

"Careful of your boots," Wren said, feeling vexed she had been discovered.

"Thank you," he replied, lifting his feet high as he walked. "I'm befogged by your going out. It's likely to rain again, you know."

"Yes, but I am going to a cousin's home where I may stay for as long as I'd like. If the weather turns poor, I'll be fine."

"I thought you usually visited the Paks on Thursdays."

Wren shot him a sideways glance. He kept better track of her schedule than she thought.

He caught the look and his ears reddened. "I stopped there first, but after a half hour of civil whiskers, decided to peep behind the cupboard."

"Oh," Wren said, trying to translate everything in her head.

"Do you go this way regularly?"

Sensing his purpose, she tried to be vague. "Oh, not recently." The last thing she wanted was Starly dangling after her every time she went to the Adleys.

Another set of hooves sounded from behind. Wren gritted her teeth and turned to see the next approaching horseman. Her jaw relaxed when she recognized his handsome face.

Casner lifted a hand for them. "Hullo there!" he called brightly, slowing his horse as he neared.

"Casner!" Wren scolded playfully. "It is not a university break. I hope you are not skipping school."

He put a hand over his heart. "I'm afraid I am. A family death has called me away—the old dowager on my father's side, rest her. And I decided to take the long way back via Tremdor. I got to Garwick just last night and am leaving this afternoon. But I had to see you. My wise uncle says I should keep watch of you—to be sure no one snaps you up." He glanced at Wren's companion. "Starly. It's good to see you, old man."

"Likewise," Starly replied with a stiff smile.

"So," Casner said, his horse shifting in the muck. "Taking a lover's walk?"

"No!" Wren cried, the same time Starly said, "Yes!"

Wren felt her face flush. "I was walking, and Mr. Starly found me. He kindly offered to escort me. But there is room for another. If you wish to join."

Casner nodded and kicked his horse into a slow walk beside them. Tension radiated from Starly, his knuckles white on the reins he held, leading his horse. But Wren wasn't concerned for him.

"How is your study going, Casner? Have you discovered anything that interests you?"

"Not a thing!" he replied ruefully. "I'm afraid I'm doomed to be a dunce."

"The boot is quite on the other leg for me," Starly said. "I found many things to interest me during my studies. Headmaster said he had never had a pupil able to display himself more than me. When one is in high society as often as I am, it pays to have a full basket."

"That's true," Casner replied. "Starly, I envy you. I'm afraid I'm forced to cut a wheedle with high society."

"Cut a wheedle," Starly repeated smugly. "I'm proud to say I've never been forced into cutting shams."

"Lucky man."

Wren looked up in time to see Casner wink at her.

"Indeed," Starly went on. "I've always naturally fit in and mingled with the height of it. Why it is a great plan of mine, Miss Amberton, to show you around Ferriton this coming social season. You need an introduction to the class of the city. What a smash you will be at all the gallywags. Why every young gentleman will have bellows to mend after setting peepers on you. To have you on my arm there would be the greatest tickle."

Wren bounced her eyebrows. "Well, I guess I should advise you once more not to wade too deeply into your plans, sir. I have no desire to go to Ferriton this season or any other."

"But you must!"

"I think," Casner broke in playfully, "Miss Amberton is quite out of touch with the workings of our world, Starly."

"I am forced to agree with you. I must say I'm quite befogged. I've never known a lady who has no desire to go to Ferriton."

"It's peculiar, indeed. But perhaps Miss Amberton has set her sights on something higher than showing off ball gowns."

Starly harrumphed and mechanically picked at his horse's coat. Wren felt a surge of gratitude that Casner had come upon them. He had only met with her a handful of times, but already he understood her so well.

The cottage soon came into view. She wanted to invite Casner in but didn't know how without being downright rude to Starly.

"There is my destination," she said. "I thank you both for walking with me."

"I'll wait outside for you," Starly said nobly.

"No! Please, don't. I'll be a great while. And I would invite you to join me, but I'm afraid that would be bad manners. My cousin is not fond of crowds."

A Pretty Game

Starly bobbed his head submissively. "Very well. I would do nothing to displease you, Miss Amberton. Until I see you next." He took up her hand, and with a discreet glance at Casner, smooshed his lips into her knuckles.

Wren smoothed her grimace as well as she could and gratefully watched him mount his horse. But instead of going away, he sat there, obstinately waiting for Casner to bid her goodbye as well.

Casner took the cue. "It is only another six weeks until the start of season break. I believe Mrs. Brayford is hosting a ball the very first weekend—for those still in the county and others on their way to Ferriton for the social season. It'll be quite a crush." He fleetingly glanced at Starly with a devilish sort of look. "I have a plan forming in my mind that I think you will be very eager to be a part of, Miss Amberton, and I must ask you not to do anything rash until I see you again." He bounced his perfectly shaped eyebrows.

Wren pressed her lips together to prevent a grin. "Of course."

He nodded and tipped his hat. "Come Starly. I've been in need of a challenge. Race me back to town."

The two young men turned their horses and jolted into a gallop down the muddy road, flipping muck at Wren. She shook it from her skirts and fairly skipped through the Adley's front door.

"I'm here!" she called.

"In the lab," Mr. Adley shouted back merrily.

Wren found him standing at the desk, swirling a little cylinder of brown fluid. "Just in time. Is the weather all right then? Come. Look at this."

Mrs. Adley mumbled a few nonsense words from her corner chair and smiled broadly at Wren, who went directly to her side and took her thin hand long enough to give it a reassuring squeeze.

"What is it? Have you made great headway?" she said, moving to the desk.

"No," he replied. "But I have discovered a way to repair cavities. See here." He dumped the cylinder out onto a folded piece of linen revealing a human molar.

"Is that…one of yours?"

He chuckled. "Certainly not. I would have kept it in my head. It's from a spent cadaver. A colleague sent a few to me. When it came, there was a rough brown hole here. I've been swishing it in this concoction daily for a couple weeks. And now, the hole is gone. Rather amazing for a dead tissue."

"What's it made of?" She sniffed the solution and stifled a gag.

"Oh, various things. And like everything I've made here, probably not very useful. I doubt any living person could be talked into swishing it. Most would rather the tooth be yanked and be done with it."

"Do you think you are getting close?"

He tucked his hands into his pockets and rocked back on his heels. "No," he answered quietly. He looked at his little wife, now sound asleep with her mouth slightly open. "I'm afraid quite the opposite. I've gone backward. Nothing even seems to be helping anymore. The brain is…complex. It is not an easy organ to mend. In fact, I'm beginning to doubt it's even possible."

"No, don't think that way. Mrs. Adley was sure there was a way to perfect it, wasn't she?"

He smiled and began to tinker with a few little test tubes. "True, she was. And there was no telling her any different. She disagreed, but I always felt our science philosophies worked against each other. Mine is the study of life. And with that death. For all things living must eventually meet an end. Among other certainties, it is a hard-fast rule.

A principle we cannot change, no matter the compounds we ingest or the fertilizer we blend into the flower bed soil. Death is inevitable. But Mrs. Adley's science was the science of breaking the rules." He inhaled a deep breath and released it slowly.

"Many times. Many times at the onset of our relationship, I told her some idea she had was impossible. But she always waved me aside to go on and make a liar out of me. She didn't believe that anything existed for only one purpose and shunned the idea that good things must always come to an end. She was sure—so sure!—that everything had the power to go on living. And she almost had me convinced."

Wren took a moment to think about the idea. She had always believed something similar to that. Seeds and offspring perpetuated the life of their parents, didn't they? And what about the divine life after death? But it was hard to be sure of anything.

"And do you not believe it anymore? At all?"

"No. If there were, surely one as wonderful as she would have been spared this—" He waved his hand in his wife's direction.

"But maybe—"

He slammed down a beaker, shattering it in his hand and making Wren jump. Muttering curse words as Wren hastily wrapped his bleeding hand in a towel, he made it clear he didn't want to talk about it anymore. Wren glanced at Mrs. Adley still sleeping in the corner. Her mind hadn't even responded to the abrupt noise.

As Wren walked home hours later, she pondered the Adleys' situation. It was clear Mrs. Adley was rapidly worsening. She was so thin, Wren was certain the woman wasn't eating as she should. She would surely benefit from a nurse, but her husband wouldn't hear of it, insisting he could care for her. Maybe on her next visit, she'd try to make Mrs. Adley eat.

Jill Turner Claybrook

When she arrived home, she found a note waiting for her.

I know it is bold of me to ask so far in advance, but may I request the honor of being your partner for the first dance at the upcoming Garwick Ball? I could not ask it in front of your doting Mr. Starly, for he surely would have begged you for the following five. But nothing would give me more pleasure than to lead you out for that first song.

Yours,
Casner

CHAPTER SIXTEEN
A Girl's Second Ball

Lyn,

Do you think it would be proper for me to wear Mr. Forner's work boots to the ball? I was just thinking that I've not much experience dancing at a ball, and I don't know how to spot a toe-stomper. What if my feet are crushed wearing my dainty slippers? Let me know what you think.

Wren

The morning of the Garwick ball dawned gray and gloomy, but the weather soon cooperated with the hostess's wish (as it usually does for the well-to-do) and brightened into a glorious early April day. Wren could hardly touch her breakfast, her excitement leaving little room for anything else. What a different experience this ball would be from the last!

She would be wanted at this one.

A ball didn't exclude one from daily demands in a household such as the Amberton's. Wren aided Plucky in the kitchen for an hour or so, then went out to feed the chickens and her wild birds. She was anxious for Mr. Forner to return from town. Her new ball gown was supposedly ready.

She was not disappointed when the lanky man rounded the hedge gate with a tailor's bag draped carefully over his arm. She ran to meet him, and he reverently handed over the burden with a smile.

"Right ready for you, Miss. And there was a post for you as well."

She took the envelope he held out and brushed her gaze over the address. Eillie. She thanked Mr. Forner and hurried into the house and up to her room. Surely her mother would want to see the gown, but Wren wanted to be the first. Carefully, she unfastened the bag and pulled back its folds. A grin could not be suppressed.

Lavender silk, with an empire waist and a square cut neck. Narrow ribbon trimmed the daintily puffed sleeves. It was just as she ordered it. It was perfect.

She wrapped the bag folds around the dress again for safe keeping and turned to the letter.

Dearest Wren,

How are you? I hope you are well. Thank you for your last letter. Despite the length of time it has taken me to write back, it was a bright spot in my day!

I'm sorry I didn't make it home for the winter holiday. Aunt has grown accustomed to my companionship and could not spare me. As Mum made no protest, I decided it didn't matter where I was. It feels like ages since I was home. Another lifetime even. I plan to come soon, perhaps in May.

What excitement has befallen you in recent weeks, Sister? Have you had any fun? How are your drawings? Have you learned anything interesting? I miss hearing your animal facts and wish I could remember half of what you do.

Some days I really wonder. This change in me has altered all of my plans. I used to be so sure of my future, and now there are just so many uncertainties. I wonder if I would make a good governess. Or maybe a shop girl? Oh Wren, what am I going to do?

Please don't mention my ideas to Mum. Or to Papa. I don't think they will be pleased.

I miss you. Give Charley a kiss for me.

With love,
Eillie

Wren refolded the letter and tucked it into a drawer. A governess? Picturing poor, silly Eillie herding wet-nosed children and trying to keep order gave Wren a pain. What disappointment she must feel.

She shook her head and moved to occupy herself. Pity (or guilt) would not ruin this day for her.

The day crept by with Mrs. Amberton oohing and aahing over the new gown every hour, Charley capering about trying to scare Plucky, and Wren trying to be calm.

Finally, the long-awaited time arrived!

The Amberton barouche pulled through the Garwick gates exactly three minutes late, and the family waited an eon-long ten minutes as the carriages before them cleared. Wren was certain the whole town was inside, and probably much of the county. Suddenly the excitement in her stomach evaporated.

"I have a pretty face, I have a pretty face," she whispered to herself, though it didn't seem to be helping.

"What's that dearest?"

"Hm? Oh nothing, Mum. I was just talking to myself."

"Why, Wren? You aren't nervous are you? You are radiant my child, isn't she Mr. Amberton?"

"What? Yes. Of course. I have great expectations for this—"

"Don't forget, dearest," Mrs. Amberton cut in. "At a private ball, everyone is considered introduced. There will be a heap of eligible young gentlemen in there. They will all be watching you. On your best behavior! It's a relief you have turned out so pretty. Not one of them would want a plain mischief maker for a wife."

Wren nodded, trying to deflect the sting. She could not decide what was worse—to be the plain mischief maker no one bothered to look at or the embodiment of perfection at which everyone stared. After alighting from the carriage, Wren took her father's offered arm and repeatedly reminded herself not to crush it.

Her nerves were soon allayed with the warm greeting she received at the ballroom door.

"Mr. and Mrs. Amberton," said Mrs. Brayford warmly, taking Mrs. Amberton's hand. "So glad you could join us. And Miss Wren. I hope this ballroom holds nothing but pleasure for you, my child."

"Thank you, ma'am," Wren replied, curtsying.

While her mother went into praises about the house to Mrs. Brayford, Wren moved on to greet Gideon. *He has grown some since I last saw him,* Wren thought. Indeed, his shoulders were broader under his perfectly cut coat, and he was perhaps even a little taller.

He bowed. "I'm glad you're here. I hope you won't run off before the night ends."

Wren laughed, recalling the excuse she had given him for her early departure at the Tremdor Ball. "No, I've given up the habit. I shall not be gambling at any tables tonight."

"Good. Then you will save me a dance?"

"Well, I'm afraid I've moved from cards to pastries, but I could probably be away from the cake table for one dance, yes."

He smiled and bowed again.

Lucy stood regally over her brother and had evidently not found much humor in Wren's jokes. "Good evening, Miss Amberton," she said frostily.

"Miss Brayford."

"I hope you enjoy the ball. I'm sorry you won't find any mud to play in here."

Gideon shot his sister a look, but she seemed not to see it, her gaze still trained on Wren.

"A shame," Wren said calmly. "As I'm sure Gideon would agree, mud does such wonderful things for one's humor." She curtsied quickly and hurried away before the young lady could reply.

Wren relaxed further when, not far from the door, she found Lyn waiting to take her arm.

"Have you ever seen anything like it?" Lyn gushed. "I thought the regular Tremdor ball was fantastic. It pales compared to this."

Wren agreed. The dark wood finishes of the enormous room were brightened by chains of white flowers and drapes of creamy silk. Wax candles flickered in bunches on tall candelabras illuminating the room with a warm, sunny-like glow. It was like walking into a dream.

The two girls wandered the room searching for familiar faces. Starly sniffed Wren out like a bloodhound and tried to engage her for the first two dances. His handsome face flickered with irritation when Wren informed him she had already promised the first dance to another but would accept him for the second. He thanked her and engaged Lyn for the third dance before bowing gracefully and disappearing into the waves of people.

Wren smoothed her fingers across the nape of her neck. "I haven't seen Casner anywhere, have you?"

"I haven't. I'm sure he is here, though. Let's find Lord Garwick. He'll know where to find him, if they are not together."

"No, he is still at the door greeting his guests. I am sure he'll be there until the music starts. I should have asked him when I came in but didn't think to."

"Well, let's just find a place to stand. If I were to guess, Mr. Casner's looking for you. We are probably making circles around each other."

So they found a good place to root themselves, standing between two polished columns where the crowd seemed thinner. The friends chatted easily to fill the time—commenting on the decorations and picking out their favorite gowns as women sauntered past. Presently, the gentle cursory music started, and couples began to take the floor. Wren looked around anxiously for her partner. She was offered to four times, but all were refused. There was still hope Casner would materialize. The younger Bofferd son came for Lyn, and Wren found herself standing alone.

All those inclined to dance were now on the floor.

Resigned to miss the first dance, she stepped back to watch. Lucy was poised to lead off with a young gentleman unknown to Wren, and Gideon stood second with Lady Julia on his arm. Wren was curious to see how her friend would move about the dance floor.

The last time she had seen him dance, he had been thirteen. His mother insisted learning at a young age would make him a better dancer and began giving him and Lucy lessons. Quickly, Lucy had grown frustrated with her brother's clumsy movements and refused to practice with him any longer. Miss Carly was only seven at the time and far too short to be a suitable partner. So Mrs. Brayford had sent for Luke and Wren.

Neither of the Amberton children knew how to dance but both picked it up easily with the woman's instructions. Lucy was happy to have a competent partner, and Gideon had been glad to have a forgiving one. Wren had not thought Gideon so terrible, though he frequently turned the wrong way, kicked into her toes a few times, and his hands were damp. Luke had jeered him ruthlessly, and Mrs. Brayford picked at his form. Despite his smile, Wren could tell poor Giddy was frustrated.

"Don't worry if you step on my toes. It doesn't hurt," she had whispered as they made a side-by-side pass. "Just pretend you're boxing."

He looked at her doubtfully. "Boxing? I don't think Mum would be pleased if I threw you a jab."

Wren grinned. "I'm too quick. You'd never hit me. But I meant your feet."

He nodded, understanding dawning. And soon, what he lacked in grace, he made up for with agility, allowing him to relax enough to concentrate on the coming steps.

"There," Wren assured him. "Now you're not moving like a wounded goose."

He had laughed and missed his turn, but the rest of the lessons had been easy fun.

Wren smiled to see Gideon moved across the ballroom floor in much the same way as she remembered—stiff and athletic—though admittedly with more confidence. Not once did he look to his mum for reassurance. Lucy was the epitome of cold grace and moved just as Wren expected her to, demanding everyone admire her soft steps and keen eyes. Wren imagined her tripping and falling into the nearest gentleman, shredding his coat with her claws.

The dance ended with still no sign of Casner.

"Wren!" Mrs. Amberton said, coming up swiftly behind her. "How did you come to stand here on the side? I saw several boys approach you. Did none of them ask you to dance?"

"I promised the first dance to Mr. Casner, Mum. I was waiting for him to find me."

"Well, I have not seen him. I don't want to see you standing here like a post again. You are planning to dance this evening, are you not?"

"Yes, but—"

"Then you'll not refuse another partner. I'll not have a daughter behave so rudely. Really, Wren, I thought you understood proper decorum."

"But Mum, what if—"

"I said you shall not refuse another. You will dance every dance you are asked, and surely that will mean all of them. Aside from insulting an eligible young man, whom I daresay many here are—the wealth in this room—I won't have my daughter looking like no one would stand up with her. Some might get the idea you have become embroiled in a scandal."

"But Mum, no one asked me at the last ball, and you weren't concerned."

"Not another dance!" Mrs. Amberton said firmly. "Oh! Mrs. Parsel, how lovely it is…"

Wren watched her mother swish away and turned just as Starly materialized to claim his dance, a smug smirk on his face. "Miss Amberton. I noticed your first partner did not come to claim you. But I assure you *I* have not forgotten. I don't know how one could."

Wren took his arm and allowed him to lead her to the floor. Starly was no Casner, but the dance was still enjoyable. From there dance

A Pretty Game

after dance, Wren was occupied. Lady Julia happened upon her once and introduced Wren to her brother and a group of young gentlemen who had come with him. She danced with them all and was delighted to discover a few even shared her interest in science.

Several times Wren tried to reach Gideon, to claim her dance with him and ask him where his friend was, and once she saw him making his way toward her, but always she was snapped up and moved to the floor. It seemed none of the young gentlemen wanted to give her the opportunity to refuse.

As far as Wren saw, Gideon only danced thrice more after the first dance—once with some girl, once with Lyn, and *again* with the lovely Lady Julia (Wren wondered how she had never before realized how particularly annoying Gideon's smile could be). The majority of his time was spent standing on the side stoically watching.

Dinner was announced, and the large gathering moved to the dining tables, which spread into two adjoining rooms and had been set with thick cream cloths, sparkling dinnerware, and trimmed with pink flowers and candles. Wren took advantage of the seated crowd and swept her gaze around the room once more for Casner. He was not to be seen, even at the head table with Gideon.

Seated by her parents, with the Paks across for them, the dinner conversation began.

"Wren, dearest, it has been such a delight to watch you dance this evening. I do hope your feet can keep up."

"They are hardy, Mum. Like regular horse feet."

"Hush!" her mother said quietly. "Do not compare yourself to a beast. Really!" She looked across the table at Mrs. Pak. "Wren has danced twice now with the young Lord Ashwood. I think he is starting to prefer her."

Wren felt her cheeks color and looked about to make sure the said lord was not nearby. "Mum, shh. Someone he knows might hear you."

"Well, it doesn't matter if they do, dearest. He has made his interest quite clear to everyone in attendance."

"He's made nothing clear. We talked about shrubs."

"Shrubs?" Mrs. Amberton laughed loudly. "I am sure there was some hidden meaning in his words. Shrubs. Anyway," she turned to Mrs. Pak, her volume contradicting the secretive hand placed to the side of her mouth, "I think our daughter is safely the most admired young lady of the evening." She elbowed her husband. "Wouldn't you agree, Mr. Amberton?"

"As you say," he replied, attending to his asparagus cream soup.

Wren looked at Lyn in alarm.

"Mrs. Amberton," Lyn began. "We are to go to Preston in a couple weeks, and Wren has promised to go with us. If I remember correctly, you have family near there?"

Wren unclenched her napkin, grateful for the rescue and change of subject.

"Why yes, I do. My brother and his family…"

Mrs. Amberton prattled on, and Lyn bore it all magnificently until she was able to pass the conversation to her mother. Wren wished her friend was beside her rather than across the table. They couldn't say anything without being heard.

"Lyn, I'm going to get more punch. Will you join me?"

Lyn consented and both young ladies hurried to the long table set with three enormous bowls of strawberry punch.

"This is sure your night, Wren. I think your mother has a point. You've successfully gathered every heart, free and otherwise."

"Have I?" Wren glanced around innocently.

Lyn snorted. "For one so smart, you aren't very observant. Are you having fun?"

"I think so. I haven't seen Casner, though. Have you?"

"No, I heard Lucy say that he had been expected earlier but must have been held up. Sorry he's not here."

Wren squelched her disappointment. "Well, you should know I'm not the sort of girl to have her evening ruined because she's been jilted. I've been enjoying meeting you on the floor. You're the lightest dancer here!"

Lyn smiled weakly. "I had to sit out a few times."

"You did?"

She straightened. "There seems to be a shortage of dancing males. But *you* haven't sat out since the first, have you?"

Wren didn't like this topic. "I think we better finish eating. I see the custard coming around already."

When the meal finished, the music once again floated about the ballroom. The dancing continued, and Wren found herself twirling and bouncing with partner after partner. Once she spotted Lyn sitting to the side and wished she could break away from the middle-aged gentleman who kept burping in her face to sit by her friend.

While Wren waited her turn to move down the line, Lyn caught her eye and pointed to the door with wide eyes. Wren felt a thrill in her heart when she spied the tall, handsome figure standing in the door. The music ended and the dancers politely clapped. The last tune for the evening was announced. At once, Wren saw several young men rushing toward her. She felt an impulse to drop to the floor and crawl to safety, but before she could make the attempt, a firm hand took her by the elbow.

She was relieved to turn and find Gideon.

"It's the last dance, Wren. Are you engaged? I mean for the dance, not…"

Wren smiled. Before she could answer, Casner reached them.

"Garwick! I had the devil of a time getting here, as you can very well tell. Had to take a horse at Rembly and ride the rest of the way myself. Nearly flying, I tell you. But I see like a good fellow you've saved my dance partner for me." Without waiting for a reply, he took Wren's hand and kissed it. "Miss Amberton, you look divine. Shall we?"

Wren swallowed and looked back at Gideon. There was something, a fleeting look, in those serious eyes that she found she could not tolerate. As much as she wanted to hold onto Casner's hand, she pulled hers free.

"Actually, your dance was the first," she said. "And I'm sorry you missed it. But this last one I have saved for Gideon."

She was gratified with an unhindered smile affecting Gideon's stony expression. He held out his arm, and she instantly took it.

The first measures were played as the dancers took their proper positions for the quadrille. Wren and Gideon found themselves in a quad with Lyn and her partner. Wren's feet were tired and possibly blistered, but she hushed their complaints, feeling sure this dance with her friends would be the best of the evening.

The movements began, and the rustle of fabric rivaled the lively music. She didn't know why, but Wren had the strangest urge to laugh. When she joined hands with her partner and moved in a small circle, he leaned slightly nearer to her ear.

"I still hate this."

"Why? You are doing well, my lord."

He half-smiled. "My mother has worked hard to refine me."

"Poor woman's fingers must be worked to the bone. But don't forget you had a very talented practice partner."

"That I did," he agreed as they momentarily parted.

The dance continued and did indeed prove to be the best of the night for Wren. Gideon's arm stretched out inches from her back created a familiar feeling of protection, and her hand pressed to his was easy and natural. Lyn was all smiles and laughter, and the dance ended too soon.

"Thank you, Miss Amberton, for the dance," Gideon said with mock properness.

"You are very welcome, my lord," she said, dropping into a low curtsy. "I'm very glad my toe bones are still intact."

He smiled and was about to speak again when he was summoned by Lucy. They were to bid their guests good-bye at the door. He bowed and left her feeling completely satisfied with her second ball.

CHAPTER SEVENTEEN
A Ride to Remember

The morning after the Garwick ball, Wren had gone downstairs to find the sitting room a garden. Bouquets in vases and jars were on every table, the mantel, and even on the floor. As the day progressed, the dining room filled up, as well as the hall. Mrs. Amberton had gleefully stacked up the notes, dividing them into piles of those simply wishing to bear her goodwill and those from eligible young men (which were deemed "absolutely necessary to respond to before they become discouraged!").

Wren couldn't even remember dancing with so many boys and laughed mirthlessly at the absurdity of it all. It had taken her an hour to read through every note and write out short, discouraging replies. Mr. Amberton grumbled at the expense, as many letters were destined for Ferriton.

Wren was relieved that most of her swains were now miles away, and that she would not be joining them. She hoped Ferriton was full this season, and they'd quickly move on to brighter stars.

In the weeks following the ball, she was thrust back into a busy social schedule, though she was surprised to find it was all pleasure.

A Pretty Game

Many of the Tremdor families—including the Toones and Starlys—had gone to Ferriton and would hopefully be gone until June at least. Most of the remaining residents had no young folks at home, making weekly card parties very tolerable.

And to Wren's further delight, either Casner or Gideon sent for her nearly every day—always in the afternoon so she could attend to the Adleys and Clamp children in the morning. They went out on rides and picnicked, strolled through town popping into the little shops to see what was new, and—when Gideon was busy—walked about Garwick's gardens or lounged in the library, allowing Miss Carly to join them. Then Wren was returned home in the evening in time for whatever her mother had planned.

Each morning Wren sent PJ with a note to Lyn inviting her to join, but more than half the time, the bird returned with a declining reply. Once she had the Garwick carriage stop at the Pak home to collect Lyn anyway.

They had spent the day on a picnic in the hills, and Wren thought it had been wonderful. Casner had been excessively funny that day, his impersonations of her mother spot on and his rather warm poetry borderline ridiculous. Wren had never giggled so much in her life. But the next morning Lyn refused to go out again, shoving Wren into the sole female companionship of Miss Lucy.

"I don't understand why Lyn refuses to come out with us!" Wren exclaimed one day, walking through town beside Gideon. "You like her company, don't you?"

He shrugged. "Yes."

"And she likes you, of course. So it isn't like she wouldn't have someone to walk with her."

"No."

"And she isn't shy. I've always admired how gracefully she moves in familiar and unfamiliar crowds. She is the same whether there are five people in the room or five hundred. So why should our little group put her off?"

He rolled his tongue against the inside of his cheek and shrugged again.

"See? Why is she being so pudding-headed? Maybe she's just busy with something. I haven't been to see her for a little while. I bet she has a big project she is working on. That's probably it." Satisfied, Wren eyed her companion in a sidelong glance. "You are rather quiet this afternoon."

He shrugged a third time and looked through a shop window.

"When are we going to the hills, Garwick?" Casner said, coming up behind them with Lucy. "I'm anxious for refreshment and Miss Amberton's company."

Wren turned just long enough to catch Lucy's daggers. Gideon gave no reply.

"Miss Amberton!" came an excited call from down the lane.

Casner turned round. "Dash it. It's that maundering woman." He took Wren by the arm just as she made eye contact with Miss Nelly. "Hurry and you won't have to talk to her. I've found she's not too difficult to leave behind."

Though his words made her laugh and she went with him willingly, she couldn't help feeling she had done something wrong when she looked over her shoulder to see Gideon and Lucy speaking kindly with Miss Nelly.

It was some time before the Brayford siblings joined Wren and Casner at the barouche. Gideon handed Lucy into the vehicle, then lightly sprang up beside Wren on the bench.

"Did you have to hear about her little toe?" Casner asked merrily from the cushioned seat.

Gideon snapped the reins.

Soon, they reached their destination—a pretty little meadow with plenty of wildflowers. A blanket was spread out and each took a spot, Gideon and Lucy radiating gloom from one side and Casner and Wren playfully bantering on the other while he fiddled absently with the hem of her skirt.

Wren tried several times to rope her melancholy friend into the fun, but he eventually laid back with his hat tipped over his dark eyes and his arms folded across his chest.

Casner surveyed the green as if for the first time. "I am glad you chose this spot, Garwick. A great farewell."

"You are leaving?" Wren asked with disappointment as clear as she could make it.

"Maybe. I am toying with an idea that would take me away just as soon as I can manage."

"And what, sir, is that idea?"

"Ah!" he replied, tipping his hat roguishly on his head. "*That* is a great secret. One that may bring happiness to many. But I do not intend to keep you in the dark long, my little pretty one."

"Well, now you must tell me."

He inhaled a deep breath and moved his head side to side, considering. "All right. But this blanket of company is not the place. Will you join me on a walk?"

Suddenly Gideon shot upright and glanced at his pocket watch. "The time. I forgot I am to meet with a barrister from town."

"But we've just arrived," protested Casner. "And I've brought this book of poetry that is most amusing." He grinned slyly. "Are you sure this doesn't have anything to do with the charming Lady Julia arriving today?"

Wren noticed Gideon's ears redden.

"I'm afraid there's no time for poetry," Gideon said coolly, rising to his feet. "Or a walk."

Lucy took his offered hand. "Yes, I'm impatient to see Julia, as well. She really is a favorite in our house, isn't she Gideon?"

"She is," he agreed.

Lucy, as always, refused to ride on the bench, and Gideon refused to hand over the reins, so the short-lived adventurers resettled in the barouche just as they had come.

The day suddenly didn't seem as cheerful to Wren. She wanted to ask how he had come to forget about an important meeting—his kind never forgot such things—or, even more keenly, why he should be anxious to see Lady Julia. A vague notion of what it might mean needled her brain, but she decided against satisfying her curiosity and instead scowled into the teasing, bright woods.

Before she was left at the hedge gate, Casner bid her the kind of farewell he gave when he'd be away from her longer than seventeen hours—kissing her hand and reminding her how well he thought of her, how he would miss her. And so she felt resigned to not know his great secret any time soon.

Which was why the next afternoon, an hour or so after she returned from being with the Adleys, Wren was surprised to see his dapper form pull through the gate in the single-bench gig.

"Where is Gideon?" she asked him from the front stoop.

"He had some business and could not come. Miss Brayford is also tied up."

She eyed the high carriage. "So…it is just the two of us?"

"Yes," he said smiling widely. "One last hoorah."

She knew her mother would not approve of an unaccompanied ride so clambered up as quickly as she could. He snapped the reins and away they went, Plucky frowning from the clothesline. Wren hoped she wouldn't tattle.

The road was still rutted from winter and after several large bumps, Wren was forced to loop her arm with Casner's, fearing she would otherwise tumble off the seat and into the spinning wheels. But she was mostly comfortable holding his arm, and he smiled down at her approvingly. The day was warm and clear, and Wren breathed deeply the country air.

"How do you do it?" he asked suddenly.

"Do what?"

"How do you make me forget everything around me? You are stunning every time I see you."

Wren felt heat creep up her neck, but she boldly replied, "I could say the same of you."

"Ah. I pinch my cheeks," he replied with a wink.

She laughed. "Well, I give you permission to end that habit. We are well known to one another now, you know. There's no need to be impressive."

"I quite agree," he said comfortably.

Ahead, a horse-drawn wagon rounded the bend. As it neared, Wren realized it was Mr. Clamp. Casner exhaled and pulled their smaller gig to the side to wait for him to pass. The wagon slowed to a stop beside them.

"Hello, Mr. Clamp!" Wren called brightly.

"Afternoon, Miss Amberton," Mr. Clamp replied. "Sir."

Casner bobbed his head and twitched at the reins. Wren glanced curiously at the load Mr. Clamp pulled—various cuts of lumber and a barrel of pitch. Mr. Clamp followed her gaze and grinned.

"For the house," he said. "Lord Garwick's ordered some men out tomorrow for repairs and to even add a room."

"Has he?"

"Yes, ma'am. Bless him! Says he weren't told of the condition of some of his tenant homes. Now that weather's let up. I think he's even ordered some work on them other houses, too."

Wren felt a little surge of pride. And she was very pleased to see a smile on Mr. Clamp's lonely face. As the wagon rolled away, she promised to visit to see the improvements. Casner shrugged when the wagon was behind them.

"What a waste," he muttered.

"What is?"

"Nothing," he replied, squinting his eyes. "Remind me again how to get to that spot."

Wren directed him, and they drove on to Pirate Pond, where he helped her down with two hands on her waist. They walked about the bank for a bit, chatting lightly about mutual acquaintances and other little things.

It soon became clear to Wren that Casner was not completely at ease. He seemed to constantly be on the cusp of saying something significant, then would cut in with a joke or some light comment. The longer this went on, the more nervous she became. Finally, as they were returning to the gig, he broke through his reserve.

"Wren, I must speak with you about something. You know, my uncle is the Duke of Mendshire."

"So I've been told."

"He is a very bored man. Unmarried and very lonely. I feel sorry for him, poor wretch. I think he may be reaching his final years."

"And you hope to not end up the same way?" Wren said encouragingly.

"Me? Of course not. I shall play my cards better."

Wren felt pleased by this. "A shame there hasn't been a duchess all this time. Why, almost any girl would give up a hand for it. Though hopefully not her right hand. I can only imagine how hard it would be to flutter a fan with the left hand." Wren tried it for a moment and knew she was correct. "Unless she was already left-handed. Then maybe it would be all right. But anyway, it would be an honor indeed. And I'm sure it is hard for him to not have anyone to care for him."

"Oh, he has more servants than I have cravats, but yes, a wife is the only thing he has ever been in want of. But I must confess my pity for him does not go as deep as what I hold for myself."

Wren was confused. "Why should you pity yourself?"

"I'm tied down, Wren. To all the dictates of my deceased father, rest him. A penniless fop riding about the country—scavenging at the mercy of friends. Right now I have to hold back in everything I want." He glanced at her significantly. "You know, it is within my uncle's power to make me very secure for a number of years."

"Really?" Wren bit her lip. She remembered Mrs. Harper once saying the only time a careless young gentleman feels the need to be financially secure is if he is contemplating marriage.

"Yes. I am tied now, but he could open the way for me to achieve all my hopes."

How many more years did he have left at university? Two? That seemed like an awful long time.

"Well," she said, hoping her next words weren't too bold, "I think it's always a good idea to see the shiny side of a penny. I am willing to help you however I can, even if it is just to sit and wait prettily."

At once they stopped walking and faced each other. He smiled in his dazzling way. "Then as his ward, may I have your permission to see him about you?"

Wren blushed hotly and ducked her head to hide it. Casner was ready to ask his guardian permission to become engaged. To her! Of all the girls in the world, he had chosen *her*.

She bit her lower lip in a smile but kept her face down. "I suppose if you really want to see him about me, yes. You may."

"Excellent. Thank you, darling. You'll not regret it."

He twitched a little closer. He was so near, a shiver moved down her spine. She looked up at him, and as if swallowed by fire, she realized she wanted him to kiss her. He was perfect in every way—charming, handsome, funny. She wanted him to be her first real kiss. Her last kiss. The only one she would ever kiss.

"Kiss me," she breathed.

He put his hands on her waist without hesitation, leaned down, and pushed his lips to hers. Wren felt hot and giddy in the full ten seconds his lips touched hers. Then he pulled away and grinned.

Wren tried to grin back.

She hoped her face didn't show what she felt. All the fire, all the excitement, all the heart-pounding, mind-numbing glee—doused. That was it? She wanted him to lean down and kiss her again. To give her another chance. But he didn't.

He cleared his throat awkwardly and started walking again. "I best get you home."

"Yes," she replied quietly.

She was bewildered. Casner had just kissed her. Really kissed her! That meant he loved her. He was even going to ask her to become the future Mrs. Casner. She should be over the moon and dancing through the tulips. But somehow she seemed to have fallen flat.

He helped her onto the gig bench, then smoothly slid up beside her. He chattered the entire ride home—commenting on the woods, how much he enjoyed his visits to Garwick, how he loved the rides with her. Wren nodded and 'uh-huh'-ed, but all her real thoughts stayed inside her head.

She was struggling with a feeling she couldn't name. Something akin to disappointment? But how could that be? It wasn't that the kiss had been repulsive. No, she hadn't even been close to gagging, which she had always feared would be her reflex response to someone's lips touching hers.

She stole a sidelong glance at the boy seated beside her. He was still handsome. She liked the way his hair curled slightly from beneath his hat. And the way his eyes sparkled when he was enjoying himself.

But that kiss? What was it about?

When he helped her down at the hedge gate and placed one more kiss on her cheek followed by the words, "I will miss you terribly," she knew she was just flustered. She was new at this, and he was so perfect. She watched him drive away and waited until he turned to wave.

"She swoons over her swain and feeleth like she hath been hit in the head with a brick!" Charley said philosophically from the tree. "How doth love feel so resplendent and awfuleth, like a sugared fork stabbed into the heart?"

Wren said nothing for she did not have an answer. She merely looked up into the tree, smiled, and went into the house.

"Wren? Is that you, dearest?"

"Yes, Mum," Wren said quietly as she approached the sitting room where her mother's voice had floated out.

"I've been—that is…everything all right?"

"Yes. Why?"

"Nothing. I just wanted to be sure he didn't—that you are all right." Mrs. Amberton smiled, relief clear in her expression.

"Yes. I'm just going to go to my room."

"Of course, dearest."

When Wren sat down at her desk, her hands neither reached for a book nor picked up a pencil. The letter from Eillie peeked out from under a pile of papers. Wren wondered what her sister was doing.

Daylight was beginning to fade, casting long shadows across her room. Slowly, she reached up and pulled the cloth from the mirror. The reflection held her gaze for a long moment. She knew the nose, the mouth, the eyes. But something was amiss. She had the distinct feeling it was a stranger who looked back at her. Mechanically, she recovered the mirror.

Dear Lyn,

I received my first kiss today. Casner, of course. It was quick but not unpleasant. I feel a bit fast for kissing him before he's decidedly declared himself, but he all but said he intends to. Am I the only one who feels like she has no idea what she is doing? Governesses ought to teach something about this. Maybe I'll write a book: "Courting Tips for Girls with No Commonsense Regarding the Opposite Sex and Other Things I Learned While Being Admired." I suppose I'll have to gather more material before I get started. So far all I have is 'Don't talk about his toes rotting off' and 'Do flit your eyelashes but only if you can manage it without looking like you have dirt in your eye.'

Wren

CHAPTER EIGHTEEN
Take it Back!

A carriage crunched down the drive, and Wren saw her sister anxiously looking toward the house. Their aunt was seated beside her, a serene smile etched into her long face.

"My girl, my girl. My poor girl!" Mrs. Amberton clucked as she hurried out to meet the hired carriage. Mr. Amberton let out a harrumph before striding out to join his wife.

Eillie's face brightened ever so slightly. "Mum, Papa. It is so good to see you," she said as she climbed out of the carriage.

Wren held back, studying her sister. How changed she was! Her hair was pulled back beneath her bonnet with not a curl to be seen, and her glasses were perched on her nose, no doubt a permanent fixture. However, the dress she wore was very fashionable, though a bit sophisticated for a girl of not yet sixteen, Wren thought. Aside from her appearance, her movements were almost rigid and her smiles obviously forced. Wren winced.

"Eillie! Eillie! Eillie!" Charley squealed as he ran from the barn. He jumped into Eillie's arms, and she held him for just a moment before setting him down on his feet. Behind her, in a billow of plum satin,

Aunt Fanny gracefully removed her tall, willowy figure from the carriage and began making her greetings.

Eillie leaned to see around Mr. Amberton and smiled. Taking the cue, Wren walked out to meet her little sister.

"Wren!" Eillie exclaimed, taking her sister into her arms in an embrace that put their mother's to shame.

"I, um…" Wren returned the squeeze. "I'm glad you've come home."

Eillie stepped back, holding Wren at arm's length. "Are you?" Her eyes searched over Wren's face, trying to detect a lie.

"Yes, I am." And a piece of her truly was.

"Well, it is only for a short time. Aunt would like to visit Ferriton before going back home, and I can't say that I am disappointed. I hope to only be here a couple weeks. But Wren. Gracious, you've changed. I love how you've pinned your hair."

Wren rubbed her foot on her ankle. "Ah. Thanks." *It's yours Eillie,* Wren thought with returning shame. *The loveliness is all yours.*

Eillie swallowed and forced another smile. "Well, I'd like to go rest. It's been a long day." She looked nervously at the house. "Am I to have my old room, Mum?"

"Of course, dearest! Of course. Plucky has changed up the linens fresh for you and everything is ready, my poor girl." Mrs. Amberton crushed Eillie to her bosom again.

The party made their way into the house, and the visitors were soon settled in their rooms for an afternoon rest. Wren tried to sit at her desk, but Eillie's sad eyes haunted her memory, making it impossible to draw a single line. Her sister was miserable. That was plain to see.

'What am I going to do?' Wren recalled her asking in her last letter.

"A governess," Wren breathed aloud, remembering her ideas. "Or a *shop girl!*" Their family might not move in the highest circles, but their father would be mortified to have a daughter enter a trade. And poor, delicate Eillie. What she would suffer.

Over the next several days, Wren was forced to witness just how delicate Eillie had become. She had always been quiet but was now timid as well. She shook when she picked up her teacup and nervously looked about the rooms as if she should be living in the barn. She jumped whenever their father spoke and teared up when their mother fretted and lamented over her.

What a wretch Wren thought herself to be. It was easy to forget what she had done when Eillie was away, but watching her sister's constant state of misery was overwhelming. The burden she had long forgotten returned tenfold, like a boulder crushing her heart.

Several days of observation were more than Wren could bear. When the Garwick carriage failed to roll through the gate on the third day, Wren begged her mother to allow her to visit Lyn for an entire afternoon. After a relentless morning's effort, Mrs. Amberton consented.

At the door of the Pak home, Wren exhaled an enormous breath of relief. The home had always offered her kindness and made her feel her best self.

"Wren, I'm so glad you've come!" Lyn exclaimed when Wren was ushered into her bedroom. "I'm so anxious for Thursday. Have you packed yet?"

"Packed?" Wren asked without thinking. She looked at the large trunk on Lyn's floor.

"Yes, you goon. For our trip!"

"Trip." Wren felt a twist in her stomach. The trip to Preston. "Oh Lyn. I've forgotten."

The silk shawl in Lyn's hand unfolded to the floor. "Forgotten? But I reminded you two weeks ago."

"I know! I know you did, but I…it slipped my mind."

"Well, never mind. I'll forgive your flutter-headed self. We aren't leaving for another two days, so there's still time for you to prepare."

"Oh, but I can't go. Eillie is home," she said, realizing it would be the perfect escape. "And Casner will be returning soon."

Lyn put one hand on her hip. "Casner? What's he got to do with anything? I asked you to come with me months ago. I can't live with my mother's family for three weeks without you by my side! I'll positively shrivel!"

Wren wrung her hands. "Lyn I'm sorry, but I can't go."

"You can't go, or you don't want to go?"

Wren shrugged.

"I see." Lyn cocked her head to the side. "I guess I shouldn't be surprised—you've gotten good at breaking promises."

"What's that supposed to mean?"

"Exactly what I say. You promised to go with me, and now you're backing out. *For a boy.* And you promised me you wouldn't let this," she motioned at Wren's face, "change you. But it has. I've hardly seen you on Thursdays. Your notes are mostly halfhearted. You're always going to parties and out for joy rides."

"I've invited you to come along on the rides. Don't act like you haven't avoided them."

"I won't because I know I have. I don't like your precious Casner. And I can't stand who you become when you're around him."

"Who do I become?"

"And," Lyn continued without answering, "I don't like feeling like the spare friend, solely there because you feel guilty leaving me out."

"That's not true and you know it. And maybe now you know how I felt every time we were in public before *this*." She dramatically mimicked Lyn's gesture indicating her own face. "No one ever spoke to me when you were there."

"Well maybe you should have said something worth saying, instead of whispering half-witted jokes for no one to hear."

"Because I know you always laugh at my jokes, I'll pretend you didn't say that. And forget the outings. I can't help you feeling like a stump. But I've missed Thursdays because I've been going to help Mrs. Adley. She's really ill, and they need me. I told you why I wasn't coming so often."

"You've changed."

"I haven't."

"Your priorities, hair, your face—"

"I haven't!"

"How did you get them?"

"What?"

"You did something to Eillie. Admit it!"

Wren straightened. The accusation was an arrow she hadn't expected. How did Lyn know? Had Wren slipped up somewhere? No. It was nothing more than a theory posed as certainty, and Wren would not be cowed into a confession like a thief in the stocks. Stubbornly, she pressed her lips together and cocked her head.

"Well," Lyn said. "You know what they say about old friends. If they don't age like a fine wine, they rot like last week's rubbish." She was silent for a moment then stood and moved to her trunk to rearrange her stockings. "I have things to do. You can show yourself out, can't you?"

"Like the queen of Langley," Wren said, turning on her heels.

Wren marched home with a bitter taste in her mouth. Who did Lyn think she was? A saint sent to cleanse the Amberton household? How Wren had ever come to think of such an insult-slinging, two-faced girl as her best friend was beyond her. And furthermore, she was thrilled not to be going all the way to Preston. Who invites someone on a trip they themselves have deemed vomit-inducing anyway?

Wren stormed up the stairs, much to Mrs. Amberton's chagrin, and slammed her door. With deliberate steps she crossed the room, ripped Lyn's gifted dragon piece off her wall, and crumpled it into a tight ball to be tossed into the rubbish bin. She then yanked the cloth from the mirror to admire her shiny, stolen hair. In a few days, Casner would return on his white horse and rescue her from all the other miserable creatures trying to drag her under.

A quiet knock sounded at her door. "Wren?" Eillie gently called out. "May I come in?"

Wren made no answer but slumped down at her desk. The door popped open, and Eillie showed herself in, cautiously sitting down on the bed.

"Where have you been?" she asked softly.

"To see an *old* friend."

Eillie pressed her lips together and nodded. "It didn't go well?"

Wren snorted. "No."

Eillie held very still and gazed at some of the drawings pinned to the wall. Looking at her by way of the mirror before her, Wren could see her sister's face, pinged with melancholy. The weight stretched and settled again. It was getting so heavy.

Was Lyn right? Was she so changed?

Wren turned in her seat. "Eillie. You are different from when you left home."

Eillie nodded her head without looking up.

"People often change as a result of someone else. You know, like when your friend—"

Eillie turned her head sharply. "I have no friends here."

Wren wrinkled her nose at what was probably the truth. Eillie had cut ties with everyone in Tremdor. In fact, she was never even spoken of at parties anymore, no doubt her friends had been burned by her lack of interest in them since developing her…issue.

"Anyway," Wren continued, "say you did. Say you have a good friend who gets mad at you—turns on you even—because of something you did. Or multiple things you did. And let's say all these choices you have made hinged on one other significant choice. How would you go about fixing it?"

Eillie pulled at a loose tendril near her ear and shrugged. "I don't know. Apologize?"

Apologize. Maybe if she apologized to her sister and then to Lyn, the boulder on her heart would roll away. Would it be that simple?

"Wren, I don't really know what you're talking about, but I will say I've noticed a change in *you* since we've been apart. You remind me of me. Before I left home. I don't know how, but it's like we have…switched something. A trade. Do you know what I mean?"

Wren nodded and licked her lips. "Like we traded looks?"

Eillie tilted her head to one side. "Yes. Like that."

Wren looked at her feet. Apologize. Just apologize. "Eillie, if I could give back some of…" Wren stopped.

"Give back some of what?"

Wren inhaled a deep breath. "That is, I took…I ate something with your hair in it. And I took your…"

Eillie rose to her feet. "You took my what, Wren?"

"I took your beauty," Wren choked out. "For myself. I concocted a potion of sorts that allowed me to take it from you."

Wren watched her sister's face grow pale, then flush with a color quite unbecoming. "*You.*"

"I didn't mean to. Honest. I didn't know what would happen."

"How? How could this happen? All this time. You knew what was going on. And you didn't tell me! How could you, Wren?"

"I'm sorry."

"You're sorry?" Eillie snatched a pillow and hurled it at Wren's head. "How could you?!"

Wren jumped when Eillie's door slammed shut. She rubbed a hand over her heart and hunched forward. The weight had not budged. There had to be something to be done. Some way to fix everything.

The basket!

If Wren could make a pudding and eat it to steal her sister's beauty, then certainly she could make a pudding with her own hair, pour it down Eillie's throat, and switch back. Then Eillie would be happy, and Lyn would see that Wren valued their friendship enough to sacrifice her blended face and glossy locks.

She did, didn't she?

Yes, deep in her heart she did. She dropped to her stomach and stretched her arm into the far reaches beneath her bed, sneezing when her nose tickled. The dusty basket was safely drawn out.

With a pair of sewing shears, she cut a thick lock from behind her ear. Again, it was probably more than necessary, but there was no room for error. The switch had to be complete.

Wren rapped on Eillie's door.

"Go away," her sister said in a quavering voice.

"Eillie, it's me. I need you to come with me."

The door opened a crack. "Why? Wren, I still need to think about this."

"There's nothing to think about." She reached out and grabbed her sister's arm. "Just come on. Hurry!"

Eillie did as she was bid and submissively allowed Wren to drag her down the stairs, out the door, and across the yard toward the woods.

Wren stopped. "Wait, no. Not there. I don't want you to end up drowned in the pond."

"What?" Eillie whispered as Wren turned their direction toward the barn. It would be much safer.

Once in the loft, Wren cleared a patch in the straw and emptied the contents of her basket.

"Wren, what are you—"

"Shhh. I need to think. I must get this right."

The formula was followed precisely, a gag commenced once or twice, and the mixture was set to simmer and bubble and thicken. Eillie shifted uneasily on her knees as she watched her sister work. When it was finished, Wren cackled gleefully and turned off the burner to allow it to cool.

"There," she said, shoving the pudding under Eillie's nose. "Now, eat this and you'll have it all back."

"What?"

"You'll have it all back—your face, hair, everything. Don't ask how, just trust me. I took it, now I want you to have it back."

Eillie leaned away from the pudding and blinked. "But I don't want it back."

The little pot lowered a few inches. "You don't want it back?"

"No! I don't. That is, I don't *need* it back." She glanced down at the pot. "Even if I thought I could stomach that. I don't completely understand how this is real—it's too fantastic. And if I didn't notice the change in you, I wouldn't believe you at all. But I promise, I am fine as I am. I want to be *seen*. Not my face or my body, but *me*."

Hm. So Eillie had felt that, too. "But you're miserable," Wren pointed out.

"What? No, I'm not. I mean I am a little miserable here. Because I know Mum and Papa are so disappointed in me. They seem to feel I've lost the chance of marrying well. And also, I've no friends here."

"No friends? The whole town loves you. Everyone always sought you out and sent you gifts."

"Flattery and that's all. I tried to pretend I didn't see it, but deep down I always knew it was all a front. False. I was never really allowed to go out and make any lasting connections, not like you were. It was still wonderful being praised and what some would call loved before, but now…it's different."

"But you hid yourself away. And cried so much. Don't tell me you haven't felt misery."

Eillie reached out and clasped Wren's hand in hers. "Sure, I did at first. I was scared. I thought something was seriously wrong with me, all that talk about a plague. I wish you had said something. And then, when I didn't die, I thought if everyone said I wasn't pretty, my life might as well be over. But going away and living with Aunt. I've changed. It took some time and work, but I like my face. My hair. I'm still me. I dance every dance in Forthshire. And with Aunt, there's no pressure to marry someone I do not love. I can wear my glasses instead of bumbling around blindly. And if I want to eat a second pastry, I do."

"But what about your letter? You are hopelessly lost, wondering what you are to do."

A Pretty Game

"What?" Eillie thought for a moment. "Oh. Yes, I *do* wonder what to do with my life. The possibilities seem endless. For the first time I can see what I'm capable of besides being a decoration. I could be a governess and teach little ones their letters and numbers. Do you know how much I would love to teach? I had never even thought of it until recently."

Wren slumped back. How had she not seen all this before? She thought of the times Eillie had skipped out on cake. The times the girls in town had stopped her with shallow praise, then carried on, never truly inviting her to join their circles. The falsehoods, the jealousy, the pressure for perfection. Eillie had felt these her whole life, and Wren had been too concerned with herself to notice.

"Eillie. I don't even know what to say. I didn't understand before. What you felt."

She shrugged. "You hardly talked to me Wren. How could you have known?"

That stung. It was true. Since the time she was old enough to know jealousy, she had shunned her sister. Separated herself from one who could have been her greatest friend.

"I'm so sorry," Wren said pathetically.

"It doesn't matter. We shall go on as we are, if you are all right."

Wren grimaced. Knowing everything that was inside of her, she wasn't sure.

"I hope we can be friends from now on," Eillie whispered. "True sisters."

Wren tugged her sister's hand and pulled her into a hug. "True sisters," she agreed.

Eillie pushed her away and beamed. "Now tell me, when under heaven did you become a witch?"

CHAPTER NINETEEN
The Letter

Dearest Lyn,
 I am sending this knowing it will come back to me unopened. I hope your trip is going well. Play a game of Takka for me.
   Your hopefully still friend,
    Wren

On the sixth morning after Eillie's return, a letter arrived for Mr. Amberton. He snatched the envelope and left the table so abruptly Mrs. Amberton hadn't even the chance to lean over to see the seal. Within two minutes such a shout erupted from his study, the whole table froze.

"Wren! Wren, come quick!"

Of course a summons like that failed to draw only the one named, and the whole table scrambled for the study.

"What is it, my love?" Mrs. Amberton begged to know.

Mr. Amberton stood behind his desk with such a smile, Wren almost didn't know him. Absolute triumph smothered his face.

"Such news!" He looked directly at Wren. "What do you suppose is in this letter? I ask you! What do you suppose?"

All eyes turned toward Wren, who was completely flummoxed.

"An offer of free cheese?" she ventured to guess.

Mr. Amberton laughed, an almost crazed sound that made her step back. "Cheese? Free cheese. No, come in child. Come in. It is an offer of marriage!"

"Marriage?" Wren whispered. "For me? From whom?" Her heart gave a hard, unsettled thump. Casner.

"My girl! From whom? As if she hasn't a notion that she might attract even the farthest of men. With a face such as yours, Wren, I'm surprised it's not from the king himself, offering to abandon his wife. But it is from a very respectable gentleman, indeed. The *Duke of Mendshire,* my child. The Duke of Mendshire is requesting the opportunity to offer for your hand."

He delighted in the gasp that went round the room and dropped into his chair, pulling his stationery from the drawer. "Of course, I've had several offers for you, but—"

"Several?" Wren cried. "You've never told me of any."

"Never mind. None of them were local, though I chatted with two of them at the Garwick ball. All fine prospects, but I knew we could hold out for better. And better has come." He waved the letter like a victory banner. "He says he has heard great things about you and has decided to take the plunge. You'll be bathing in diamonds," he cried, dipping his pen into the ink pot. "And we'll be quite comfortable here, I am sure. You'll not forget us. Yes, there's a good girl."

Wren couldn't move. *The Duke of Mendshire?* She had heard his name, sure, but that was hardly an introduction. "Papa," she said with a thick tongue. "What are you doing there?"

"Sending my reply, of course! He must know his prize is secure."

Wren swallowed, feeling her head begin to swim. "But I don't even know him. I've never even seen him."

"What does that matter? He says he'll begin his journey as soon as he receives a reply. You'll meet him soon enough."

"But…what if I don't want to meet him?"

Her father's pen stopped, and he drew in a heavy breath without looking up.

"Wren," her mother whispered. "Consider, my dear…"

The pen remained frozen, hovering over the next stroke. "It will make for an odd marriage if you never meet the man."

Wren lifted her chin. "Not if I never allow the marriage at all."

The pen dropped, and Mr. Amberton shot up. "Not allow?" he barked. "Not allow? As if you have any say in the matter. How can you be so selfish? I never thought you capable."

"Brother," Aunt Fanny broke in. "Think of the poor child—"

"Poor child? There isn't one in this room. I have put a roof over all my children's heads and food in their mouths. And what answer do I get? A son who never writes, a daughter who whimpers at the slightest trouble, a boy who refuses to act properly, and worst of all, a selfish, stubborn little chit who is refusing to give a little of herself for the comfort of her family. We would all benefit from such a connection, and she wants to refuse us. No! I'll not have it. She will meet the duke, and she will marry him. I'll see to that!" He dropped back into his chair, fuming noxious anger and scratching horribly at the paper.

Wren clenched her fists but could not loosen her tongue after such a speech. Was she ungrateful? Selfish? Stubborn? She had mourned what nature had given her, taken what had been bestowed on her sister, jilted her best friend, and stolen from a couple who trusted her implicitly. At the very moment it should have come to her rescue, her pride failed her. She could not argue. She was those things.

All of them.

A Pretty Game

The wax was dripped, and the seal was pressed. Wren felt a hand take a hold of hers and looked down to see Eillie's fingers wrapped around hers.

"Plucky. Plucky!" Mr. Amberton bellowed. The woman appeared behind the little group. "Take this to the post this minute. Send it express. Do not let it out of your sight until you have paid the stamp, whatever it costs. Understood?"

"Yes, sir," Plucky said with a small curtsy before going away with her head down.

"Well," said Mrs. Amberton in a quaking voice. "This calls for a celebration, then. Wren, dearest? Shall I have Plucky make—"

"No," Wren whispered. "I don't want anything. May I please be excused?"

Mrs. Amberton swallowed, nodding her head. Wren glanced at her father's stony face before slipping her hand from Eillie's and brushing past Aunt Fanny and Charley. To her room she flew for the solace of her little pillow.

The Duke of Mendshire. Was there any fate worse than this? To be forced to marry the ancient uncle of one she might have chosen on her own accord. What will Casner think of this?

A soft knock came at the door. "Wren?" Eillie called.

Wren gave no answer, so the door opened. A slight pressure befell the edge of the bed, and Wren felt a gentle hand stroke her hair.

"I'm sorry, Wren."

Wren pushed her face further into her pillow. This was not how it was supposed to be.

"I have heard Aunt speak of him before. She said he is a most charming man. She met him long ago and seems sure he wouldn't have changed. Maybe it won't be so bad as you suppose."

"I don't know how it could be any worse."

"Oh but think of it. You'll be able to travel, maybe see some of the animals you've drawn. You'll not have to work in the kitchen or in the garden. Or empty latrines. Think of all the good you will do with your wealth. And you'll be able to have a whole library all to yourself, I bet."

Could she trade her freedom for books? No! A fresh wave of tears washed over her.

"It should be me," Eillie whispered. "Wren. I will…I will eat that pudding. Then he would take me instead."

It was true. If Wren hadn't meddled, Eillie would be the one being primed to be a duchess. And she'd be just as miserable except no one would know it. At least Wren had spared her sister that pain.

"No, Eillie. I deserve this. Stupid, selfish girl that I am!"

"Don't speak like that, it isn't true. I will always be grateful you are my sister. I'm only sorry that this has fallen to you. Oh Wren, there must be some way to fix this."

Wren launched upright. A fix. The Adleys! Agitation pushed away the tears, and she raced to her closet. The time had come for a confession of a very desperate nature. Mr. Adley was a resourceful man. If anyone could help her, surely he would have mercy and discover a solution to her troubles. A jacket and bonnet were thrust into place and the basket was looped over her arm.

"Where are you going?" Eillie squeaked.

Not wanting to garner attention from the rest of her family, Wren threw open the window.

"Wren, what are you doing?"

"Going to see our cousin. Cover for me. Tell them I am resigned but wish to stay in my room. And I'm not hungry."

A Pretty Game

"Not hungry? Plucky will never believe—"

Wren didn't pause to listen to her sister's protest. She swiftly scrambled her way down the hooks, leaping to the ground when she came to the missing mount. Before anyone could stop her, she ran across the yard and ducked through the hole in the hedge.

Unable to make her legs walk, she fairly ran down the road. Her heart pounded within her chest, but she was determined. She would not persuade her tongue into another lie. The truth this time, she vowed. Only the truth.

Presently, she was at the locked front door, rapping her fist firmly against the solid wood.

"Mr. Adley! Mr. Adley!"

A shuffle from the other side told her he was there. It opened and his startled face peered out at her. "Wren. Why whatever—?"

"I stole her bottles, Mr. Adley!" she shouted as if he were clear across a field. "I stole Mrs. Adley's bottles!"

"What? Bup, bup, come in, dear child. This is—come in and sit."

He led her into the sitting room where Mrs. Adley was in her chair, staring blankly out the window.

"Now, I'm afraid I didn't understand a word you said. What is all the kerfuffle?"

Wren inhaled a deep breath and folded her arms across her middle. "I stole bottles from Mrs. Adley and made a hairy pudding and now I'm to be married to an old man and I don't think I can go through with it."

Mr. Adley stared a moment, then dropped into his chair.

"You did *what?*"

Wren opened her basket and held it out. "I took these. And a formula. And I'm so sorry to have deceived you. I was desperate."

He was silent for a few excruciating minutes, then finally said, "My dear girl, desperation does not justify betrayal." He snatched the basket from her hands and dug about to see what she had. "Yes, I noticed this burner was missing. I thought Mrs. Adley had hidden it. Well, I'm at a loss. I don't know what to say." He lifted the torn notebook paper and his eyes widened at the red X. "Oh dear. Oh dear, dear." He read through the formula, then slowly looked up at Wren. "You made this, you say?"

"Yes, sir. About eight months ago."

"Eight *months*. And the hair?"

"My sister's."

Mrs. Adley laughed in her absent way.

"Oh dear." Mr. Adley set the basket on the table and pressed his clasped hands to his forehead. "Miss Wren. I heartily wish you had consulted me."

Wren almost laughed, too. What would she have said? 'Oh Mr. Adley! I desperately want to be as pretty as my sister so that everyone will notice me, fall at my feet, and love me.'

He dropped his hands. "My wife's research and discoveries are not for girlish games. You always seemed like an intelligent young lady. I'm surprised at you. Such silly, thoughtless behavior."

Wren nodded as her heart plummeted to her feet.

"Oh dear, dear. I remember this one, yes I remember. And your sister? I suppose you realize by now what you have taken from her?"

"Yes."

"Well, this is a problem indeed. I'm sure Mrs. Adley would know what to do, but I am quite at a loss."

"Mr. Adley, please. I can't marry this man. The only reason he wants to marry me is because of my face. Is there anything to change me back, maybe just for a time until he has forgotten me?"

"Miss Wren. Our bodies are not embroidery cloths that we can simply undo and redo stitches. Not like clothes we can take on and off willy-nilly. What you have done is permanent. Which explains the red X. Mrs. Adley recognized the danger of stealing looks from another. She experimented with rabbits to find it worked, but she knew it was wrong. Wrong for any human to do it! She could never bring herself to destroy her findings. But these methods are not for playing. Why do you think she kept so much of her work secret?"

Wren looked at her feet and tried to scrape the dirt from her boot tip with the other.

"Aside from the obvious ethical problems we are facing, many of her later discoveries are incomplete. As I've told you, she began to be suspicious someone would steal them and left out ingredients or steps, marking with little codes known only to herself. So if there is something to help you, it will likely be incomplete."

"Maybe in her older books. Couldn't we look?"

Mr. Adley covered his face with his hands and inhaled a deep breath. "I do not think I should," he said through his fingers.

Wren slumped in her chair. Beauty swapping had been so easy to do. It didn't seem like it should be so difficult to reverse.

Finally, Mr. Adley dropped his hands. "This is most distressing. I like you, Wren. You are our closest friend here. You are family. But I am very disappointed. I never suspected you could use us this way. I do not know if we can continue to trust you to come."

"Oh! Don't say that. You may trust me. I will never take anything again. Ever. I have learned my lesson."

"You have, have you?" he said doubtfully.

"Yes, I'm sorry. So terribly sorry. I feel wretched about all of it!"

He nodded and rose to his feet. "Yes. I am sure. But I am afraid, my girl, you've only just begun to feel it."

Wren left the house with instructions to return in three days time to allow Mr. Adley time to think. She wondered at Mr. Adley's last words. What could he mean? She felt awful for stealing from Mrs. Adley and deceiving Eillie so long. Her best friend hated her, and she was to marry a man she had never met. Her world was rapidly crumbling. How could she ever feel worse?

CHAPTER TWENTY
A Damsel in Disguise

Casner had been at Garwick for three days now, and Wren had not heard a single word. She burned to speak with him. To see his face. Though she dreaded his reaction (she had read all about lover's rage), her one hope stood on the possibility he considered his semi-proposal a prior claim to his uncle's.

And so, prepared for the long walk to Garwick with Eillie at her side, Wren marched forth without invitation.

The two sisters used the time well, filling the entire distance with conversation. Despite herself, Wren smiled and laughed, astonished to discover Eillie had a great sense of humor. She told Wren about all the friends she had made in Forthshire and imitated some of the fancy gentlemen as they pranced about the town.

They talked about music and biology and picnics and treats. They were making up for years of self-made separation, and Wren felt a love growing for her sister she never knew was possible. And, with lively blue eyes and a warm, genuine smile, she realized Eillie was still one of the loveliest girls she had ever seen.

Wren almost forgot her troubles.

But as they neared, the uncomfortable tickle in her stomach grew. Now that the house was in view, she wasn't sure how she was going to announce their visit.

'We are concerned for Mr. Casner's health' seemed silly. Why not send a note? 'We were in the neighborhood' was outrageous, as they were a good four miles from home. 'I'm engaged to an old Duke and am hoping to hear of his demise' seemed…inappropriate.

They were spared having to supply awkward excuses when Casner himself walked out the main doors.

"Why, Miss Amberton. Miss…"

"Eillie."

"Yes, Miss Eillie. This is a happy surprise. I was just going out for a ride. I didn't know you were expected."

"We're not," Wren said hastily. "But I need to speak with you."

"Of course. The sitting room?"

"No!" Wren looked around only to find a groomsman and a gardener. None of the family had seen them. "I'd like to speak with you privately. Outside, if that's all right."

Casner tugged his jacket straight. "Of course. I always hope for everything to be as you wish it, love."

Did he? Poor boy. He was in for a terrible surprise. A great upset to the plans he had been dreaming for them.

He held out his arm, which Wren gratefully and painfully took, and led the girls into the labyrinth garden on the far side of the yard. They came to a bench, and he invited both sisters to sit. Eillie stood uncomfortably for a moment, then mumbled she would just wander over to some roses a bit further down the path. Casner took her seat.

Wren was very still, fighting the urge to say, 'never mind' and return home. She knew she must choose her words carefully.

A Pretty Game

"This path is very neat," she managed. "They must rake it often."

He smiled. "Yes, I believe they do. But come, darling, you didn't walk all this way to comment on the gravel. What troubles you?" He reached a hand up to her chin and made her look at him, leaning his face near hers.

She opened her mouth to speak, but a firm tread crunching on the path drew her attention behind them. She felt herself wilt as her eyes locked with Gideon's. She hurriedly stood, conscious of how close Casner's face had been to hers.

Gideon's jaw flexed once, enough for Wren to see from where she stood. "I'm sorry," he said shortly. "I did not realize anyone was here." He turned to go back the way he had come.

"Gideon, wait!" she called out, suddenly wishing she had joined him to the conversation from the start.

"Never mind, love," Casner said soothingly. "Let him go. I'll talk to him later." He pulled her gently back to the bench. "Now, what is it that's troubling you? You look like a frightened kitten!"

Wren inhaled a shaky breath and shook her head. Something felt all wrong.

"Good lack, you are beautiful, even when you're upset," he said, raising her hand to his lips. "I'm going to have a hard time calling you Aunt."

"Oh, don't kiss my hand! You're only making it…wait." Stop the cart. "*What?*"

"You are a devil of a girl. Teasing me and looking like you do all the time. It will be hard to pass you to my uncle."

Wren leaned back. "Pass me? So. You know?"

"Of course I know. How do you think my uncle heard of you? News of a beauty travels far but not one hundred miles."

231

"I'm sorry. I think I've missed something. Weren't we...don't you...I thought we were a thing."

"Well, we are, darling. Or were rather. Our outing to Pirate Pond was our last hoorah. I told you so."

"Yes, you said a last hoorah before your going to school."

He chuckled and took her hand, which she promptly withdrew.

"Wren, I'm sorry. I think you added those words. I never said that. I said, 'Our last hoorah,' because I was almost certain my uncle would offer for you soon. I couldn't be completely frank. He still was a little undecided—I hadn't your permission to encourage him yet—and I didn't want to falsely raise your hopes." Some of the humor slipped from his face. "I really am sorry, love. I thought you understood."

"But you kissed me!"

"You asked me to. How could I turn you down?"

"By saying 'I can't kiss you because you're going to be my auntie.' You—this is—" Wren stood and set to pacing.

He crossed his arms and watched her. "You are upset."

She looked at him wide eyed. "So you never meant to come back for me. *This* was your plan?"

"Well, yeah. I mean, I kind of said as much. What did you think?"

"I thought you were going to propose."

"Propose? No, darling. It's been fun, but I can't commit to anything, even lovely as you are. And I'm not sure I could manage you anyway."

"*Manage* me?" she nearly growled.

He quirked his lips into a smile and raised his eyebrows as if she had just proved his point. "And besides I'm not sticking around. I'm going abroad on tour."

"Tour?"

"Yes, see some places I've never been. Gain some culture. I'll soon come into some money. From my uncle. I've been corresponding with him about you. He's had all my cousins doing so when they meet a woman who would make him a worthy companion. I'm sure one look at you and the deal will be sealed."

"Sealed? He doesn't even know me."

"Doesn't need to. I told him you were the most gorgeous creature to have ever hit the ground and a bit of a handful though very fun, and he's set on it."

"You've sold me."

"Well, no, don't put it like that. You make me sound like a cad. I've considered you, too. Think of it, Wren. You'll be a duchess."

"I don't want to be a duchess."

"Every girl wants to be a duchess. You said so yourself."

Wren narrowed her eyes at the crafty fox. Like bits of sand falling in to fill the cracks between bricks, it all began to make sense. He didn't know her at all. He never had. Never listened to her. Never pieced together her character.

Be a duchess! As if she would sell her soul for it.

"And of course," he continued unwisely, "if you are not ready to sever our relationship, I'd be more than willing to let it continue whenever I'm in Langley. I'm not opposed to a fling with a married woman now and then."

There were no words. Nothing coherent came into her head. His confident smile faltered. He leaned back and swallowed.

With both hands she reached out and shoved him. Hard. And sent him toppling backward over the bench.

"Darling, now really…" he stammered, lifting himself up with one arm and holding out the other.

"You—don't—get—to—say—anything!" She pushed his legs to the side, rendering him completely off the bench. Hot, angry fumes rolled off her countenance.

"Then I'll be off," he said quickly, scrambling to his feet, bits of bark clinging to his jacket. "I'm in a bit of a hurry. My uncle will be in contact."

"I would rather he be at the bottom of the sea. Tell him he can keep his title. I don't want it."

"But Wren—"

"Do not call me by name. Miss Amberton to you. You used me!" She gave him another shove.

"Hey, it isn't my fault you didn't understand half of what I said. I thought you were clever enough to realize we were just having fun."

It would have been better for Casner to have held his tongue for this added insult to injury, and Wren really wasn't good with pain management as it was.

In times like these ladylike behavior is not required, neither is a lady required to act like a gentleman. A gentleman might engage in fisticuffs or a duel—with set rules of conduct and a clear definition of a winner. But a lady behaving neither like a lady nor a gentleman is unbound by any sort of rules.

Wren pulled a bottle from her pocket.

"What is that?"

"This? This is Swine Juice."

"What?" he said with a teeny, baffled smile.

"You've never heard of it before?" She gently swirled the bottle, pretending to analyze its contents. "Hm. Do you think *you* are clever enough to escape your own fate?"

"My what?"

"I always keep a bottle with me. One never knows when she will encounter a real pig."

He glanced around and tugged at his cravat. "I really better be off."

"Oh, no. You must stay. As your future auntie, I insist." She popped off the lid. The surface fluid began to fizz and pop. "You don't mind swill, do you?"

"I don't know what you mean."

"How about smells? Do they bother you?"

"Wren, I can't…put that away."

"I really am sorry to do this. You have such a nice nose."

"Wren…" he began backing away.

Wren twitched the bottle at him. He jumped. She twitched again. He jumped further and laughed nervously. Then she let him have it. She thrust the bottle at him and allowed the entire contents to slosh over his chest. As soon as the solution met the open air, it crackled and whizzed, popped and sparked.

Casner yelped and stumbled backward, tripping over his feet. He jumped up, swiping madly at his sparking suit. In a burst of panic, he sprinted for the fountain, where Eillie stood perplexed, and flopped in, a terrible slap as he sank into the water.

Wren waited until his soaked figure sat up in the knee-deep water to be sure he wasn't going to drown, before summoning her sister, disappointed she couldn't even produce a snicker for her victory.

Somehow, it didn't feel like a victory at all.

Eillie waited a mile of brisk walking before she spoke. "So, what did he say?"

"What did he say? He said he would be happy to hold my flowers at my wedding. He knew, Eillie! Not only did he know, but he is the one who brought it all about. I've been so blind."

"Oh," Eillie replied quietly. She slipped her arm through Wren's. "I'm sorry things didn't work out between you."

"What? Oh, *that*. Well, hold your pity. I am suddenly aware how little I wanted to be Mrs. Casner."

"Really? But I thought—"

"I know what you thought. I tricked myself into it, too." It was true. She felt no loss where Casner was involved. None. She was ferociously upset, yes. But not because it meant she was nothing to Casner. No, she was upset solely because she had been duped. Betrayed. Trapped. "I'm sure he'll make a fine husband for some prancing pony, but that girl isn't me. The nerve! Popinjay, dirty pig…man. He thought I aspired only to be a duchess. Me!"

As if her only goal was to procure the wealthiest husband. As if her soul wasn't capable of any real feeling. As if she were just a pretty face. The whole point of being a perfect beauty was to be seen, but this proved a terrible turn.

She was *still* invisible.

CHAPTER TWENTY-ONE
An Unexpected Encounter

Dearest Lyn,

I know you are not home yet, but I find myself needing to write to you anyway. Why did we not train PJ to carry messages to Preston? I hope you are well and enjoying yourself despite your misgivings. Me? I'm having a good wallow in self-pity. Truly, you should see me. I haven't brushed my hair in three days.

Love,

Wren

After shutting herself at home for several days, Wren heard through word of mouth that Casner had left Garwick the very day she had confronted him. No longer afraid of an uncomfortable meeting, she felt the freedom to come and go as she pleased.

There was a distant roll of thunder just as she stepped out her front door, but she was not deterred. She had failed to return to the Adleys on the third day and felt she could put it off no longer.

The overcast sky seemed to dampen the noise of the earth, and the quiet walk was pleasant until she saw a stocky, young gentleman making his way down one of the bright green hills on foot. For some inexplicable reason, her eyes immediately sought a place to hide.

Too late. Gideon caught sight of her and turned in her direction. Wren paused in the middle of the road, winding a thumb around a finger, as a light sprinkle of rain pattered the brim of her bonnet. It was falling steadily not too far off now, the scent in the air having already shifted.

"Hello," Gideon said, stopping well out of reach.

"Hello."

Several heartbeats passed.

"It's starting to rain."

"Yes. I'm hoping to make it to Ebdor Cottage quickly."

He bobbed his head in approval. She watched his jaw flex a few times and noticed his fist clench once.

"Just coming from Brayford Hall, I guess?"

"Yes."

She stared at her friend. He was good. So good. He was neither tall nor notably handsome, but his looks were still striking. His thick brows and strong jaw. And alert eyes that seemed to see everything. Well, not everything.

"Giddy, I want to tell you something."

He shook his head. "No, I see that you really don't. And you don't need to. Casner has told me enough."

"Oh." Casner knew some, but he didn't know all. Wren wanted Gideon to know everything. "But—"

"I hope you're happy."

Wren drew in a sharp breath. It wasn't an 'I wish you all the best in the world and hope you'll have joy in everything' sort of 'I hope you're happy.' It was more of the 'I hope you're miserable and develop a terrible, eternal rash in your underarms' sort. This was unlike her friend Gideon.

He shifted his weight and crossed his arms over his chest. "You'll be pleased to know you took me in."

"Took you in?"

"You know what I mean."

"No, I don't. Please enlighten me."

"I never thought you one to play silly games, Wren. I've watched you go around, leading a trail of fellows on, laughing at everyone with less brains than you. Even me."

"I never laughed at you Gideon."

He flushed. "I didn't mean that. I meant—for a little while, I thought you…" He drew in a deep breath. "I never thought you cruel before. You've done a good job hiding it."

"Cruel?" The accusation might be true, but in the moment, she didn't want to tax her brain with it. The word stung like a thousand slaps. Her own hands curled into fists. "What about you? You ride about the country, grumpy and solemn. It takes such an effort to be with you."

"I have responsibilities, Wren. Things I must do. I don't get to go on joyrides every day."

"Well, poor you. You have to sit in your gigantic house with all the food in the world brought to your feet and servants to brush your coats and comb your hair for you."

"I never asked for them!"

"They are still yours! It doesn't matter what you ask for and what you don't. This is the blow you've been dealt, and I'm sorry it's so awful for you, but you could at least act like you're grateful. I liked you better when you were a poor squire boy."

He leaned forward. "And I liked you better when you were a forgotten little bug girl."

His dart found its mark. A wave of heat swelled in her chest and burned in her eyes, and she knew if she opened her mouth, flames would surely roast him. She picked up a clod of dirt and hurled it at her friend turned foe. The earthen missile exploded in a spray of crumbs against his shoulder, sending him stumbling back, his eyes wide. After one stunned second, he picked up his own hand-sized clod and drew it back.

Wren dared him with her eyes, her chest still heaving under her fury. He brought his loaded hand forward and slammed the clod to the ground at his own feet, then stomped into the copse of trees, vegetation flying in his wake.

"Lost your spirits, then, my lord," she tried to exclaim, though it came out little more than choked babble.

Wren stood on the road long after he had disappeared, absolutely flummoxed, her breathing uncontrollable. Fury was slipping from her grasp, leaving an empty void in her chest.

What had just happened?

Here she had simply wanted to confide in him the nightmare she could not wake from, and it had swiftly become another layer of torment. She pressed a hand to her head, working through the spat.

Cruel? Is that what he really thought of her? 'I thought you…' He hadn't finished. What else had he thought?

She started for the cottage again, the clouds brutally opening before she was halfway, forcing her into a run. She pounded on the door, drenched to the bone, and was immediately ushered in to sit by the warm fire beside dear Mrs. Adley. A rattly cough broke loose from the little woman's throat.

Mr. Adley patted his wife's back, mumbling soothingly until the fit subsided.

Still focused on his wife, he said, "I'm afraid she's caught a chill. Last week I took her into town with me to post an urgent letter to the board. Anyway, I needed to go into a few shops, as well, and by the time we were driving home, she was so fatigued. I tried to hurry, but…" He knelt down to Mrs. Adley's level. "I'll just get the tea now, love." He wiped her nose with his handkerchief, kissed her forehead, and left the room.

Needing to feel some sort of comfort, Wren reached out and took Mrs. Adley's unusually warm hand. The woman did not look away from the fire but did not withdraw her hand either. Wren gently squeezed it, feeling an undercurrent of courage. Presently, Mr. Adley returned with the tea things and for a time, allowed the room to sit in contemplation.

"Now," Mr. Adley said gently after the long quiet, "I am not as proficient in counseling as a female may be—I know my sweetheart would far and away outperform me here if she were able. But tell me, my child. What is all the trouble now?"

Wren stared at the flames licking at their prey, and a pop of sparks flew from the fireplace. "My friend is angry with me," she replied quietly. "I think because of my engagement to the duke."

"I see. And do you not think she will forgive you?"

"He."

"Oh. Oh, dear. I'm afraid I shan't be much help here."

"I never meant to be engaged to a duke." She turned to look at the gentleman sitting behind her. "I never meant for any of this. I only wanted people to notice me."

He nodded his head and leaned forward to crack at the pile of peanuts. After a length of time, he said, "You know, I have always been a recluse. I give speeches and lectures here and there, but I often try to skip the after parties—I never want to get caught up talking about someone's personal matters. I like what I understand, and I understand the physiological part of life much better than the psychological. Anyway, for many years I lived alone, bumbling about in my studies, researching, traveling, that sort of stuff."

He looked at the ceiling and inhaled a deep breath as if breathing for the first time. "And then one day, I saw *her*. She was radiant with intellect and poise. Everything I thought a woman should be. And my heart was taken at once. Now, I have always been the kind no one—and certainly not the opposite sex—pays much attention to. I never thought she'd look my way. But she did. I learned that day that it isn't important to be noticed by everyone. What matters is to notice who truly notices you."

The room fell silent again, aside from the crackle of fire and the rain pelting the windowpanes. A gentle thumb traced over Wren's hand, and she looked up at Mrs. Adley. She still stared silently at the fire, her expression blank as a fresh sheet of paper. But Wren could feel her. She could feel the woman on the inside and knew that Mrs. Adley was someone who would have noticed her, too.

"I'm so sorry I betrayed your trust," she whispered to the woman.

Another long length of time stretched on quietly before Mr. Adley got to his feet.

"Well, now. While you were away, I had much time to think. I am still not pleased with what you have done, but I feel it right to frankly forgive you, as you have done so much else to help us. I also took some time to search all of Mrs. Adley's papers and found one I had forgotten." He grabbed a book from the table, flipped it open, and handed it to Wren.

"Beastly Drink?" Wren looked up from the book. "Oh Mr. Adley,

A Pretty Game

I might have been what some call plain before, but I don't think I was ever *beastly*."

He smiled. "Beggars cannot be choosers, my dear. I can't reverse what you've done, but I think this will be of use to us. You see, no red X. That means this one is not permanent."

Wren looked at the page again and felt a teeny spark of hope.

"I took the liberty of testing it yesterday. Not on myself of course. I used a rabbit I trapped. I didn't want you to drink it only to have your head explode or something."

Instinctively, Wren put a hand on top of her head. She hadn't realized that was possible.

Mr. Adley tossed a few peanuts into his mouth. "But it worked wonderfully. You should have seen it—all…" He put his hands forward, searching for words. "It looked much like the monsters of my childhood nightmares. In truth, I couldn't sleep at all last night. So I think this will suit your needs perfectly!"

Wren handed the book back, with a little shake of her head. "How?"

"Think of it! I'm sure this man will want to meet you before the day he says I do. So when he comes for a visit, you'll drink this up, he'll get one look at you and run for home. Nightmares, I tell you!"

Wren pressed her lips together. It just might work. "How long will it last?"

"Well, I don't know much about dosing. I would be afraid to give you too much—might work so well no one will believe it is you. Or worse, it might last years! But I gave the rabbit a spoonful, and it lasted about eight hours. He's good as new now. So for your weight, the same dose might last two? I'm no apothecary, but I think that sounds reasonable."

Wren stared into the fire again. It was a chance. A real bit of hope swelled inside her. "All right. I'll do it!"

"Wonderful," he said. "I have it ready for you. Let me fetch it."

Wren smiled. A real smile. "Mrs. Adley," she whispered. "Do you think there's a chance? Do you think this could work for me?"

No reaction came from the woman.

"Thank you. For all your research. Even if it doesn't work, I'll always be grateful to you."

Mrs. Adley's mouth twitched into what looked like an effort to smile, and Wren knew, despite her inability to respond, Mrs. Adley heard her. And she understood.

Mr. Adley returned with a little vial of murky, purple fluid and held it out to her with a trembling hand. "Careful now. It's all measured out. Wait until the time is at hand, then drink the entire bottle. Understand?"

"Yes. Thank you, sir."

He nodded. "I hope this does the trick. We'd hate to lose you. Especially to some fancy, conceited fellow up north. Yes, I hope with every fiber of my soul this does the trick." He patted her cheek, then looked out the window that had fallen silent. "Well, the rain has let up. We've got a new spring in our step thanks to our dear Mrs. Adley's work. I think we might have a few sugar biscuits before you return home."

A small, pre-victory party was had, and Wren left the little cottage feeling lighter and dryer than when she had come. If this new plan worked, she would be free to turn all her endeavors to regaining Lyn and Gideon's good opinions.

Her little gleam of tranquility was snuffed out midway across her own yard.

"Hail!" Charley called from his tree. "The strange duchess is come home at last. She'll be spitting glad—or mad—her betrothed doth come three days hence."

Wren stopped mid step and turned. "What?"

"Her great papa hath received a notice of the impending coming forth of that important man—the Puke! Three days hence, I say." He climbed down a few branches, and his face took on a worried look. "Is he going to take you away, Wren?"

"Not if I can help it."

He grinned. "I was hoping you'd say that," he exclaimed and climbed back into the leaves. "Oh! And beware of the storm that rageth in the house guts."

Inside, Wren discovered just what her brother meant. The house was in an uproar, with little maids Wren had never seen before darting from place to place, drapes and rugs stripped from their places, and a loud banging coming from somewhere unseen. Above everything, Wren could hear Mrs. Amberton. "Scrub, Mr. Forner! No, not like that. Scrub as if your life depended on it, for it very well may."

Wren stepped into the dining room to see Mr. Forner scrubbing one of the upholstered chair seats at the table. Mrs. Amberton was perched on top of the table, polishing the lower crystals on the chandelier. She looked down to critique Mr. Forner again and caught sight of her daughter in the doorway.

"Wren!" she exclaimed, climbing down. "Thank heavens you are here. Take this cloth and work on the doors of the sideboard."

"Why? What are we doing?"

Mrs. Amberton reared her head back and rolled it forward. "The duke, dearest! The duke is coming! It's lucky Mrs. Thorte could spare some of her staff today, or I'd wish myself in a grave."

"Is he to inspect the closets? Seems rather forward."

Mrs. Amberton squinted one eye. "Anyway, I hate to use your hands, but everyone must work. Do stay low to the ground, though. No standing on the chairs or tables."

"Yes, Mum, but why?"

"Why? Of all the—do you think I want my daughter—soon to be Duchess of Mendshire—falling and breaking her pretty little neck? Because she was *cleaning?* No! I shall not have it. You will stay low to the ground as you are told. Eillie. Eillie!" she shrieked.

"Yes?" Eillie said, appearing at the door. Her face was smudged with soot, her hair was tucked up into one of Plucky's caps, and she had several rags tied to her apron strings.

"Are you finished with the hearth yet?"

"No, Mum," she replied, pushing her glasses up the bridge of her nose. "I started only ten minutes ago."

"Well, scoot then, child. What are you standing here for?"

Eillie said nothing but bobbed her head submissively, glanced at Wren with an apologetic smile, and disappeared.

"Plucky!" Mrs. Amberton shouted, passing through the servant door to the kitchen.

Wren went to the sideboard and began rubbing the smudges off the darkly finished wood. She smiled as she listened to the groundskeeper mutter to himself about working indoors, scrubbing chairs as if he were a fancy butler. Aunt Fanny came into the room, evidence of having been hard at work dotting her person.

"Wren, dear, how are you feeling? Are you all right with him coming so soon?"

She shrugged. It had to happen eventually. It would be better to get it over with. "Yes, I think so."

"Good. Then it won't cause you any distress if I take Eillie in two days?"

Wren stood to look the woman in the eyes. "If either of you are wanting to go, I shouldn't hold you back. I would like Eillie with me, but I know she isn't happy here."

Her aunt smiled. "There's a good girl. Yes, Eillie is much better away. I'm glad you understand that." She picked at a loose thread on the rag in her hand. "Well, back to work. Thank you, dear."

The work continued into the evening. Mrs. Amberton asked that dinner be served in the kitchen so as not to undo all they had accomplished. Mr. Amberton put up a brief fight, but in the end, lost the battle. However, he would not lose the war. When Mrs. Amberton insisted they not have a fire in the sitting room, he put down his foot.

"Are we not to live until the man comes? If this is the case, why did we not wait until the day before to purify the house? By the devil, I'll have a fire at my feet!"

Wren pressed her lips together to hide her smile. If Aunt Fanny were not visiting, her father would be in his cold study, content as a squirrel ready for winter and not bothered a bit by his family's discomfort of no fire.

When the house was still for the night, Wren sat at her desk staring into the mirror. "Is this the face of a duchess?" she whispered. Maybe it was. But was there a duchess on the inside?

She sighed and re-covered her mirror. She plaintively looked over her desk, settling on the text Gideon had sent to her. She traced her fingers slowly over the title before taking it up and over to the bed with her. The room was dark, with only faint silver moonlight seeping in through the window, but she opened the book anyway and thumbed through the pages.

A soft knock came at the door. Wren stuffed the book under her pillow and bid Eillie to enter. Her sister came in and climbed into the bed beside her, as if they were small children again. It had never been comfortable before, but now that things were different between them, Wren felt herself relax into her mattress.

"I hope you are all right," Eillie whispered. "I've never seen Mum in such a flutter. You'd think the king was coming and he'd have her head if he found a spot of dirt."

Wren snickered. "I wonder what would happen if I forgot to clean my boots at the door the morning of his arrival and tramped mud all through the house."

Eillie giggled. "You wouldn't!"

Maybe not, Wren thought. *But I am willing to ingest Beastly Drink.* For the first time, Wren thought about the reaction she was going to create in her parents. She swallowed and tried to forget it.

"Aunt said she told you we are leaving in a couple days," Eillie said. "I really wish I could be here to support you, but I think she's anxious to continue on. She wants to stop and see a few friends on our way to Ferriton. I wish you could come."

Wren reached through the blankets and found her sister's cold hand. "I don't deserve you, Eillie. I've been horrible to you, but you love me anyway."

"Of course I do. You're my sister. You don't know how many times I dreamed we could talk like this. That we could be friends and tell each other all our secrets and jokes. You'll write to me, won't you? And more than just news from town. I really don't care to hear any of that. I want to know what is happening to you." She giggled a pretty little sound. "I loved when you wrote me about you and Lord Garwick wrestling in the mud."

Wren gasped. "Eillie! We weren't *wrestling*."

"Say what you will, it sounded like wrestling to me. You are good friends, aren't you? You and Lord Garwick. I remember him coming for you and Luke and wishing I was invited to go, too. I would sit by the window and listen to you all laugh as you disappeared into the woods."

Wren smiled painfully at the memories. She had been glad to escape Eillie all those expeditions into the woods. And now that she would take her, there were no more adventures to go on. "I'm afraid Gideon and I are not friends. Anymore."

"Why?" Eillie asked innocently.

"He is angry at me. For being engaged to a duke. And other things."

"Yes, that makes sense. He's jealous."

Wren snorted. "Jealous? No, I don't know why he would be jealous. He's angry because he thinks I've changed. Like Lyn is. But I haven't. Not really."

Both girls were quiet for a while before Eillie rolled over to look Wren in the face. "No. That might be why Lyn is mad. But I think Lord Garwick is jealous. I bet he was hoping to keep you always."

"Eillie, I think you are quite mistaken."

"Maybe. I guess you know him better than I do. But I saw the way he looked at you after church. I stared because he wasn't paying any attention to me. He looked like…what's the line in that poem? *A man whose heart hath been opened, Whose every look and deed proclaims it.* That's how he looked at you. I think that's how he's always looked at you."

Wren closed her eyes and tried to envision what Eillie described. An image of Gideon at the Garwick ball came to mind. His sharply pressed coat and soft cream cravat. Coming forward and back, as the dance moved gracefully on. And the feeling of him leaning close, his words in her ear. She *had* felt something different that night.

"I'm sorry. I shouldn't have said anything."

"No," Wren said softly. "No, you shouldn't have."

CHAPTER TWENTY-TWO
The Puke

Most loving, wonderful friend,

Tomorrow is it! I shall either come out free and victorious or seal my fate as a duchess and forever wear chains of diamonds. But don't worry. If I fail, I will always have a bowl of bonbons ready for you, and you may borrow my coach and six any time you'd like. Just be sure to give me two weeks' notice so I can have them to you on time, as I will practically be living in the outer limits of the civilized world. I wish you would come home and save me.

Your terrible, penitent friend who deeply regrets her faults and inability to see things as they are,

Wren

In the early hours of morning, Wren opened her eyes. The sky was still gray and only the birds outside her window stirred the silence of night. It was *tomorrow*.

Come freedom or cruel fate, she would know her future this afternoon. And somehow she felt relief in that. The worst part of everything that was happening was the uncertainty. The feeling she was standing on a fence, teetering one way and then another. She was ready to just fall and be done with it.

Breakfast three hours later was unusually quiet. Neither of her parents spoke more than a few words, and with Eillie and Aunt Fanny having left the day before, the table felt empty. His Grace was expected by the afternoon, and Wren had specific instructions to stay indoors to primp for the next four hours. She assured her mother she could primp alone and asked to be banished—or excused rather—to her room.

She sat down at her desk and decided to draw a while to better pass the time. Selecting her pencils that could easily be washed off rather than ink, she let her hand create what it would.

Lines with no rhyme or reason.

Bits and pieces of creatures.

Scrawly letters (she grit her teeth when she traced out a G).

She tried to remind herself over and over she was not going down without a fight, but the sinking feeling pressed at her from all sides. Oh! that the man would just come and get it over with.

After several hours, she slowly washed her hands and face, searching for calm in the cool water. It wasn't found. Then she repinned her hair neatly about her head (vanity of hair was hard to overcome), covered her mirror, and changed into her simplest muslin. The crunch of gravel under what sounded like an entire fleet of horses told her the time had come. She had better be quick. Sitting on the bed in the event it would make her ill, she closed her eyes and gulped down the little vial of Beastly Drink.

For a moment she felt nothing, but when a firm knock at the front door reverberated through the house, her face began to tingle, then burn. She laid back as countless muscle spasms overtook her.

A knock then sounded at her own door. Wren sat up to better see Plucky's reaction. "Come in," she called as casually as she could.

The woman stepped in, her face flushed. "His Grace is here, miss. Your mother—" She choked and grasped the door. "Cover me in feathers. Child, what have you done to your face?"

"Nothing," Wren replied, fighting a smile. It was working. She felt her features. Interesting. "What's it look like?"

Plucky carefully pried her fingers from the door. "I'll fetch your mother."

Within a minute Mrs. Amberton burst into the room and gasped before turning an interesting color of purple.

"Wren. He is here!" she said huskily. "I do not need to tell you how important this is. We don't have time for these games." She reached out and tugged at Wren's nose.

"Ouch!"

"Take it off."

"My nose?"

"No. Yes. I mean your pig's nose. Take it off this minute."

"I can't Mum. This *is* my nose." Wren gave it good a tug. "See? It won't come off."

Her mother narrowed her eyes. "I don't know how you have done it, but it must come off." She reached up again, pinched it hard, and twisted.

"Ow—Ow-Ow! Mum, stop!" Wren jerked away with tears stinging her eyes.

Panic washed over Mrs. Amberton's face. "Then you are sick."

"No, I have to go down. He has to see me."

"Absolutely not. You will stay here or to the undertow with you."

Rot! Feeling disgruntled, she would not be showing off her face to her betrothed, Wren plunked back onto the bed and crossed her arms.

An unladylike cry escaped her mother's lips, and she rushed away in a swish of fabric. When the door clicked shut, Wren dropped her ear to the floor and listened.

He was announced. "The Duke of Mendshire," Plucky said in the most dignified manner Wren had ever heard her speak. "And Mr. Casner."

Mr. Casner! What was he doing here? Wren had half a mind to fly down the stairs and beat him with the poker.

Mrs. Amberton's exuberant welcome and gushing praises for the duke nearly made Wren gag. The only thing her mother really knew about the man was his wealth. As if that were enough to make a good husband.

Then Mr. Amberton's voice came through the floorboards.

"And where is our angelic daughter, Mrs. Amberton?"

"She is unwell, my love. I'm so sorry, Your Grace. To have come all this way and not see her. Won't you be seated?"

"Nonsense," Mr. Amberton claimed. "She was well enough when I saw her this morning. Plucky! Plucky, send Miss Amberton down."

"Oh dearest. Pray, let her rest. She *really* is out of sorts today. I think it best if she stays where she is while we get to know His Grace."

"I said she is to come down," Mr. Amberton said with finality.

For once in her life Wren was overjoyed her father ruled with an iron fist. Plucky's heavy steps began to climb the stairs. Wren looked up at her clock. How much time did Mr. Adley say she had? Two hours? Nearly one quarter of an hour was already wasted.

Another knock at her door. "Come in," Wren squeaked.

Plucky poked in her head. "Your father—oh!" She moved herself through the door entirely and pushed it shut behind her back. "It's worse!" she croaked. "What curse has befallen this house?"

Wren grinned. "Am I beastly?"

"That's a word for it. But what—your lovely skin! You're almost green, Miss Wren. And you've got hair—no *fur*. And your nose. Oh, he's not going to like this."

"I hope not Plucky. I should hate to marry a man I do not know."

"I meant your *father*. I'll tell him you're clearing your stomach."

"No! No, I am going down. This is my chance." Wren brushed past the flustered woman and breezed down the stairs. This would be the performance of a lifetime. So much depended on it.

In overdone grace she entered the room. This man wanted to make her a duchess. With all her airs and poise, would he still want her for one if the face did not match?

"Here she…"

Mr. Amberton cleared his throat in a sort of wheeze. The daggers her father unleashed with his eyes thunked into Wren's chest. She was sure were it not for the gentlemen in the room, he would have strangled her right then. Mr. Casner let out a surprised cry.

Then the stooped, gray-haired man turned and started. It seemed they were equally surprised with one another. Wren never knew a duke could be so tiny. Some aged men are still pleasant to gaze upon, but time had not been kind to this one. Though she hated to judge by looks—she of anyone knew the brutality of it—she felt no self-control. If he had come to be her grandfather, she might have loved his mouse-like features, but given the circumstances, she judged away.

Mr. Amberton manfully stifled his fury and evened his tone. "Your Grace, may I introduce Miss Wren Amberton."

The duke shot a questioning look at his nephew, then, recovering his dignity, bowed deeply.

Casner broke his silence. "This is not Miss Amberton. What games—?"

"Good afternoon, Mr. Casner," Wren said sweetly. "I am so pleased to see you again. Has your tail sprouted yet?"

The memory and her voice were enough to convince him she was indeed Miss Amberton. With a bewildered expression, he stumbled through a polite apology. Then everyone was seated, and tea was brought in. Plucky exhaled heavily when she entered—obviously relieved Wren was still alive.

While her cup cooled and Mr. Amberton and the duke discussed the weather, Wren couldn't keep her eyes from darting to the clock. Minutes ticked away. The man was keeping his seat far too long. She would have been satisfied with him running from the house (if he could manage it) screaming. No matter the lashings from her father, she would take them. But there he sat. Calm as a lazy cat, glancing at her strangely every so often.

Mr. Casner squirmed like a fly in a spider's web, periodically wiping his long hand over his face or resting it on his jaw or scratching his neck.

Wren looked into her cup and stirred. Perhaps it was just good breeding that kept the duke there. He had not jumped up and proclaimed a wedding date yet. Perhaps he would finish his tea then kindly dismiss himself from their lives.

As she watched him nibble his scone—bringing to mind a mouse even with just one paw holding the morsel—she thought of Eillie. If Wren had not conjured herself into her sister's shoes, Eillie would most likely be sitting here, lovely as the day she was born. She would be listening to the nasally voice, taking the looks that eyed her like a prized ham, and saying nothing. Surely her sensitive heart would have broken to be forced into such a marriage. And she would never have spoken a word of it. Because she knew her duty.

Wren felt a pang of guilt. She was not so selfless. What was she sacrificing for her own comfort? Peace and prosperity for her parents, connections for Eillie and Charley. A way out for Luke. She was throwing the happiness of her entire family under the carriage wheels. What kind of wretch—

The duke sneezed, and a spray of soggy scone bits covered his lap.

Guilt was gone. Wren smiled serenely. Duty or not, she could never marry this man. Perhaps if she had loved him before she would be happy to wipe up his spewed mess, but she hadn't and now it was impossible.

She stirred her tea some more and looked at the clock. Forty-five minutes had elapsed. Suddenly a tingle ran up her nose. Then it became an itch. She reached up to delicately scratch it and felt sloughs of skin scrape off under her nail.

Get out! She had to get out. As she hunted for a way to excuse herself, her cheek began to itch as well.

"Wren, dearest," Mrs. Amberton broke into her panic. "The duke's cup." She widened her eyes and nodded toward him.

"Oh! Yes. Beg your pardon, Your Grace." Wren reached out and took his offered cup and saucer.

She didn't dare look at her father but glanced at her mother again. Her eyes were still wide and her lips were pinched tightly together as she stared back. Something was happening.

Wren put her head down and carefully poured the hot tea. "Sugar, Your Grace?"

"No. Just cream."

She could feel his steady stare and turned slightly to shield herself. Time seemed to slow down. Why was he still here? Why have another cup? She leaned forward to take up the cream pitcher. *Plop!*

Her heart stopped. Wren looked down into the duke's cup in time to see her nose bob to the surface like a dead fish. Afraid her face now lacked a centerpiece, a hand flew up to find her real nose intact. With a hand pressed to her face and the disgusting snout still floating in the duke's tea, Wren was frozen. She certainly couldn't hand it back to the man. He would—or maybe yes, she—no! No, she could not. She felt her heart jolt into double time and glanced at Mrs. Amberton who was now near fainting.

With no other choice, Wren flung the cup over her shoulder. The hot liquid rained onto the carpet and the dainty cup crashed against the wood floor. Mr. Amberton turned his daggers on her.

"There was a fly in His Grace's cup, and it surprised me," Wren said through her hand while rising to her feet. "I must go. It has been a pleasure, Your Grace. Don't come again." In three strides she was at the door with her hand grasping the knob.

"Stop," a nasally voice commanded before she could turn it.

Her whole face itched as if it were engulfed in flames. Sloughs of skin and fur dropped all around her.

"Turn around," came His Grace's next command.

She did as he bid her. He might be tiny, but there was a note in his voice that made him impossible to ignore.

"Put down your hand, my dear."

She again did as she was told, though not without hesitation, and raised her gaze to meet the others in the room. Mrs. Amberton's eyes were rolling in her head, and Mr. Amberton's were trying to murder her where she stood. But the duke? His shoulders were shaking and tears were streaming down his cheeks. He was laughing! Of all things, the man was laughing—or chortling rather. He mopped his face with a pristine handkerchief pulled from his coat pocket.

"What a show, my dear. What a show. Do come and sit." When she didn't move, he commanded. "Sit!"

Wren obeyed, scratching at her face and peeling off layers hanging loose. Two hours? Mr. Adley had grossly underestimated her time.

"My deepest apologies, Your Grace. My daughter—"

The man raised his small hand to hush her mortified father. "Wonderful, wonderful. What a mask. I was told you are very pretty my dear, quite out of the way, but this! Such spirit. Wonderful. I am sure it was not in your plan to marry an old goat like me, was it?"

Hope sprung up like a child with the promise of cake. She had misjudged the little mouse-man. He was not heartless. He would release her!

"We shall cut the engagement down to two weeks. Tomorrow would suit me better, but I'm sure your mother would like a little more time. I promise I'm not so bad and will take the greatest care of you. You shall have everything you want, my dear. Everything! Oh, I like this. I like it immensely."

Good thoughts gone. The man was not a mouse. He was a rat. A half-dead, sharp-toothed, beady-eyed rat. Her face dropped (not just more of her nose and skin dropping, but her whole face looked down). She couldn't bear looking at the horrid, merciless man.

Her parents forced her to stay as they bid His Grace goodbye. He asked that the engagement not be announced by the family until after it had been posted in the papers in Ferriton, and her parents consented, though Wren knew her mother would have preferred shouting it from the rooftop as soon as he stepped out the door.

Before scurrying off, the duke made the engagement ironclad with one brief kiss on her hand.

When he and his nephew were gone away with all their finery and the carriage out of sight, Mr. Amberton unleashed his pent-up fury. He stormed, he raged, he slammed his fists into the furniture. But Wren heard none of it. Her thoughts were somewhere else. She held her peace until he finished his tirade with an exasperated, "What have you to say for yourself?"

Rising to her full height and meeting his eyes, she calmly and quietly replied, "Nothing Papa. But I am two weeks shy of being a duchess. You will treat me as such," and left the room.

CHAPTER TWENTY-THREE
Fisticuffs!

Wren didn't want to go up the stairs. She didn't want to be shackled to the prison any longer. She flew out the kitchen door and rounded the house, striding toward the hedge gate. Was it all over? Her life as she dreamed it.

Was it really over?

It was. Like a swift and decided death blow, the duke had ended it with his sharp, selfish words. She swiped her palms across her eyes, willing them to release no tears. Feeling more skin coming off, she lifted the hem of her frock and furiously scrubbed at her face as she moved. Her breath felt choked by her burning throat.

None of this would have happened if Casner had never set eyes on her. Why had Gideon ever brought his terrible friend home?

She dropped her skirts just in time to bump into a firm chest.

"Miss Amberton!" Toone said blithely, holding a bouquet of hot house roses. "I've just returned from Ferriton and was coming to call on you. What a delight to find you already out. May I escort you?"

She sighed. There was no end to this day's misery! "I'm just on my way to see a cousin, and I'd rather—"

"I'm going that way myself," he said, offering his arm. He looked over his shoulder then hastily helped her put an arm through his. "This way, isn't it?"

Resigned to a life of orders, she allowed him to drag her in hurried steps toward the bend.

"Miss Amberton!" Wren thought she heard another voice call. She tried to look over her shoulder, but Toone bumped her with his hip, causing her to slip a little on the damp road.

"Despite all of yesterday's rain, a lovely day," he commented in forced calm, squeezing her arm tighter in his and speeding up. They rounded the bend. "Just perfect for a walk for two."

"Miss Amberton!"

Now she was sure someone was calling her. Before Toone could distract her again, she turned to see Starly hurrying toward them, a bouquet of roses also in his hand.

"Overdressed puppy," Toone muttered under his breath.

"Out walking, I see," Starly said, much pleased with foiling his friend. He held out his roses. "For you, fair one. Yes, I'm glad I've caught you."

"What's your game, Starly? You can see I've already got Miss Amberton on my arm, so if you would kindly creep off—"

"A young lady should not walk alone with a gentleman," he returned, looking coolly at Toone. "The slapshop idea. I'm surprised you would compromise Miss Amberton in such a way."

"He's right," Wren agreed. "I really would rather walk alone."

"We are on a public road, and I am merely escorting her to her destination. I see no harm in it."

"Spoken exactly like a cakey, pramping pinnywizzle."

Wren extracted her arm from Toone's. "Really, I'd like to be—"

A Pretty Game

"You know, Starly, I feel like I should be insulted, but the trouble is I have no idea what you are saying. If you'll excuse us."

"If you had any pleasure of the society I have—let me explain to your tiny, bumpkin brain. You're a dandy. A dandy with zero style and even less wit. No wonder Miss Amberton is trying to escape you."

"Actually, I'm trying to escape you both so—"

Toone squared his broad shoulders. "Well, she runs from you!"

Starly growled and threw his roses to a ghastly death. "Fisticuffs!"

The two young men dove at each other, fists and curses flying. Wren rolled her eyes. She was much too exhausted for games. She turned to leave them to it but froze, releasing a bitter laugh as Gideon rode up on his thoroughbred to complete the spectacle.

"Miss Amberton," he said.

His sarcastic tone nettled her. "Lord Garwick," she replied in like manner. The sting of his abandonment burned anew. "How nice of you to join us."

"What stir have you caused now?" He stood up on his stirrups to better view the scuffle.

"A duel for my hand."

He laughed. "More simpering casualties to add to your count. Gratified? In the nose, Starly! In the nose!"

"You'll never have her," shouted Starly.

"And I suppose you think your childish swipes will prevent me," his opponent cried.

With one failed cross swing, their boxing turned into a wrestling match, and they tousled to the muddy ground. Rips of shirtsleeves, cries of anguish, and Gideon's jeers filled the air.

"Cheap shot at the whirlygigs, eh?" Starly growled.

"Unfortunately, easy to miss," Toone grunted.

Wren looked at Gideon and raised her eyebrows. "How long should I let them continue?"

"What do you mean?"

She raised her voice to better be heard. "I mean how long should I let them continue this farcical scene before I inform them that I am already engaged?"

The scuffle paused, Starly in a headlock and blood oozing from Toone's nose.

"You what?" he said through the stream of red.

"Not that I did anything to encourage either of your attentions besides having a face, but I feel I should inform you, yes, I am already engaged."

"Engaged?"

"You know. To be married. I am claimed. Taken. Unavailable. Bought and sold. Off the market. Very soon to no longer be Miss Amberton. How many more ways shall I say it?"

"To whom?" Gideon asked, his face pure confusion.

"The Duke of Mendshire," she said with spiteful significance. "All thanks to your friend, Mr. Casner."

"A duke?" Starly said, loosening himself from Toone's hold.

"Yes. A duke. According to my father, I had to accept the highest bidder. The king is married already, and the prince is still in diaper cloths, which I find I might even prefer, but he didn't offer. So, a duke it is. Now, if I may be excused, I will continue on and practice my duchessing."

She turned on her heels and headed toward the cottage in long, undignified strides.

"A duke," one of the duelers said again.

"Wren. Wait." She could hear Gideon slipping in the mud, trying

A Pretty Game

to catch her. He placed a hand on her shoulder, but she shook it off. He caught up and fell into stride. "Why didn't you tell me?"

She looked the other way and tried to pretend he wasn't there.

"Don't pretend like I'm not here. Why didn't you tell me?"

She stopped and crossed her arms. She had wanted to talk to him about this days ago. Not now. Not today. "I tried to, but you said you already knew. That Casner told you."

He shook his head. "He didn't say anything about you being engaged. Among other things, he said you were very good at playing your game. Gathering piles of hearts or some such thing—you know how he talks. He said you were a clever girl who would settle for nothing less than being a duchess."

So Gideon had not known. Hadn't been jealous as Eillie had supposed. Wren broke into her strides again. "A soothsayer indeed. Set the pieces and make a prediction. Famous."

"Wren," he said, falling into step once more. "Wren. Stop!" He grabbed her wrist, and she stopped, fighting the impulse to slide her hand up into his. "Do you know the Duke of Mendshire?"

She yanked free. "No. But I've just had the pleasure of meeting him. He's very grand."

Gideon pounded a fist into his hand. "That's why Casner has brought him. The bacon-brained, rat of a man."

"That was my impression of him, too," Wren said, trying to sound thoughtful. "Or wait, did you mean Casner?"

"What the deuce possessed you to accept? Wren, you cannot go through with it. That man is not right for you. He's old and backward and grumpy."

"So he's you but old."

"No!"

"You're right. You are taller. And you dress better." She really did like the cut of his coat, the set of it across the shoulder. And his simple, clean style. But that was neither here nor there. "I have a responsibility, Gideon."

"What kind of cockamamie—?"

She had heard enough. "Don't lecture me about cockamamie responsibility. You've got heaps of it. The fact is, I'm no longer the 'forgotten bug girl,' remember? I'm the pretty face, my lord. This is all your fault anyway."

"*My* fault?"

"Yes. If you had never brought Casner here, my betrothed never would have discovered me. And if you had gone out with us the other day instead of having cockamamie responsibility, Casner wouldn't have had the chance to ask if he might speak with his uncle about me, which I so stupidly assumed meant he wanted to propose himself and gave permission."

"Did you want him to?"

Wren clawed her fingers into her hair. "That doesn't matter! It has never mattered what I want. I'm cursed. Invisible. No matter what I do or say, I end up trapped. Forever a disappointment. And I'm sick of it. I don't want this." She gestured dramatically at her face. "I don't want a face of any kind anymore."

"That's absurd. What trouble is your face?"

She almost laughed. "It's every kind. You can't understand." She tilted her head to one side and looked up at him, feeling a pain when their eyes met.

"Tell me what to do," he said earnestly. "As your friend, I'll throw them both out if it will make you happy."

Wren drew in a sharp breath and felt her quick-burning anger snuff out. Friend. That was all he wanted to be to her. But now he couldn't even be that. She was engaged, very soon to be married. And a friendship such as theirs must be put to an end. Especially if her heart was at risk.

She smiled weakly and slowly resumed her steps. He followed.

"I'm hopeless, Gideon. If a duke with all his wealth and power can't make me happy, then who can?"

He looked down at his boots, silent. Her last little spark of hope went out.

"If I marry the duke, he will take me far, far away from everything and everyone." Away from her parents. Away from shallow suitors. Away from all reminders of her shortcomings. The duke, little and old as he may be, could at least spare her from hurting anyone she loved ever again. What had she told Gideon the other day? 'You could at least act like you're grateful.'

"And I'll never have to come back," she added in a near whisper.

"And that is what you want?"

She wiped a hand across her face. "Yes. That is what I want."

His steps stopped, and she could no longer force hers to walk. With a heart facing the harsh gallows of reality, she ran. She ran and didn't stop until she reached Ebdor Cottage.

"Come in, child, come in," Mr. Adley whispered. "I'm glad you are here. Dr. Maphis has just gone. Mrs. Adley is not doing well today, I'm afraid. Oh," he said, tipping his head back and looking at her appraisingly. "You look flustered. Are you all right?"

"Yes—no—I don't really know. I've just met the duke. And he has set a date."

"Oh dear. So the Beastly Drink didn't work. Oh dear. I'm sorry to hear this."

Wren nodded. "But Mrs. Adley. She is ill?"

"Yes, I'm afraid so. She was terribly feverish through the night, and the doctor is sure she has developed pneumonia." His voice cracked. "Of course I let him do whatever he could, and he bled her, but it only seemed to be made worse."

By this time they had reached the bedroom door to find the frail woman tucked neatly under her sheets. She was so still Wren had to watch carefully to see her shallow, quick breaths. Wren's heart sank into her toes.

Mr. Adley walked over to the side of the bed and poked at the pillows. "There, dear. That's better, is it? Quite comfortable now. Miss Wren is here to see us." He looked back at Wren. "I'm sure she is happy you're here. Come," he said, placing his hands on the back of a small chair. "Come sit by her for a minute."

Wren took the offered seat.

"I'm just going to get myself a snack. I haven't eaten since last evening and am beginning to feel the need."

He left the still room, and Wren reached under the smoothed sheets to take her friend's hand. For the hundredth time, she studied the face that had become as known to her as her own. But it was still now, almost foreign without the expressions that changed as rapidly as the quick snapping of her mind. And something else wasn't right.

"I don't know if you can hear me," Wren whispered. "But I've come to see you. I'm still engaged, and I'm so fickle, I can't decide whether I want it or not. I met him today. The Duke of Mendshire. Do you know him? I was hoping he'd at least be a charming old man, but he's quite the opposite."

Wren gently squeezed Mrs. Adley's hand and let out a short, soft laugh. "Gideon compared him to a rat, just like I did in my head. But

A Pretty Game

I bet his house is so large, I'll be able to avoid his scurrying most of the time. I hope he doesn't want an heir." She pictured herself chasing after a little rat-faced baby with a tail and shuddered. "But we haven't discussed that yet, obviously. Anyway. I suppose I should be grateful. My parents are ecstatic about the match. It will provide them with connection and comfort and me the means to live as I wish. And maybe my brother, Luke, can come home. That could make it worth it. But if I am being completely honest, I want to be selfish. I wish you could tell me what I should do."

The little breaths crackled, and Mrs. Adley began to cough violently. Wren held a nearby handkerchief up to her mouth and when the fit passed, wiped away the thick, pink-streaked spittle and settled the feverish woman back onto her pillow. Looking at her again, as if struck in the gut by a hot iron, Wren saw the truth.

The something more she had always seen in Mrs. Adley was gone.

Even though Mrs. Adley's emotions and words made little sense, there had always been an air of confidence about her. A defiance of nature. Something neither time nor suffering could alter.

But death could. And it felt dreadfully near.

A sob broke from Wren. "I'm so sorry you have to be ill. Here I am complaining about my engagement, and you don't even get to know where you are. Nothing is fair. Nothing is as it should be. I wish I could have known you before you came to be like this. I wish we could sketch and hypothesize and experiment together. I should have liked to have tasted your special tea. Mr. Adley says it was the best. And I wish I could have your help now. I know you would understand me."

Wren dropped her head on the edge of the bed.

A board squeaked behind her, and a soft hand touched her shoulder. "She understands," Mr. Adley said gently. "She does."

Wren stayed with Mrs. Adley for another hour, drawing courage from the weak hand and feeling a balm on her heart that only comes from the pure love of another.

That evening a knock sounded at the Amberton front door. After a quick and quiet exchange, Plucky brought in a note with a little bottle of clear fluid delivered by Dr. Maphis.

Dear Wren,

I wanted you to know that Mrs. Adley has passed. Do not come to me. As much as I enjoy your company, I would like to be alone. I've been looking through her books and discovered this. It is called "Flat Tonic." Once ingested, this amount should make an individual emotionless and unmotivated for a year or possibly more. I think you know how it might be of use to you in order to buy some time. I cannot bear the thought of you going away from me, too.

Please consider,
Wilfred Adley

CHAPTER TWENTY-FOUR
To Free or Not to Free

"Wren, why are you dressed black?" Mrs. Amberton asked the next morning. "Is that from my closet?"

"I am in mourning, Mum. I thought it would be appropriate for a few days at least."

"In mourning? Oh, for that Mrs. Adley. Dearest, she was hardly known to us."

"She was known to me. And she is, after all, our cousin."

"I suppose that is true. Well, you'll need to change. I received an invitation from Garwick today. Evidently His Grace is still in town, and we have been invited to a small dinner in honor of your engagement."

"Oh no, Mum. I don't think I can go. Please."

"Not go? Silly girl. Why would you not be able to go? Of course you are going. Not go to Garwick on invitation, indeed."

"Please, Mum, don't make me."

"If she won't, I will," Mr. Amberton said from behind his paper. "There is no discussion here, Wren. After your intolerable antics yesterday, you shall correct the impression you gave of yourself."

Wren stared at her plate. Couldn't he see? She had given the correct impression of herself. She was an antics-prone, funny-faced girl who could never be a duchess. She looked up at her mother with pleading eyes.

Mrs. Amberton's face softened. "Wren, I am sure you are nervous about the task before you—"

"Task? A marriage shouldn't be a task, should it, Mum?"

"No, but in some cases it is. I am sure you are nervous, but I'm sure it will turn out well. You have disappointed us over and over, but you somehow always manage to be unscathed."

Wren was not sure if the comment was intended to make her feel better or worse.

"Make no more fuss, dearest. Please. We have been bestowed with a great honor. On all accounts, the duke is a fine man. I certainly would not marry you to a rake."

"I didn't think the puke was very fine," Charley mumbled.

"Charley! You have been raised better than to speak like that about Wren's betrothed. You—"

"May I be excused?" Wren begged.

Her mother nodded—a tenderness still in her eyes—and Wren left her meal untouched. In her room, she climbed back into bed fully clothed and tucked herself into a ball. She remained that way for the rest of the morning, drifting in and out of sleep.

When her legs grew restless and the sun too bright, she got up and reorganized her wardrobe three different ways before she gave up ever being satisfied with it and left half the things out mid-fourth organization. Then she tried to sketch out a few types of reptiles and several different species of foreign trees, but all of the drawings made her think of Lyn. Finally, she dropped her pen.

Oh, how she missed her friend! She pulled out a little scrap and took up her pen again.

Dearest, kindest, bestest friend,

I am in such a state! Mrs. Adley has passed, and I'm not allowed to feel it. Eillie is gone, and I have discouraged Gideon from speaking to me ever again, so now I'm all alone. On top of it all, I'm engaged to a rat-grandpa, and I'm not even allowed to refuse to see him. I have been provided a possible fix. Do you think it would be so terrible to not feel anything? Or not want to do anything? Like get married or something? Would that be so bad? At the moment, I don't think so. So I might try to help His Grace feel the same with a little drink of sorts. None of this probably makes sense to you, but it doesn't matter. I'll burn this note like the rest when PJ brings it back.

I need you, Lyn. Please come home before I'm swept away.

Wren

She gently took PJ from his cage—stroking his feathers with her thumb—and tucked the note into the small tube. When she released the bird, she imagined she had tied a string to him, and that he pulled her along with him. High into the sky, then to wherever Lyn was at the moment.

The dreaded time of the dinner party drew near, and Wren prepared herself for the evening of torture. Not only would she need to endure the duke, but Casner would be there. And Lucy. And Gideon, too. Was there any evening destined to be more miserable?

The Ambertons arrived at Garwick precisely three minutes late and were ushered into the sitting room. The duke eyed Wren with dignified relief, Lucy with thinly veiled disdain, Casner with a hint of fear, and Gideon impassively.

"Wren, we are so happy for you," Mrs. Brayford said tightly, coming forward to take her hands. She gave them a little squeeze. "I hope you will be very happy."

Wren nodded and remained at the door while her parents moved to sit on an open settee. Mrs. Amberton looked at Wren wide-eyed and jerked her head toward the duke. Wren inhaled a deep breath and traipsed across the room to sit beside her betrothed while the entire room watched in silence.

"Pleasure to see you again, my dear," the duke murmured to her. "I know those combs in your hair. I'm glad you like them." He looked over her face, amusement brightening his eyes. "I see your nose is quite healed up."

Wren reached up and scratched her sniffer. "Yes, Your Grace. It's still a little itchy."

Mrs. Amberton cleared her throat.

The duke smiled widely. "Yes, I'm sure." He shifted to face her father. "I'd like to know a little more about your family, Mr. Amberton. I've been told you have two sons and another daughter?"

"Yes. My eldest son serves in the King's Navy, fourth unit. On the *Victory*. My younger son is still at home. He'll be going to secondary school within a couple years. And our other daughter is currently in Ferriton with my spinster sister, Fanny. I believe you are acquainted with her?"

The duke looked taken aback for a moment then replied, "Fanny Amberton. I do not recall."

"Fanny Richter, actually. She is my half-sister."

There was a pause. "Richter, you say? Yes, I believe I remember her now. Lovely woman. Well, it certainly is a small world. Reynard, I wish you had informed me I had a connection to the family. I wouldn't have been negligent in asking after mutual acquaintances."

"I—I had no idea, Uncle," Casner stammered.

"Never mind. Tell me, Miss Amberton. Do you prefer rubies or diamonds? I would like to select a ring for you as soon as possible."

"I've never really thought about it, Your Grace."

"Not thought about it?" he replied skeptically. "Well, if you've no opinion, I'll select it for you. Would that suit?"

"Yes, Your Grace."

Dinner was announced, and the awkward group rose to remove to the dining room. Mrs. Brayford took the duke's arm, and Casner hurried to take Lucy's, leaving either Gideon or Mr. Amberton to take Wren's. She moved closer to her father, but before she could slip her arm through his, Gideon offered to escort her. Hesitantly, she accepted.

Her heart gave a painful thump. Though she felt him firmly beside her, somehow he felt miles away. Wren wasn't sure how to bridge the distance that had sprung up between them.

Suddenly he tipped his head toward hers and whispered, "Why didn't you tell him you prefer willow vines?"

She released her held breath and tried to smile. "Well-made willow jewelry is so hard to come by. I don't wish to be too demanding."

"Ah. And what was wrong with your nose?"

"Oh. It fell off," she replied, as if she were talking about a lost shoe.

He gave her a puzzled look, but she turned her head away. She wouldn't have time to explain everything anyway.

They reached the dining room. Gideon pulled out her chair and waited for her to be settled before taking his seat at the head of the table. She watched him for a moment and rubbed her foot against her ankle where the vial of Flat Elixir was tied.

As the soup bowls were placed, Wren tried to form a plan. The duke was seated beside her, giving her easy access to his bowl or cup. But Casner was the only one who seemed disinclined to stare at her periodically. How was she to empty the little bottle without notice? She didn't want to be suspected of poisoning her betrothed!

As minutes passed and the conversation carried on in a relatively natural manner, her hands began to tremble. Twice she dropped her fork into her lap and once did she knock over her glass. Mrs. Amberton pursed her lips and seemed to be on the cusp of scolding her daughter but each time held her peace. The duke pretended not to notice the mess on her lap and refilled her glass himself.

"I shall take good care of you, my dear," he said gently as he poured.

As often as she dared, Wren glanced at the head of the table. Gideon conversed in his usual concise way, but Wren could tell he was uncomfortable.

She imagined herself leaping to her feet, flinging handfuls of peas at the duke and then her parents, shouting, 'You'll never take me alive! To the woods, Giddy!' Her friend would then meet her at the door, and they'd run for it, grabbing dessert on their way.

"Wren!"

She looked up at her mother, who smoothed her irritated features and smiled warmly. "His Grace is speaking to you," she said almost through her teeth.

"What?"

"I was merely wondering if you are at all musical."

"Oh, I play a little."

"Well, I should like to hear you this evening."

A Pretty Game

Wren looked around the table. Lucy smiled at her benignly, almost encouragingly. The walls were getting closer all the time.

Wren cleared her throat as delicately as she could. "Ah, well, I don't think I'm really...good enough to...play for a group."

"A shame," replied the duke, turning back to his plate.

The room fell brutally quiet. Wren shifted in her seat. She was frighteningly on the verge of pouring her bottle down His Grace's throat for all to see. Then it would be over. If she were sent to prison for the murder of his personality, at least she would go knowing full well she was guilty.

Mercifully, Mrs. Brayford declared the meal over. As the women rose to leave, a fierce panic seized Wren's heart. Every idea escaped her. Every eye watched. It was over. Opportunity had been lost. Miserably, she trailed after the others, a failure in her scheme.

And then a miracle!

Out in the hallway, a lonely tray set with a decanter and glasses rested on the side table, waiting to be taken in to the men. In a split second, Wren made up her mind. This was it! Now, for an excuse.

Consciously, she lagged behind the group, then hastily pulled one of the combs from her hair and let it slide quietly down her dress to the floor. When she entered the sitting room, she put a hand to her head and gasped. "Oh, my combs. I've lost one. I better go find it."

"Send Rawlings," Mrs. Brayford said. "He'll—"

"No! No, it's no trouble. I'm sure I lost it somewhere between here and the dining room. I'll be right back."

Retracing her steps through the gaping passages, she returned to the abandoned hallway and tiptoed past the dining room, failing to resist a peek. Her gaze collided with Gideon's through the gap in the doors and with a little "Eep," she hurried to the table where the tray still waited. What honors she gave the footman for being so lazy! Hastily, she grabbed the little Flat Elixir bottle from its hiding place on her ankle and froze as one of the dining room doors slid open.

"Lost?" Gideon whispered, coming toward her with a hesitant smile.

She closed her fingers tightly around the bottle and straightened. "No, I...er, not *me*. I lost one of my combs."

He looked around and spotted the piece on the long runner where she had dropped it. He retrieved it, and when she took it from his hand, her fingers brushed his, which seemed to linger around the accessory longer than necessary.

He swallowed hard. "Wren, I'm sorry. If I've said anything our last few meetings that hurt you."

She feigned indifference with a small shrug. "Oh, I haven't given any of it another thought."

"Haven't you?" he asked, his eyes intensifying.

And for some inexplicable reason, her eyes welled with tears. She furiously blinked them away and tucked the comb recklessly back into her hair.

"And I really do...want you to be happy," he continued. "You deserve to be. You have always been a great friend to me."

"Thanks. You, too," she replied lamely.

He bobbed his head and glanced at the tray. "I better go." He backed away a few steps then turned and disappeared through the door.

Wren exhaled a heavy breath and looked at the tray. Four glasses gleamed in the sconce candlelight. She stamped her foot. Rot! Which one was for the duke? She couldn't very well contaminate the whole decanter. Shaking her head, she tried to think clearly.

"Dora, stop!" said a laughing voice from somewhere around the corner. "I'm sure the master is waiting. I have to get back."

Quick!

Wren uncorked the elixir, emptied it into one of the cups, then sloshed some of the amber liquid over the top of it. There! It looked normal. It could work. The honored, lazy footman appeared from around the corner, a beaming scullery maid hanging on his arm.

They stopped and abruptly separated. "Good evening, miss," they said in unison, bowing or curtsying.

"I was just pouring my betrothed, the puke—duke! The duke. His drink," Wren finished as confidently as she could manage. "Will you be sure he gets it?"

"Certainly, miss."

"Thanks."

Satisfied, she turned to go back to the sitting room, the sound of the dining room door sliding open behind her. She had done it! She now only needed to wait for the elixir to take effect, then plant ideas in the duke's head ('You don't want to marry me. It's too much work. Just go back to your enormous nest and have a long, long nap').

'I really do want you to be happy,' Gideon's words echoed in her head. '*You deserve it.*' She stopped.

Did she?

Did she deserve to be happy? Her mind flooded with memories of the last nine months since that fateful day Mrs. Adley's laboratory was discovered. Sneaking. Stealing. Enjoying. Crowning her acts of selfishness, she had just sentenced a man to feel nothing for an entire year—perhaps longer—so that she might painlessly make an escape. She was not a girl. She was a snake. A selfish, devouring snake.

"I'm a terrible person," she whispered to herself.

Without hesitating another second, she bolted for the dining room and burst through the doors.

"AVAST!" she shouted.

The men startled and stared at her. Her father's veins throbbed threateningly in his neck, but Wren didn't care. The footman had just handed the duke his glass. The rest were still empty on the tray.

"Uh…I noticed one of the cups had a gross chunk of something on it. Ope, yep, here it is."

She took the duke's glass from his hand before he could examine it. The footman gave her an odd look but so did everyone else. She emptied the glass into a potted plant, shaking it vigorously to get every last drop, and set it on the table.

"All right, well, crisis averted. Thanks," she said, tripping over the carpet. She fairly flew to the sitting room and took the seat next to her mother, her heart pounding in her ears.

"Are you all right, dearest?"

"Fine, Mum. I'm fine." And she was. She was still engaged, which was awful, but she had not harmed anyone. She had saved someone from herself!

The evening went on, with perplexing friendliness from Lucy and small but not unkind gestures from the duke. Casner never said more than a few words, and though her mother did force her to sit at the piano, Wren fumbled through a couple childish tunes and returned to her seat feeling as if she had done her duty.

When the party finally drew to a close and the guests were filing through the door, Wren was surprised to find herself caught up in an embrace from Lucy.

"I want to congratulate you on your engagement," she said in a low tone. "You'll not forget to have me at Mendshire, will you?"

"Um."

Lucy pulled away but kept a hold of Wren's arms. "Love really seems to be in the air. Only fancy—two weddings in one summer!"

"Two?"

"Yes, of course. Gideon is all but engaged, you know. It's been arranged for some time." She cocked her head. "Or didn't you know?"

"No. I hadn't heard."

"Well, I guess I don't know why you should have. Gideon is so quiet about things. But we expect him and dear Julia to announce it publicly before summer. Mother is so pleased."

Wren forced a smile and mumbled a reply she couldn't remember minutes later. Gideon engaged to Lady Julia? Wren suddenly felt pushed from the proud little pedestal she had put herself on. Maybe she was not so selfless. She couldn't eke out even a button of happiness for her friend.

Before she passed through the large mahogany doors of Garwick, the duke offered Wren his arm and looked up at her, telling her casually about his vast estate. She tried to listen to the descriptions of ancient woods and sprawling hills, but her ears wanted to hear what Gideon was saying to her parents behind her. She couldn't even muster a smile as she listened to them talk happily about Luke.

"Well, good evening, my dear," the duke said, handing her up into the barouche. "I am leaving in the morning for Ferriton. I shall send my carriage for you and your mother in a few days time, and we shall shop for your trousseau together, hm? Everything you want will be yours. Will that please you?"

"Yes, thank you, Your Grace," Wren said without looking at him.

"And you shall do nothing that is distasteful to you. You have my word."

She nodded. He hesitated a moment, then opened his mouth to speak but was interrupted.

"Oh, Your Grace!" gushed Mrs. Amberton. "You are too kind. I cannot tell you how pleased Wren is with your offer. She's a trifle willful, you'll find, but she is so grateful you have pursued her. In truth, she is extremely shy and quite beside herself, you know. She never dreamed of being a duchess and now in just a few weeks time. You've made us all very, very happy. We shall await the carriage anxiously and will be delighted to oblige you in any way."

"Thank you, madam."

As they pulled away, Wren turned to see the duke scurrying up the steps. But Gideon still stood in the drive, watching them go.

CHAPTER TWENTY-FIVE
Dead Schemes and Things

The hour was late when the Amberton barouche pulled into their drive, and Wren went directly to bed, taking time only to remove her shoes before climbing under the blankets.

She laid awake in her dark room considering the events of the past few days. The dinner party. The duke's patient attentiveness. Her near escape. Gideon's apology and pending engagement. And just yesterday she had sat by her ailing friend's bedside. Now she was gone. The pain was still very fresh in her heart, and she wondered how Mr. Adley was getting on.

A spring wind was blowing over the house, plinking bits of something against her windowpane. She wished it would rain so the sound could soothe her into painless sleep. Another plink, louder than the first. Then another.

Plink, plink.

Wren yanked off her covers and threw open her window to find someone was indeed trying to get her attention.

"Lyn!" she whisper shouted. "Meet me at the door!"

Her friend nodded and both girls hurried to meet in the middle.

When the lock was unfastened and the door swung open, Wren threw herself into Lyn's arms.

"What are you doing here?" she whispered into Lyn's shoulder.

"I got your note. We just arrived home late this afternoon. I came earlier but Plucky said you had gone to a party. I took a gamble and guessed what time you would be home."

"Did you walk?"

"No, Papa drove me."

Wren leaned around and peered into the darkness until she made out Mr. Pak. He waved from their gig.

"Can you come in?"

"Yes, for a few minutes." Lyn stepped inside, and they tiptoed to the parlor. "Wren. What on earth does your note mean?"

"I'm so relieved you got it. I've been so anxious for you to come home. I'm so sorry I didn't go with you!"

She launched into the whole story for her sympathetic friend—nothing of the last nine months was left untouched. From the Adleys, alchemy, and beauty thievery (which understandably took some time to explain satisfactorily) to all things Gideon, Casner, and the Duke of Mendshire, including the plan with the Flat Elixir.

"So, how did it go?" Lyn asked anxiously.

"You forgot to say the 'Your Grace' part."

"Then you're still engaged! What happened? Didn't it work?"

Wren shrugged. "I couldn't do it! I started thinking too much. I thought about Eillie and how I hurt her. I thought of my family and the disappointment they would feel. The little duke in his giant house, sitting alone, feeling nothing…and I just couldn't do it. Ugh. What sour luck. Of all the times to strike up a conscience."

"But you can't marry him! What are you going to do?"

"I don't know. He's staying at Garwick tonight and returning to Ferriton in the morning. He has asked me to meet him there soon. To get my trousseau." She slumped back in the chair and clasped her hands over her crumpled dress.

"And what about Gideon?"

Wren sighed. "What about him? I don't think he needs the duke to buy *his* bridal things." She tried to laugh.

Lyn stared a moment, then crossed the room to kneel before her. "What is the matter with you?"

"I'm engaged to a rich rat grandpa and have imploded all of my personal relationships, though most seem to be on the mend."

Lyn snorted. "Wren, be serious! I can't believe you're just going to roll over like this."

"What choice have I?"

"I don't know, but you're forever coming up with a plan. You've always gotten out of scrapes. Remember when you accidentally poisoned all your father's chickens?"

Wren gave a short sort of laugh. "Yeah?"

"Did you just run away?"

"No. I buried all the chickens and said a fox got them."

"Exactly!"

Wren gasped. "Lyn. Will you help me dig a hole then? It will have to be big. Do you really think anyone will believe the duke was attacked by foxes?"

Lyn grabbed her by the shoulders and gave her a shake. "I meant think creatively."

"Wild boars then? You know their tusks can grow up to nine inches."

Lyn put her hands up to her forehead. "You're impossible. I don't know how you can joke about this. My point is you figured a way out of trouble. There's got to be *something* you can do." She dropped her hands and softened the hard lines that had suddenly formed on her face. "I better go or my father will come after me and wake the whole house." She took up both of Wren's hands. "*Think.* Think hard. I know you can get out of this and still keep your reputation intact."

Wren said nothing but nodded in agreement. They embraced, and Lyn quietly slipped out. Wren sat in her chair for another hour before she got up and locked the front door.

When she was snug in her bed, she let her wheels turn wildly. She could run away to somewhere overseas—Royce maybe. But she was certain she would get unforgivably seasick, and they'd have to throw her overboard.

What if she faked her own death? No, she wasn't good at holding her breath. And it was a horrid thought to be buried alive.

Or perhaps she could swindle the duke into marrying Lucy instead? She sat up. Yes, that could work. Lucy would make an excellent duchess. And she would probably drink her own mother's blood to get the title. But the poor duke. Wren would have to give him the emotionless elixir in order for him to survive the ordeal. And then she'd be right back where she started.

She dropped back onto her pillow.

Her feral ideas continued to run wild for some time before a gradual shift came about, and she began thinking in the context of what her friend would have done in a similar situation. Wren was certain Mrs. Adley's character was far more reasonable than her own. Mrs. Adley had been wise and concise in her actions.

What had she chanted to herself that one day so long ago by the herb garden? 'Be brave, brave. Be brave.'

Mrs. Adley would be brave. She wouldn't scheme, wouldn't run. Wouldn't toss round rocks into a well hoping to still get her wish.

She would reason. She would speak up. She would be clear.

Wren threw her legs over the side of the bed and went to her wardrobe to dress but paused, trying to think rationally. If she went to the large house now, with its impossible number of windows, she would never find the duke's room. And she certainly couldn't bang on the front doors in the moonlight.

She climbed back under her covers to wait for dawn, her mind never quieting enough to allow sleep. When the first glimmers from the sun lightened the dark sky, she put on her boots and coat, then quietly slipped out her window.

Reciting her speech for the hundredth time, Wren walked toward town. "...but I shan't marry you, Your Grace. No, not for all your rubies..."

The little town was already showing signs of life. The breeze floated the smell of freshly baked bread, and the blacksmith shop glowed through filmy panes. A rooster crowed somewhere nearby.

Wren inhaled a deep breath and began her speech again. Ahead, a carriage rolled toward her. She straightened. Six horses, if she wasn't mistaken. The carriage turned down the road that would eventually lead to Rembly, and she caught the flash of a crest. The Mendshire crest. Wren broke into a run.

"Wait!" she cried. "Your Grace, stop!"

She rounded the corner and raced after the carriage, but it moved too swiftly, the gap ever widening. She gave chase until her chest burned and she could shout no more. She stopped, gasping to catch her breath, and watched the carriage grow smaller and smaller.

"I don't want to marry you!" she bellowed, raking her fingers into her hair. But it was too late. She kicked at the dirt. "Wretched rot!"

She turned back toward town, feeling the words of her speech rolling away with the carriage. They wouldn't keep until she next saw the duke. She had to get the words out now. Before she burst with anxiety. Before the papers proclaimed the match or the duke had time to purchase a ring and a license. But how?

She considered stealing a horse. Or borrowing one rather. (Not a thief.) But when she peeked over the fence of the community stable, the only specimen not in a padlocked stall was Mrs. Harper's goat. Even she found it difficult to imagine its short legs being speedy enough to catch His Grace's coach and six.

"Miss Wren!" a voice called from above. "Is that you?"

Wren looked up to see Miss Nelly leaning out her window.

"It is you! I thought so. Out so early. But are you well? My, worn through, poor dear. I'm up as well, as you see, but I'm just having my tea and writing a letter to my brother in Ferriton. I must finish before eight so I may send it, but the teapot is still hot, and I can make time for a visit if you'd like. Won't you come in?"

Wren pressed her eyes shut. And then…

"Miss Nelly. It is Saturday. The mail doesn't run again for another two days."

"Oh, I'm sending it with my sister. Save the postage, you know. She is leaving today to visit some friends. Just one stop planned, so she should reach town by Monday. My, the weather is pleasant this morning. Seems all the birds are feeling free."

"Miss Nelly, do you have paper and ink I may have?"

"Of course. I've just bought new stationery. Exactly the color of lilac. Very pretty, indeed, though it smells a bit like ham. I shall be glad to lend you some. I'll send Millie down directly to let you in."

A half hour later, Wren sanded the paper and read through her letter to the duke again. She thanked him for his offer, as was appropriate, then very clearly expressed her desire to be released from the engagement and firmly stated she would not be persuaded otherwise. Feeling like there was nothing else to be said, she folded the paper and tucked it into the envelope.

Her parents were going to be bitterly disappointed. The second half of their lives would not be full of cushions and bonbons. But she would take care of them. She would take care of them even if she ended up rubbing creams on their feet all the rest of their days.

Of course the sisters were curious as to why Wren Amberton would be sending a letter to the Duke of Mendshire, but she managed to keep her purpose secret, rattling off something about a sandwich recipe she promised to share with him.

Mrs. Harper solemnly promised to deliver the letter, and after prying herself away from Miss Nelly, Wren began her slow walk home, crossing every finger and toe that her straightforward honesty would bring the desired outcome. She only had to wait.

CHAPTER TWENTY-SIX

Revelations

Wren watched from her window as her father—dressed in his black suit—pulled the barouche through the hedge gate, heading toward town. It was Langlish custom for only men to attend a funeral, which was fine with Wren. She didn't want to go sit with a bunch of strangers anyway.

She whiled away the time creating a watercolor of the life cycle of a rose, using three little rose hips Mrs. Adley had given to her some months ago as inspiration. They were wrinkled and dry now, but she remembered when they were smooth and red, fresh with life.

After her father returned and disappeared into his study, she waited an hour more, then set out for Ebdor Cottage. No answer came to the door, so she quietly let herself in and found Mr. Adley sitting in his parlor before a pile of untouched peanuts.

"Hello," she said.

He looked up in surprise, then rose to his feet. "Hello, my dear girl. I didn't hear you come in. Please sit."

She crossed the room and embraced him a moment, whispering her sympathies, before taking a seat.

"It is all right. I think I've known it to be coming for some time. I just didn't want to see it. You should have seen her. So peaceful."

"I'm glad."

"It's quiet here, with her gone. I thought I'd be able to get more work done if she wasn't forever moving my books and shuffling my papers. But I would have her do it again." He pushed the pile of peanuts around the table. "I'm glad you've come. I've been thinking. Probably too much. But we once talked about Mrs. Adley's ideas and I said I doubted her. That nothing could go on after its time. Do you remember?"

"Yes." She was sure she remembered all their conversations.

"When her casket was lowered and the dirt began to fall, it occurred to me quite forcefully that Mrs. Adley was not in that box."

Wren looked at Mrs. Adley's empty chair.

Mr. Adley chuckled at her confusion. "That is to say the entity that is Mrs. Adley was not in that box. Do you understand?"

"I think so." They were both quiet for a few minutes. Wren smoothed her skirts. "But what about her goal? Perfection. Do you think that exists?"

He smiled warmly and leaned back. "That remains to be seen. You know, Mrs. Adley was a seeker by nature. And it wasn't vanity that made her so. I don't think she wanted to live here forever or make mounds and mounds of gold. That is the traditional idea of alchemy. But it wasn't hers. You know several of her discoveries are on the shelves of apothecaries all over the world."

"No, I didn't know."

"It's true. But far too many of her discoveries are not for the average person to use. We can be selfish beings—possibly doing more harm than good with the powers of the Divine Governor in our hands. So

I think it is good that we close up her little lab for now. I shall keep her things, of course, but shall work no more." He withdrew his handkerchief and wiped his eyes and nose. "It does me good to see your face, Miss Wren. She loved you so."

"And I loved her. So very much." Wren wiped her own eyes with the heel of her hand, then moved from her chair to sit beside him. "What will you do now?"

"Well, I shall stay here, I think. There isn't any reason for me to go anywhere else. Except…were you able to—you know—get out of your engagement?"

Wren pressed her lips together. "No. Thanks for your gift, but no. I discovered a conscience and couldn't use it."

His face brightened slightly. "I'm glad to hear it. I was so desperate when I sent it. But after a day or so of thinking, I regretted my rashness. I'm glad you thought better of it than I, though I shall be so sorry to lose you."

Wren nodded. "Well, I hope to have a chance yet. I sent him a letter this morning—telling him directly I wished to be released. I think that's what Mrs. Adley would have done."

He cracked at a shell and put a few peanuts into his mouth. "Yes. She would have been direct. I never had to wonder what she was thinking. I think you've done the right thing. I hope he has a heart and listens to the pleas of such a young thing."

The room fell silent aside from the ticking clocks. Wren ached for the comfort of her former visits. Mr. Adley was clearly distressed, brave as he was trying to be. It would not do to leave him feeling as she found him. "I used my Spark Juice to teach a boy a lesson."

He stopped fiddling with the shells and looked up in surprised amusement. "Did you?"

Feeling he was hoping for a good diversion, she went into the Casner and the Fountain story. Mr. Adley was shocked at the young man's behavior, as well as the duke's hiring his nephews to do his wife shopping. He laughed heartily at her retelling.

"Well done, Miss Wren. You are a quick thinker. I had hoped you would never have need of the juice, but that was a case it was surely needed. I hope the young man learned his lesson."

"He hardly looks my direction," she said with a laugh.

She told him the full beastly story as well and soon they were in his study, sorting books and papers, and feeling quite at ease. When Wren announced it was time for her departure, Mr. Adley took her hand and gave it a fatherly kiss.

"Thank you for coming to me. You have been a balm to my heart. Come to me again soon, will you?"

"Of course. I shall look forward to it."

She left the little cottage and took the long way home, tromping through the cheerful woods, past Pirate Pond and other childhood landmarks. It was funny how dead trees and wandering brooks could feel like a part of one's soul.

His Grace had said his home was surrounded by woods, as well, but she hoped never to see them. It was an unnerving feeling to have all her hopes attached to a piece of paper.

Wren reached home and decided to continue walking to Lyn's. She was welcomed inside, and Lyn was informed of the letter. Wren sensed a little disappointment from her friend—she was skeptical of the simple plan—but Wren was still certain it was the best course for the situation.

They spent the afternoon catching up, Lyn reenacting her aunt's overbearing orders and her cousin's pompous declarations. Wren laughed so much, it felt almost like nothing had disrupted their lives. They spoke no more of their spat, both content to know the other still cared. Theirs was the kind of friendship that could weather any storm given the right amount of time for the turbulent waves to calm.

Though the next several days dragged like an anchor at the bottom of a sandy bay, they were not wasted. With uncertainty dangling over her head, Wren discovered certainty by reclaiming her independence—eating breakfast at the table as she pleased, wearing her comfortable frocks or fancy silks when she wished, and even on occasion folding her arms without shame. It was as if something had awakened inside of her, a sense of self unlike anything she had ever known before.

Finally, on the fifth day after sending her letter, her walk to the post office was rewarded. With a trembling hand, she accepted a letter with a finely scrawled address, as well as one in Eillie's neat hand, from the postman and ran toward home, exclaiming hello and goodbye to acquaintances as she passed.

Fearing her mother would see the letter from the duke, Wren went directly to the barn. There in the loft, she dropped into the straw and forced herself to breathe. The seal was deep purple—the duke's insignia pressed into it. She shut her eyes and slid her finger under the wax.

For a few minutes she sat there, eyes closed, letter open. Her stomach turned, and she almost lost her breakfast. Then gathering courage from thoughts of Lyn and Mrs. Adley and Gideon, she opened her eyes and read the letter.

My dear Miss Amberton,

I have received your letter and thank you for your directness. My circumstances have been incomprehensibly altered in the last few days, and I find I am rather relieved by your request. You are a lovely girl, and I was afraid to disappoint you. We shall dissolve our engagement in a mutual truce, and as it has not yet been announced, I imagine there will be no complication. I wish you all the best in your life endeavors.

    Sincerely,
    W. James Nest. Duke of Mendshire

Wren reread the brief letter, forcing its contents into her mind. He had agreed to release her. She was free. She pressed the letter to her chest, her breath light and quick. It had worked. How she didn't really know. A green face and odd behavior should have been more effective than a letter. But it had worked! She dropped back into the hay and let out a scream of victory.

Suddenly she remembered Eillie's letter, and with a light heart, tore it open.

Dearest Sister,

 I hope I am not stepping out of place, but you will never guess what has happened. Aunt has eloped! And I am the instigator. Me! I am near fainting to explain!

 The entire journey to Ferriton, Aunt was very reserved. I could tell she was agitated, but I assumed she was just anxious for you. It wasn't until she had again mentioned her acquaintance with the duke, that I began to think she had feelings for the man. Acting on my suspicion I made some inquiries and found out his residence in town. I felt very bold.

 He was not at home when I called, so I left my card with a note asking him to call on me, claiming I was anxious to meet my future brother-in-law. The very next day, he came. (Such a small man for a duke, I thought he was a messenger.) Anyway, I knew at once I was not mistaken. You should have seen the way they looked at one another. (Kind of an odd pair, really, but I assure you there was chemistry!)

But it was so awkward. While we conversed politely I asked myself, 'What would Wren do?' I stewed for some time over this, and finally it came to me. I pretended to faint and dropped my teacup in my lap (not very creative, I know, but I haven't much practice in scheming. And do not worry, my legs were only slightly scalded). When I "came to" I excused myself to clean up and asked His Grace not to leave before I returned.

I dithered for about an hour, and when I returned, oh! there was a change. Aunt was bright pink, and the duke very agitated. I was worried they had quarreled, but when His Grace took his leave, he kissed her hand so long I began to blush myself. My heart nearly broke for them. Aunt immediately excused herself to her room for the rest of the day.

I went to bed with such a heavy heart that proved completely unnecessary. For what happened next you'll never guess. Except you might, I suppose, because I already told you. They eloped! I awoke to find a letter left with her maid. It was long, but the gist is when Aunt was working as a very young governess, she met the duke and they fell madly in love. But she refused him, insisting they could never marry due to his reputation and his title, marrying so far beneath him. And so they parted. And neither ever forgot the other. Isn't it romantic?

Just this last year, the duke decided he had enough of being lonely and, spoiled into thinking he could have his way in just about anything, began seeking out the most interesting of young ladies to find a companion. (His pride kept him from seeking out Aunt, fearing being twice rebuffed or she had long ago married and forgotten him. Why he didn't try to find out I don't know. I suppose that's a man for you.)

Anyway, the duke went home last night and found your letter asking to be released. Oh Wren, what timing! He had begun to question his motives at the dinner party, but then Mum said something at parting that made him hold his tongue. He is too much a gentleman to have ever broken off the engagement himself and disappointed a young lady and her family.

Your letter has saved all of you! He returned last night after I had gone to bed, and they formed their hasty plan. Is this not a shocking turn? I am packing my trunk as soon as I finish this letter as I have been left in the care of a Mrs. Yale who is in need of companionship. I have met her several times, and she is very kind, so do not worry for me.

Oh Wren! Are you happy? I will never forget your face when we left. I have seen you miserable but not like that. You've been a constant thought to me. And now, you are free! I don't know how you will break the news to Mum and Papa, but it is all true and there is nothing that can be done now. I hope to return home for a visit before the month is out.

Much love,
Eillie

Wren screeched and fell back into the straw. It was too good to be true! Surely Mum and Papa would not be angry at the duke for marrying someone so close to the family. They would still receive the connections they hoped for and would probably be invited to visit. And she was free!

She kicked her legs into the air a few times, her entire body leaping with glee, then gathered up her letters and hurried out of the barn. She was too excited to talk to either of her parents just yet but had others to inform.

"Where are you going?" came a call from the beech tree as she passed through the hedge gate.

She looked up at her little brother. "To Lyn! Charley, you shall be the first to know. I am not leaving. I am staying here!"

"Really?" he cried. "So you aren't going to marry that old puke?"

"Duke, Charley. He's a duke."

"Not to me if he was going to take you away. Boy is Mum going to be surprised!"

Surprised was not the word Wren would have used. "Yes, but don't tell anyone, all right? I'll tell them when I get back."

"I make an oath," he said with a fist over his heart.

She ran all the way to Lyn's house and breathlessly related the good news. The two friends jumped around in circles, banging on the floor so loudly Mrs. Poole came flying up the stairs to scold them for shaking dust from the ceiling. The girls dropped onto Lyn's bed and laughed at nothing in particular.

"You saved me, Lyn. When I was ready to sink into despair and shutter myself up forever, you saved me. Thank you."

Her friend smiled. "I'll always be here to tell you when you are being stupid."

"I'm glad for it. Because I'm afraid it happens often."

After an hour of giggles and some Karian tea, Wren left her friend. For a few steps she went toward Garwick, but a flutter in her stomach turned her the opposite direction in favor of a cottage.

Tired from running, Wren took the road at a relaxed pace, winding through town and then the woods, feeling herself in easy contemplation. What a turn of events. Perhaps the Divine Governor didn't hate her for setting fire to the belfry after all.

How perfectly amazing that all of those she loved so well—and had at one time or another betrayed—had aided in her rescue. Lyn had made her mind begin to turn again when it was resigned to being hushed. Mr. Adley had provided her with concoctions and words of wisdom. Gideon had opened her heart to feel more. Sweet, lovely Mrs. Adley had inspired her to be brave.

And Eillie.

Eillie who she had used most abominably. Who she had neglected and avoided and scoffed. Who she had stripped of natural loveliness for her own use. All this, and Eillie had not abandoned her in time of need. She would never have guessed how swift forgiveness would come from her sister. What she now knew was her sister loved her despite all her faults, and that she, Wren, deeply loved her sister.

And for the first time in her life, Wren realized perhaps she had always had what she really wanted.

Mr. Adley was overjoyed by the news his young cousin brought. It was a great comfort to him to know she would be around to keep him company, at least for now. They spent the rest of the afternoon that glorious day, reminiscing about Mrs. Adley, sifting through old material and discussing ideas for his forthcoming paper. Wren knew that theirs was a friendship meant to endure and that Mrs. Adley's influence would always be felt.

As could be supposed, Mr. and Mrs. Amberton were not as delighted by the news as everyone else.

"Jilted! You have been jilted," cried Mrs. Amberton as her husband promptly removed himself to his study, his face purple. "Odious man! Leaving my daughter at the altar."

"Mum, I didn't even have a ring. And I haven't been jilted. I asked for the release, and he gave it to me."

Mrs. Amberton waved her handkerchief in Wren's face. "I've told you before, a girl in love does not act rationally. You didn't know what you were doing."

"I assure you love did not warp my brain. I knew full well what I was doing when I sent that letter."

"Oh! But you didn't. Think of the gowns and the jewels and the connections! Wren, you have lost it all. He has denied you of all the happiness you might have known. And now you will never have any of it. Not a drop. You shall be miserable."

"I won't. Believe me, Mum. I am not at all disappointed. And think of Aunt Fanny. How happy she will be."

"Well, she is beyond the age of providing him an heir. I daresay they'll regret their choices."

"I think they both knew what they were doing."

Mrs. Amberton pursed her lips in contemplation for a moment. "I suppose I cannot say I am completely bitter about the match. I'm sure *I* will still get to ride in his coach and stay at Mendshire. And I suppose there's still hope you'll catch the eye of someone favorable. Someone you will like better. Maybe one who does not live quite so far away. I admit it was a trifle difficult for me to see you so unhappy, though I think it was in ignorance. How fortunate we have not announced it. I should have hated to retract such a declaration." She quieted for a moment, pulling at the edges of her handkerchief, then asked, "Is Mr. Casner still in town?"

Wren shrugged.

"You know he's fourth in line."

Wren snorted. "For the dukedom, maybe," she said, taking up her favorite novel and plunking languidly into her chair. "But for me, he is dead last."

CHAPTER TWENTY-SEVEN
As it Should Be

"He's coming! I see him! I see him!" Charley scurried out of his tree, slipping on the last branch and falling the last five feet to the ground with a rumpled *oomph*.

"Wren!" Mrs. Amberton screeched, straightening her skirts and smoothing her hair. "Hurry! Go fetch your father. They'll need a moment."

Wren squealed—an expression of nerves and anticipation—and sprinted to the front door. "He's here!" she yelled without entering more than a few steps. She wasn't about to miss seeing him ride through the hedge gate.

Footsteps alerted her she'd been heard, and Mr. Amberton appeared just as Eillie ran lightly down the stairs. The servant door of the dining room swung open, and Plucky blustered out, shaking flour from her apron.

Wren grinned and ran back out the door just as a trim bay with a tanned, handsome rider rounded the hedge gate.

"Luke!" Charley cried, bouncing alongside the horse. "Luke! It's me! Your brother Charley!"

Luke threw a leg over the horse and alighted, tossing his naval hat aside. "Are you sure? I thought I had a baby for a brother. No, you can't be!"

Charley dove into his arms—pressing his face into all the uniform buttons and buckles—then pulled back an arms length. "I am! I can prove it! Mum, am I Charley?"

"Yes, darling."

"See?" he said, wrapping his arms tightly around his brother again.

Luke laughed. "Yes, all right. You've convinced me. Hello, Mum."

"My boy!" Mrs. Amberton gushed. "Charley, step aside so the rest of us can have a turn."

Charley shook his head, so Mrs. Amberton was forced to embrace her elder son with Charley smashed between them.

"Sir." Luke bobbed his head respectfully to his father, and Mr. Amberton returned the gesture. "And is this pretty, little Eillie? All grown up, I see!"

"Yes, it's me. Twenty-two months is a long time. We're so happy you've come home."

"Me, too. And dear Miss Plucky. You are crying!"

"I've got flour in my eye," she replied indignantly, hugging him stiffly and patting his shoulder.

He grinned and looked over the woman's head at Wren. "And you," he said, shuffling forward a few steps with Charley still firmly in place. "Wren, how are you?" he said, taking her into his arms. He was so much taller than she remembered.

"I'm well," she said simply, but she was so much more than that. Her heart was near bursting. Luke was home! It was to be a short leave—here in Tremdor for a week only—but he was home. And she planned to make the most of it.

"Well, enough of that!" Luke said, pulling away and prying Charley from his waist. "Are we having a party? I'm famished!"

Dinner was still four hours away, but the young sailor was taken into the dining room to be fed a light snack of roasted wild pheasant, squash bathed in butter, crusty bread, and a side of fresh spiced applesauce. With his family gathered around him, he told some of his tales at sea, complimenting Plucky on the fine food every few bites.

The remaining afternoon hours were spent in the comfort of the drawing room, swapping more stories and Charley reading several of his plays, complete with dramatized voices.

As the hours passed, Wren's excitement for her brother's return was slowly replaced with anxiety regarding the approaching welcome home party. Gideon was coming. And her hands grew so clammy she couldn't keep them dry however she swiped them on her chair.

It had been two weeks since she had broken her engagement, and their only meeting—after church services—had been awkward to say the least. She had felt him scrutinizing her every move, as if he were watching for her to make a mistake. They had spoken, but not much more than '*Hello, how are you? Luke is coming home. I'm so glad—sorry about your engagement failing. That's all right.*' As they parted, she had longed for the former easiness between them.

An hour before the meal was set to begin, Wren went into the kitchen to help Plucky finish a few things. As she drizzled a thin icing over the carrot cake, she tried to work out her avoidance plan. Mr. Adley was coming. She could sit by him the entire evening. And she wouldn't need to speak much—Luke had enough stories to fill days of talk. Would Gideon be wearing his navy-colored coat or the black with plated buttons?

"Wren! You're missing the cake!"

"What?" She glanced down at the puddle of white on the counter block. "Oh! Sorry, Plucky." She grabbed the rag and wiped up the sticky mess before excusing herself to her room.

She was alerted to Gideon's arrival when she heard a well-known *whoop* of joy from Luke. She scrambled to her window and watched the two friends—who were more like brothers—reunite, complete with an embrace and back slaps she could hear through the glass. Her heart gave a little leap at seeing Gideon's wide, unsuppressed smile. He was wearing his navy coat—her favorite. That was how he should look always.

Gideon glanced up at her window, and she dropped herself to the floor, startling PJ into a fit. Oh, the misery in her heart!

A knock sounded at her door. "Come in," she squeaked.

Eillie swished into the room in her pretty peach-colored dress. "Where are you? Oh! What are you doing down there?"

"Gideon is here."

Eillie giggled wickedly. "Are you going to hide all evening then?"

"Depends on how long he stays."

Eillie took a hold of Wren's arm and pulled her up. "You'll never get away with it. Mum will find you."

"I know." Wren drew in a deep breath and exhaled. Squaring her shoulders, she held out an arm to Eillie. "Shall we?"

Eillie slipped her arm through. "We shall."

As they waited for dinner to be announced, Wren was grateful her brother evidently planned to keep Gideon to himself. Mr. Adley arrived a short time later and proved to be a magnificent distraction, full of new information from an article on sardines he had just been reading. Wren was only tempted to look at Gideon four hundred and seventeen times.

Though Mrs. Amberton wished for a grand affair, parties at Amberton were not at all formal, and when dinner was announced, the group simply crowded out of one room and into the next. Wren pulled out a corner chair beside Mr. Adley and moved to sit.

"Oh Wren, dearest," Mrs. Amberton said. "I planned to sit there with your father and Mr. Adley. Do come and take this seat."

Heat rushed to Wren's cheeks as Mrs. Amberton tapped the chair beside Gideon. Mrs. Amberton squinted her eyes once. Arguing would only make things more uncomfortable. Courageously, Wren obeyed. Gideon rose as she seated herself. Their eyes met briefly before he turned his attention to adjusting his silverware.

Wren looked across the table to find Luke staring at her, a smirk across his face. She gave her head a little shake. His smirk widened.

Salver after salver was brought out until the table disappeared. The lids were lifted, and the dining commenced.

"Well," Luke began merrily, shaking out his folded napkin and placing it across his lap. "I guess it's time for me to say the obligatory 'so much has changed since I've been away.' I foolishly expected to be the only one made new. But it seems my parents are the only two who have remained untouched by time." He smiled and winked at his mother, who blushed and smoothed her hair. "My brother is aspiring to great things, and my sisters have grown smart, lovely, and good—Wren, I shall be disappointed if you have outgrown your scheming, though. And you Giddy. Is there a Lady Garwick in the works?"

He paused only long enough for his friend to choke on his drink. "Anyway, I thank you, Mum. Sir." He leaned back and shouted, "And you, Plucky! I thank you all for this welcome. This fine food. This house! Not one of you has spit on my boots or threatened to throw me overboard. I can't tell you how good it is to sit here among you!"

Luke carried much of the conversation throughout the meal—discussing various creatures of the sea with Mr. Adley, rattling his mother by telling of the storms the *Victory* had endured, and enthralling them all with his brave admiral's life history.

Once Wren and Gideon reached for the fruit bowl spoon at the same time and bumped hands, but other than that jolt, she felt herself relaxing. Gideon, too, seemed to come to himself, and it was almost as if no awkwardness had ever been between them.

When everyone had finished their cake, Charley was forced to bed while the rest of the party retired to the drawing room. As Mr. and Mrs. Amberton visited with Mr. Adley, a game of cards was struck up, with Wren and Eillie on one team and Luke and Gideon on the other. Pitted against her mentor, Wren found herself challenged.

"Play your seven, Wren," Luke cajoled.

"No! You will only need one more set if I do. I prefer to keep you further out."

"What was I thinking, Giddy, teaching her how to play?"

"I told you to think better of it."

"That's the problem," Luke said with a sigh. "You have to speak plainly. You should have told me I'd lose to her every time. I don't know what it means to think better of things."

Wren eeked a note of delight. "Another set, Eillie! Good work. One more. Our poor lord must have a pitiful hand."

"It's lucky for you he does," Luke cried.

Eillie bent the two cards in her hand. "I hope he doesn't have anything higher than an eight," she said, placing one on the table, then covering her face.

"He doesn't. Everything in that suit has been played. It doesn't matter what you play, Gideon. You can't win."

He looked up to meet Wren's eyes and held them for a full five seconds. He quirked a heavy brow and dropped a red nine onto the pile.

"How did you hide that?"

He shrugged. "You miscounted."

"No, I didn't. We have played four nines already. You cheated somehow. Eillie, look through your tricks. Luke, you, too. Find all the nines."

"He's right, we hadn't played them all," Luke said. "Good show, old boy. That's what you get for being overly confident, Sister."

Three nines were ferreted out, the fourth still staring up from the middle of the table. Gideon played his last card, followed by the others, Luke's card winning the pile and stunning Wren with a loss.

The evening passed into night, and finally, the party was brought to an end. Mr. Forner was sought out to drive Mr. Adley home in the family barouche, and Gideon departed on his horse, promising to return tomorrow.

As soon as the door was shut, Mr. and Mrs. Amberton claimed exhaustion and retired to bed, leaving their three eldest children to themselves. Wren sank into her chair feeling unexpectedly satisfied with the evening.

Luke stood at the fireplace, his arm resting on the mantel. "So," he said, stirring the coals with his boot. "You and Gideon, huh?"

"I knew it," Eillie said triumphantly. "You think so, too, then?"

Wren blushed hotly and shot Eillie a baleful look. "I don't know what either of you mean. We are good friends, just like we've always been."

"Ha!" Luke said, turning to face her. "Nice try. But I saw your face. You are head over ears for the Viscount of Garwick."

"I'm not either! And it doesn't really matter. He doesn't think of me. In any way special."

"He does, though," Eillie said. "Don't you think, Luke?"

He shrugged. "How should I know? He's so level and I've never seen him in love before, though I know he has strings of girls pining for him."

"Thank you for pointing that out." Wren picked at the cushion, thinking of fancy Lady Julia Tounscend of Colton and wishing that entire county would sink into oblivion. Every day she expected to hear their announcement.

Luke laughed. "I'm kidding. Kind of. Anyway, know I would fully support the match. In fact, nothing would please me more."

"*Anyway*," Wren said, rising to her feet again, attempting to appear exhausted. "We better turn in. I have a feeling this week is going to be crammed."

The timing of Luke's visit was indeed fortuitous. It was Gideon's last week before the long university break ended, and therefore it was a week he had worked out ahead of time to have most of his schedule free. Luke was a tireless organizer, and the week went out just as Wren had hoped.

With a near constant party made up of herself, Luke, Eillie, Lyn, and Gideon, picnics were had in the Garwick hills, Pirate Pond was revisited and new treasure was buried, Plucky baked up sweets by the tons, and games were played every evening, indoors and out.

During this time, Wren manfully convinced herself that she was happy just being Gideon's friend. He was attentive to her all week—handing her up into carriages, partnering with her in games, and singling her out for walks around the picnic area. He never spoke about anything of importance, never tried to take her hand affectionately, but was warm and comfortable. Though the far recesses of her heart cried out for more than just his good graces, she was obstinately determined to appear just as she always had and be a friend to Giddy while she still could.

On Saturday morning, at Mrs. Amberton's insistence, Luke and Mr. Amberton left the house at sunrise for a father and son bonding ride in the Brayford hills.

Left to her own devices, Wren went out into the yard searching for a comfortable seat with her sketchpad under her arm and a plate heaped with cake for breakfast. She had just situated herself at the base of a beech tree when Gideon rounded the house, stopped, then casually came toward her.

"Luke is out with Papa," she said when he was near enough to hear.

"I'll wait—with you—if that's all right."

"Fine with me," Wren said, putting a bite into her mouth. "Cake?"

He shook his head and took off his hat as he sat down opposite her. "It's a nice morning."

The birds overhead chirped and bounced through the trees, and the freshly risen sun was already warming the valley.

"Yes, it is very nice."

After a few moments he cleared his throat. "I start university again in two days."

"Oh, that's right," Wren said as if she hadn't been keeping track. "Are you ready to go?"

"I think so. I'll actually leave tomorrow morning. Going early to make a detour to Colton."

"Ah. To see Lady Julia?"

"What? No. To escort my mum. Why do you ask about Julia?"

"Oh, I just thought you would want to see her. You know, since you are practically engaged and everything."

"Engaged? To Julia? Who told you that?"

"So it isn't true?" she said, trying not to sound too interested.

He flipped his hat in his hands, a trace of amusement in his expression. "No."

"Ah." How could she have fallen into that trap? Of course it wasn't true. Why had she believed Lucy, the queen of viciousness?

It was quiet again under the beech tree. Wren poked at her cake with every ounce of focus, pretending to work up the perfect bite.

Gideon watched her for a minute, then said, "Do you remember when you accused me of not being competitive? At that party of my mum's?"

"You aren't. Hardly an accusation."

"As I said, it depends on the game."

Wren stabbed at her cake a few more times and took another bite, struggling to understand why he would bring up that particular conversation.

He looked up into the tree. "I've been examining my hand while trying to count the cards playing against me. A bit ago I realized how fast the game could turn. That I'd wasted too much time sitting back and watching, hoping to be told which card to play. I thought I'd lost completely, dolt that I am."

Wren felt her heart speed up in her chest. She took another bite in forced calm.

"I went to Ferriton a few weeks ago."

"Oh?" she said with a mouthful. "For a haircut?"

"No. To see if I could purchase an estate. Far away from here."

"Hm," she replied and began furiously eating her cake.

"It turned out to be unnecessary, I think," he paused. "But on the way home I examined my hand again and am afraid I still stand a great chance of losing."

"How so?" she asked, still slightly unsure if they were talking about what she thought they were talking about but feeling pretty sure they were. An undefinable current of happiness pulsed through her body as she put another large bite into her mouth.

"Wren, I...will you put down your cake?" He moved onto his knees and took the plate out of her hand, laughing lightly as he did. "You're distracting me. I'm no good at this game! I don't know when to play a card and when to hold it and you don't give me clear hints. I don't even know if this is making any sense. And I know you could have your pick of anyone out there."

"Could I?"

He scoffed. "I'm not a complete fool. I see the way other fellows look at you."

An abrupt feeling of frustration ruined her euphoria. She flung her fork into the grass. "Gideon. If you're suddenly playing your hand, as you put it, because I've grown pretty, then you can take your cards to another table."

"What do you mean?"

She said nothing.

He, too, was quiet a moment, his face pinched in concentration. Finally, he said simply, "You have always been pretty to me, Wren."

She rolled her eyes, nodding, and folded her arms over her chest. Of all the times to joke.

"You think I'm joking. I'm not. Of all the girls I've met, I've never forgotten your eyes, your smile. You are funny and kind and—"

"Oh no," she interrupted. "I am not kind. If you knew everything I have done."

"I didn't say you are perfect," he retorted. "I meant you are kind on the whole. And I'll never find a girl more interesting to me than you, in all of Langley, I'm sure. *Wren.*" He put a finger under her chin and lifted her face until her gaze met his, which meant she looked at him down her nose. "Tell me we aren't just good friends. Tell me you want to be with me like I want to be with you."

"Wren!" Mrs. Amberton screeched from the house. "I need you to empty my latrine. It's too heavy for me and Plucky."

Wren pinched her lips together fighting a smile, and Gideon dropped his hand.

"Just a moment, Mum. I believe Lord Garwick is in the middle of proposing."

"Lord Garwick? Propose—oh! Oh, forgive me, I did not see you, my lord! I shall handle my…issue myself. Do continue."

Gideon and Wren both burst into a fit of snickers, struggling to keep them low. He gathered his wits sooner than she and moved to sit beside her.

"Not quite marriage yet—though I fully intend to pursue that. But for now, just that I might pay my addresses to you."

"Like you'll send me flowers and exotic candies?"

He entwined his fingers with hers. "If you want them."

"And love notes?"

"Tucked into the pages of my old books."

"Hm. It's very tempting. I've wondered before what Giddy in love would look like."

"I'm afraid you've seen him for a great while. I hope you are not disappointed. So…yes?"

"All right."

"It will be long. I still have three more years at Starton that I am expected to finish."

"I don't mind."

"And my estate is not as glorious as Mendshire. You won't be a duchess."

"I'll manage."

"And I *am* grumpy."

"I know."

"Good." He leaned his face nearer. "Then…"

Before Wren closed her eyes, she made a quick study of the face she knew so well. The face of one who saw every piece of her and loved her anyway. There was no pretense, no hiding behind a mask with Gideon.

And if that wasn't enough, she plainly felt the difference when their lips met. Like her first kiss, she was warm and giddy all over, but there was something more. No superficial fancies. No slippery intentions. His kiss was made of something.

It was made of his heart.

My dearest Lyn,

You'll never guess what happened today! Oh! I have no words to explain, but I'll try. Charley released PJ from his cage, but the window was closed. With nowhere to go, the poor bird flew into the hall and flapped his way right into poor Plucky's face!

She whirled around in circles (so Charley said), shrieking there was a bat in the house. She's terrified of bats, you know. Mum went into hysterics—certain our house was overrun (she knew she had felt one in her bed last night)—and I grabbed a chair cushion

A Pretty Game

(what I intended to do with that…?) and dashed up the stairs with Eillie, ready for battle. All was still until 'Flop, flop, flop.' The poor, confused creature flew out from the nursery stairwell and raced down the hall. We chased him all about, stumbling twice over the semi-unconscious heap that was Plucky, and finally got him settled enough to grab him. It was such an uproar!

Also, Gideon kissed me and now we are a thing. He loves me, did you know? You probably did.

Love, your most faithful, sincerest, stupidest friend,
Wren

Acknowledgments

Special thanks to Jana and Megan, my ever-dedicated first draft readers who had to read when it wasn't very pretty.

Melissa, Tara, LeeAnn, Tessa, Kat, Deana, and Lindsay, your thoughts and enthusiasm for my story propelled me forward and gave me courage—thank you.

Rachel, thanks for reading with and without your editor hat on. You gave me confidence to call it finished.

As always, thank you to my children for inspiring my curiosity, looking out for one another, and for giving me time to sit at my computer.

Huge shout out to my husband, Travis. I appreciate you.

And a deep, forever thank you to my mom. I'm sorry you weren't able to read this story, but you were with me every page. I know you would have loved Wren, too.

Other Books by the Author

The Falcon Princess

Ayra of Darkwater Quarry

Made in the USA
Columbia, SC
20 February 2024